STAR RIDERS

STAR RIDERS

CAROLINE HARTMAN

Red Dobie
P R E S S

Exton, Pennsylvania

Star Riders

First Edition

ISBN-13: 9780989387170
ISBN-10: 0989387178

Published by:
Red Dobie Press
    an imprint of Alexemi Publishing
P.O. Box 1266
Exton, PA 19341

www.AlexemiPublishing.com

Cover Design by Bradley Wind, www.bradleywind.com
Please visit the author's website: www.carolinehartman.com
Other works by the author:
    Summer Rose
    Sacred Ponies

Printed in the United States of America

Dedicated to

My son, Tom Hartman, and his wife, Pat Hayden Hartman

My daughter, Ann Hartman Shaw

*My daughter, Susan Hartman Giordani and
her husband, Michael Giordani*

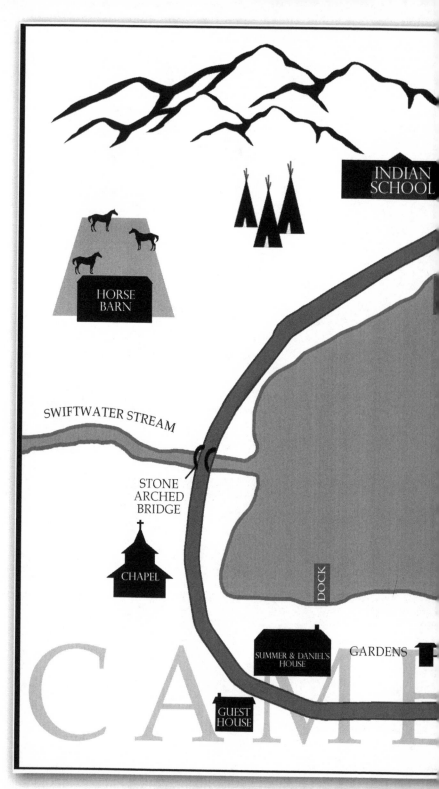

CAST OF CHARACTERS

Most characters are fictitious; however several came from history. A star precedes their name.

Louisa Lenore Charteris *Daniel's Half Sister.*

Martha Graves *Wife of the Stationmaster at Morgan's Corner.*

Daniel Charteris *Former Union Brigadier General, Co-owner of Camelann, brother of Abbey and half-brother of Louisa, husband of Summer Rose, father of Mac, Gussie, John Alexander, Lilly, and the twins..*

Summer Rose Charteris Wife of Daniel, *mother of Mac, Gussie, John Alexander, Lilly, and the twins.*

Abbey Charteris DuPree *Daniel's sister, married to Will Thunder Cloud, a half-breed Sioux, mother of Alice and Emil, formerly married to Captain Ed Kincaid.*

Big Bear *Native guard.*

Guilliame Emil Thunder Cloud DuPree (Will Thunder Cloud*) Half-Breed son of Wakanda and French Canadian fur merchant, Nicholas DuPree, married to Abbey, father of Alice and E*mil.

*Lt. Col. George Armstrong Custer (Autie) *Commanding Officer of the U.S. Army's 7th Cavalry, brother of *Thomas and *Boston, married to *Libbie Custer.*

*Elizabeth (Libbie) Bacon Custer M*arried to George Custer.*

*Major Thomas Custer *Brother of Lt. Col. Custer and* Boston, *Commander of C Company, 7th Cavalry.*

*Red Cloud *Headman of the Lakota Sioux, uncle of Will Thunder Cloud.*

Lew Graves *One-armed stationmaster, married to Martha.*

Dr. Matilda DuPree *Sister of Will Thunder Cloud.*

Mrs. Violet Montour *Housekeeper and duenna to Matilda and Emily.*

Dr. Elliott Cutter *Heart Specialist from Scotland.*

Dr. Emily St. Clair Roommate of Matilda, sister of Hal.

Hal St. Clair *Former Brigadier General, co-owner of Camelann, married to Fanny, father of Hank and Charlie, childhood friend of Daniel.*

Fanny St. Clair *Wife of Hal, mother of Hank and Charlie.*

Mrs. Helena Love *Amish housekeeper and cook for the Charteris family.*

Wakanda *Mother of Will Thunder Cloud, grandmother of Alice and Emil, headmistress of the Camelann Indian School.*

*Emmanuel and *Maria Custer *Parents of George, Thomas, Boston, Nevin, Custer, and Maggie Custer Calhoun.*

*Monaseetah *Daughter of the Cheyenne chief, Little Rock, a member of Black Kettle's tribe, rumored to be George Custer's Indian mistress.*

*President U.S. Grant *Eighteenth President of the United States, former commanding general of the Union Army.*

*Julia Dent Grant *Wife of President U.S. Grant.*

*Orvil Grant *Brother of President Grant.*

*William Belknap *Secretary of War during Grant's administration.*

*Lt. General William Sherman *Commander of the United States Army.*

*Major General Phi Sheridan *Second in command to General Sherman.*

Edward J. Kincaid *Abbey's first husband*.

*Jack Red Cloud *Son of *Red Cloud, childhood friend of Will Thunder Cloud.*

*Crazy Horse *Great military leader of the Sioux, friend of Will Thunder Cloud.*

*Chief Gall *great military leader of the Sioux, friend of Will Thunder Cloud.*

*Sitting Bull *Spiritual leader of the Sioux, Sun Dancer.*

*Rain-In-The-Face *Great enemy of Thomas Custer.*

Beau Farro (Wolf Tracker*) Sioux Medicine Man, friend of Will Thunder Cloud.*

*Bloody Knife *Col. Custer's favorite scout.*

*Captain Frederick Benteen and *Major Marcus Reno *Longtime enemies of all the Custers.*

*General Alfred Terry *Immediate commander of George Armstrong Custer, overall commander of the Yellowstone Campaign.*

*Captain Grant Marsh *Legendary captain of the river steamer, Far West.*

*Dr. Henry Potter *Surgeon to the 7ᵗʰ Cavalry.*

*Sgt. Mike Madden *Wounded soldier.*

Peter and Henrietta Newton *Bismarck telegraph operator and his wife*

Todd Ward Cutter *Son of Dr. Cutter.*

Dr Ray Stone *Local Doctor in Camelann.*

ANIMALS
Owen and Mayo *The Charteris dogs.*
Chester *Daniel's favorite horse.*
Rabbit *Summer's favorite horse.*
Toledo *Tom's favorite horse.*
Feather *Louisa's pony.*
Sooty *Lilly's pony.*
Romeo and Juliette *Great black Perchons.*
Comanche *Lone Survivor of the Little Big Horn Massacre.*

TABLE OF CONTENTS

Chapter 1

THE GENOA SAUSAGE

Morgan's Corner, Pennsylvania
November 17, 1875

Ten-year-old Louisa Lenore Charteris looped Feather's reins on the post outside the train station. She nuzzled her cream-colored pony and he nickered back. "Wish me luck, Feather," Louisa whispered with a big, shoulder-shifting sigh. She stiffened her spine as she walked up the three steps to the train station-general store-post office. Her daily chores since coming to live at Camelann included picking up the mail; she hated this particular job. She'd come to Camelann last summer when her mother died, and she did love living with Summer Rose and Daniel and her half nephews and niece, the lake, the waterfalls, the forests, the fields, all the horses, but she hated picking up the mail. She nodded to the wooden Indian guarding the entrance and stepped inside.

A bell tinkled and delicious aromas of coffee, fudge, fresh bread, and spicy Genoa sausage greeted Louisa. The door to the mysterious depths of the station creaked and Mrs. Graves emerged and stepped up to the counter as silent and forbidding as the wooden Indian. Without so much as a hello, Mrs. Graves tossed Camelann's canvas mailbag onto the counter.

Mrs. Martha Graves, wife of the one-armed stationmaster was the recently appointed postmistress for Morgan's Corner; she scowled at the girl. A big woman, Mrs. Graves glided rather than walked. Dressed in tans and grays she blended into the drab walls and dusty mountains of merchandise. Nothing about the woman suggested femininity. Uncle Hal said she looked like a man who wore women's clothing. By his tone Louisa knew Hal meant no flattery.

Louisa, in contrast to drab Mrs. Graves, wore a soft tan corduroy riding skirt and a cornflower blue hand-knit sweater with a matching scarf; both exactly matched the color of her big eyes. With her flawless, creamy skin, the girl flush with youth promised great beauty. Mrs. Graves obviously hated her. "I suppose you came for Camelann's mail."

Louisa nodded. *Is she daft? She just threw the mailbag on the counter.*

The woman reached into the nearest candy jar and pulled out a piece of fudge and shoved it in her mouth. For a second, Louisa thought she might offer her a piece—Louisa loved chocolate—but, of course, she didn't. The girl watched the big jowls mash the chocolate. The sight quickly killed any desire for candy.

Mrs. Graves snorted. "Letter in there for Daniel from your half-sister, Mrs. Abigail Charteris Kincaid Dupree. She's a bigamist, you know. Her first husband came through here two days ago." Martha sneered and faked a whisper. "A bigamist is almost as bad as a whore." She held up the letter from Abbey. "Wonder what she wants?" She muttered, "That Indian-lover always wants something, and your big brother Danny-boy always sends it. Must be nice having money." Some women knit or crocheted or quilted. Martha, however, crowned herself the queen of gossip. Feeding tidbits to the town became her duty.

"How is the Charteris' newest princess?" Her voice dripped of envy, as she eyed Louisa's blue sweater. "They sure dress you nice. Did Summer knit your sweater? It matches your eyes." She pointed to the skirt. "I bet that cost a pretty penny!" She let loose an ugly laugh and snorted. "I bet they're grooming you to be a whore just like your mama." Daniel, Abbey, and Louisa share the same father, Louis Charteris, but different mothers. Daniel and Abbey's mother, Flora, the only one of the three parents still alive, was now Reverend Tuttle's wife. Louisa's mother had been a high-class hooker in Washington D.C. during the war.

Unfortunately, Mrs. Graves made it her life's work to know all the Charteris' family history and to remind the girl every time she saw her of her tainted lineage. Now she stepped from behind the counter, shoving the long Genoa salami, which always hung from the ceiling, out of the way and held out Camelann's mailbag. She bent low, sticking her face into the girl's. "Do you even know what a whore is?"

Louisa tried to concentrate on the swinging salami, but it was difficult to ignore Mrs. Graves.

Martha grabbed Louisa's jaw, her voice rasped. "Look at me when I speak to you, you little Jezebel. Doesn't the high and mighty Summer Rose teach you any manners? In case no one ever told you, Pearl, your mamma, opened her legs and let men poke her for money—that is what a whore does. You know what I mean, don't you? You've seen them wild dogs doing it, haven't you?"

She reached above her head and unhooked the long salami from its hook, turned Louisa around and smacked the girl's bottom with it. "Get out of here, little Miss Fancy Pants. You, in your expensive clothes with half the town dressed in rags. Why that's a sin. You should be ashamed. I can't stand the sight of you.

"Take this," she said shoving the mailbag at Louisa. She shook the long sausage at the girl. "Get yourself out of here before I poke you myself. You look like a whore." She whacked the little girl again.

Louisa turned, clutching the mailbag to her chest, and ran out the door. Tears blinded her; her breath came in gulps. It took two tries to free the reins. Mrs. Graves stood in the doorways shaking the giant sausage. Once mounted, Louisa hunched tight to Feather's mane and urged him faster and faster toward the lake.

Above Forty-Foot Falls she dismounted. A fierce wind out of the north ruffled her skirt. She didn't notice the wind or the spectacular view of the lake with the fields stretching all the way to the mountains. The wind whipped her dark hair loose from her horn and wire combs. They fell to the ground as she slipped out of the wind into the narrow passage which twined down behind the falls. Daniel and Summer's children, Gussie, Mac, Johnnie, Lilly, and the Indian children from the school had shown her the grotto behind the falls last summer. Memories flashed of one sweltering afternoon when they splashed in the spray and jumped through the curtain of water.

Today she didn't notice anything but the thundering falls. She did remember vague ledges and dark crevices, good hiding places; she crawled up on a high rock, clutched the mailbag to her chest. Her hair fell over her face. She swiped it back and sobbed harder. Louisa knew what her mother had been, she'd known for years, and always she felt ashamed. A knife of pain sliced hard into her chest as she lay down on the rocks. The children in Chicago had been so cruel that Pearl had taken her out of school and hired a tutor. "Your mama's a whore...your mama...." In her head she heard their chant over and over. "Your mother's a whore; your mama's a whore; your ..."

She laid her cheek on her arm and sobbed as conflicting emotions assaulted her. Part of her felt such shame of her mother; another part ached with a deep longing. Good Lord, how she missed her mother. "Please God, take me to her." A picture of Mrs. Graves swinging the salami conjured in her head. "I hate her," she cried. She hoped to die and go to heaven with her mother.

꽃꽃

When Feather returned to the barn alone, Daniel sent out alarms. Daniel's boys ran to the Amish and the tenant neighbors. Daniel raced to Morgan's Corner to request help from the towns-people. Summer alerted the Indians. By twilight torches spread over Camelann's twelve thousand acres.

Near midnight, with the temperature hovering near freezing, a thin rain started. Daniel dismounted and stood at the top of the falls, hoping ridiculously to see through the night. As he turned, he stepped on the horn comb, snapping it. Holding his torch high, he knelt, recognized it right away, and studied the ground. A broken twig, crushed grass, a dislodged pebble led him to the cave. He almost missed her but a corner of her bright scarf peeked out of a high crevice. A shorter person would have missed the bright blue wool. He climbed to the ledge, felt her warmth, and hoisted her to his shoulder.

Louisa's small body curled into him. "I've got you, sweetheart. Hold on tight."

Once outside the cave he fired off the agreed upon three rifle shots as a signal. He pulled her close to his chest, mounted Chester, and raced through the cold rain to home. By the time they arrived they were drenched.

"She's blue with cold," said Summer as she handed her husband a big towel to mop his face and took Louisa. She nodded to Wakanda, the Indian woman, headmistress of the Indian school. Summer asked, "One of you please fill the bathtub with hot water and the other heat bricks in the fireplace. They'll warm the bed." She turned and took the girl into her and Daniel's bedroom, which was right off the dining room through to the bathroom, a recent addition for which she was, at the moment, very grateful.

As she slipped off Louisa's wet things and folded her into her flannel robe, Summer's mind raced. "Daniel, run upstairs and check on the children. If any are awake tell them Louisa is home and safe."

Chapter 2

ANSWERS AND CHOCOLATE

A half- hour later, Daniel, somewhat drier, sat on a wooden chair beside his and Summer's bed adding a spoonful of whipped cream to Louisa's hot chocolate. She had requested both the hot drink and him. Between sips, in a low voice, she said, "Mrs. Graves said bad things about Mama. Called her a whore?"

He handed her the napkin and motioned for her to wipe her mouth. At the end of Pearl's life Daniel and Summer had helped take care of Pearl and her daughter. The Sisters of Charity at Lourdes did most of the actual nursing, but Louisa trusted her half-brother above even Summer. He'd never given silly answers to her questions; he never lied or talked to her as if she were dumb, and he never told her, like some did, you are too young to know.

Now he arched one eyebrow. "I'll assume you know what a whore is?"

She nodded.

Daniel set down the cup of chocolate, the spoon rattled in the saucer. "Your question is a tough one, Miss." He tweaked her under her chin. "You've never been poor or gone to bed with one side of your stomach gnawing on the other side. Your mother as a girl was dirt poor, much poorer than you can imagine. She and her sister, Opal, couldn't leave the house at the same time because they only had one pair of shoes between them, and both were too proud to go barefoot. Often they went hungry, and snow came through cracks in the walls of their bedroom. Her mother didn't have a winter coat.

"So Pearl and her sister slept with soldiers for money. At first, they bought food and shoes and a warm coat for their mother. The war made a lot of people crazy. And women were very much in demand. Men thought they were about to die and didn't follow the rules anymore. She made a lot of money."

He paused and poured more chocolate into her cup and dipped another big glob of whipped cream from the bowl. "About the time you were born, Pearl married my father, and Pearl didn't need to make money. He was rich and a good man. I think he must have loved her a lot. They lived in Chicago, but he died."

Daniel handed her the cup and waited for her to take another big sip. "Remember Auggie?"

Louisa nodded.

"After our father died, Pearl married Augustus Vanderslice, a former Confederate captain. She needed money and I'm sure she wanted to protect you, but Auggie was not a good man. He left you and your mother when she became ill with tuberculosis. I came out to Chicago and brought you here. We took her to the sanatorium. Remember how we visited her. Remember the big veranda at Lourdes?" He added a dab of whipped cream to her nose. "And the nuns with their great winged hats?"

Louisa frowned and took another big swallow. "Did Summer tell you about the salami?"

Daniel nodded. "She did. Don't you worry. I'll pick up the mail from now on. You stay away from that witch. She won't bother you again. I plan to speak with her."

Louisa, her big eyes even bigger, said. "Maybe you'd better let Summer do the talking."

He set down the cup. "Why?"

"You might lose your temper."

Summer stepped into the bedroom. "She's right. You'd better let me talk to her." She winked at Louisa. "We sort of like you a little. We don't want to give anyone an excuse to hang you."

⚔

A steady rain drummed on the roof and a soft fire burned in the fireplace. With Louisa finally asleep in her own bed, Daniel sat at his desk, opening the mail and sipping a whiskey. Summer sat on the leather sofa trying to stay awake. Wakanda had returned to the Indian village.

Summer asked, "Can't you think of a way to have Martha fired?"

Daniel took a deep breath. "I probably could. However, I feel responsible for Lew losing his arm and he's a good man. I ordered him to take the hill at Wilson's Creek."

Summer nodded. The war, a decade past, still haunted them.

The hall clock chimed two. Daniel held up a letter. "Abbey writes that Will isn't well. She's bringing him to Philadelphia to the doctors at Jefferson Hospital. She wants to know if the children can stay here. Did you know about this?"

"No, I didn't. I'm sure Wakanda would have mentioned it if she knew. What's wrong with Will?"

Chapter 3

THE WILD EAST

November 18, 1875
Pine Ridge Indian Reservation—Dakota Territory

Abbey Dupree finished ironing the last of the children's white people clothing. She folded the shirts into tissue paper and packed them in the valise with their nightclothes and toiletries. The children would change clothes when they crossed the Missouri. Abbey smiled to herself. What a crazy incongruent way they lived. The children, with only a quarter part native blood, looked Indian, high cheekbones and tanned skin when dressed in buckskin and feathers, but dress them in white people's clothes and they looked white. Will, even with his blue eyes, was half Indian. Dressed in white men's clothing he still looked very Indian, and herself ... she didn't even try. No buckskin or feathers for her. Blonde hair, fair skin, pale green eyes, a slight cleft of her nose, a dead giveaway of her Scottish ancestors.

She smiled to herself. None of her speculation mattered. Most men, white or Indian, instantly focused midway between her collarbones and waist. What is, is, she thought.

Big Bear knocked on the outside door. She'd been expecting him and called for him to enter. Red Cloud, great leader of the Lakota Sioux, had arranged for Bear to travel with them. She appreciated all the kindnesses, but they tightened the band about her chest, because she knew why they were so kind. Her family, her friends, all feared for Will. Her young handsome husband, the best man she'd ever known, was ill. One look at him and anyone saw he was not well.

Red Cloud, Will's uncle, had traveled several times to the eastern cities—he'd met with President Grant--and knew the rigors of train travel. He sent Big Bear to help her with luggage and the children. Red Cloud also held enough clout with leading citizens and politicians to procure a private railroad car. Although the adults acted nonchalant for the sake of the children, Abbey suspected they knew their father was seriously ill. His beautiful bronze color now overcast with gray held a constant sheen of strain. He tired after ten steps, and he couldn't climb the hill beside their house here in the Dakota Territory. When she pressed her ear to his chest, his usually steady heartbeat gave a swooshing sound.

She had written Tilley, Will's half-sister and one of the rare women doctors in the United States. Dr. Matilda Dupree had studied in Paris and Philadelphia.

After Tilley read the symptoms, she wired back: BRING HIM EAST IMMEDIATELY.

Bear strapped the trunks to his back and lifted the valise. "Is Thunder Cloud ready?" Her husband's full name, which they both agreed was much too long, was Guilliaume Emil Thunder Cloud Dupree. Whites called him Will; Indians called him Thunder Cloud.

Into the room came the children, one on each side of their father. Willowy Alice Fire Cloud was but seven years old, and rough-and-tumble Emil Running Cloud, who looked more like his father every day, was only five. "We're right behind you," said Emil. "Remember the picnic basket, Mom."

＃＃

At the station, a sky the color of raw wool, stretched forever. Thunder threatened in the far west, and tumbleweeds, the size of shoats, skittered along with puffs of dirt. The air smelled of dust and rain. Lt. Colonel George Armstrong Custer, former General George Armstrong Custer of Civil War fame, and Libbie, his wife, with a half dozen of his men, clustered around the few chairs on the train platform. The general dozed; his body stretched over two chairs. Their horses, all blood bays or grays, in their gleaming tack stood further down the tracks ready to board. Band members amid their instrument cases waited beside them. Colonel Custer just about always traveled with at least a four-piece band.

The men's laughter faded as they approached. A woman as obviously white as Abbey married to a half-breed such as Will did not sit well with most of the soldiers. They could take Indian wives, but it didn't work well for American women to marry savages.

Off to the side of the station two Indian women, sitting in an open tipi on a bright red blanket, provided a touch of color to the bleak landscape. Abbey waved to the women and Will, out of breath, stopped for a moment and leaned against a post. Abbey, with her windblown blonde hair and wearing a double-breasted navy wool suit with brass buttons and a yellow-fringed shawl, stood out like a ray of sunshine. Not a soldier on the platform could look away. Everyone stared at them. Overhead the United States flag snapped.

Finally, Major Tom Custer, George's younger brother and aide-de-camp, tipped his hat to her and nodded to Will. Tom Custer helped them up the steps. Not a West Pointer, like his famous brother, Tom Custer, had enlisted as a private with the 21st Ohio infantry when the war began in order to be near his older brother. Tom, then sixteen, idolized Autie, the family nickname for George Armstrong Custer. And during the war Tom fought honorably in many major conflicts as a private then later was commissioned as a lieutenant. He moved up the ranks on merit and won two Medals of Honor, the first soldier to ever do such a thing. A few spoke of nepotism, but anyone who read the citations knew Tom deserved them. Hal and Daniel and most of the Union Army veterans highly respected him.

At the train station, the colonel, still draped across two chairs, thumbed the brim of his hat, the soldiers cleared a path. Libbie Custer came up and briefly hugged Abbey then moved toward two other women who must be traveling with them.

The train grew larger and louder as it screeched into the station. Out of the white steam stepped Red Cloud with a contingent of braves. More Indians on horses came from around the station. Abbey suddenly couldn't breathe. For a moment the opposing factions eyed each other like stallions vying for top horse. The moment passed. Red Cloud hugged the children, Abbey, then Will. The sadness suddenly became too much to bear, and tears flooded her eyes.

Would her Will ever come back here? Would she? She was so frightened at the thought of losing him. A sick knot in her stomach threatened to overwhelm her. She sat suddenly a few chairs down from the famous former general, praying she wouldn't faint. Tom Custer nodded to the men remaining on the platform, Red Cloud, and the stationmaster. He then took her arm, helped her stand, and ushered her into the private car. Bear followed with Will. One of the soldiers whistled. A snap of Tom Custer's fingers silenced him.

Tom didn't say a word. The strength of his hand, even through her sleeve, calmed her. He situated her in one of the plush red chairs by the window, fixed her a glass of water then motioned to her purse. She understood and handed him the tickets. While the sky darkened and lightening flickered, Tom Custer dealt with the stationmaster and sorted out who belonged and who didn't, situated Will, the luggage, the children, and even Owen, the dog, which the children insisted on bringing along, while Abbey wilted into the chair. Strains of *Garry Owen*, the 7th Cavalry's anthem, drifted in thru open windows. Just as the train pulled out of the station, Tom came, knelt at her side, and rested his hand on her wrist.

"Mrs. Dupree, I'll be on the train until just this side of Toledo. Don't hesitate to send for me. Owen is a big hit with the band. They'll look after him, but he must stay with the horses." He looked at the children. "When you want to visit, come and get me. I'll take you back." He squeezed Abbey's shoulder, nodded to Will, winked at Alice and Emil, then left.

◦※◦

While Abbey and Will chugged across the prairie, Summer set two Amish girls to cleaning the house and sent all the children with Lobo, a teenage Indian boy, to feed the horses and muck out the stables. As she stood with Daniel watching them race to the barn, she shook her head. "They certainly have a lot of energy. Please ask one of the boys to saddle Rabbit for me. She needs some exercise and I feel like a ride."

Her husband suspected what she had in mind. "Want me to come with you?"

"Thank you but I can manage."

Once the house cleared of people she sharpened her eight-inch Bowie Knife, and loaded her Smith and Wesson. Next, she bathed and brushed her sable hair until it crackled then pulled it back in a tight chignon. She then dressed in a new riding suit, culottes and jacket of soft cardinal red wool, and her good black boots. A flat brimmed black gaucho's hat and black leather gloves completed the outfit. She checked herself in the long mirror. She knew she looked good. She felt invincible.

Daniel brought up Rabbit and when he helped her into the saddle, he growled in a whisper, "You look gorgeous. Want to come back to bed with me?"

Just the look in his eyes sent a rush of heat through her. With a smile, she bent and kissed him on the lips, a lingering kiss she hoped he felt in his toes. "Plan to make an opportunity later.

For now, I'm off to buy some salami. No one smacks a child of mine."

"Should I worry about Martha's safety?"

She took a deep breath. "No. I don't plan to kill her." She smiled brilliantly. "I may use your name for clout, okay?"

⊰⊱

A little east of Chimney Rock Tom Custer came by Abbey and Will's private car and visited with Will. He stayed for coffee and the three of them enjoyed the visit.

Since then she's seen him a few times in the dining car and along the corridors, and once she sat at breakfast with Libbie and the two younger Custer boys, Boston, a brother, and Autie Reed, a nephew, both teenagers. The boys blushed and giggled and eyed her chest, but eventually quieted. They had enjoyed their holiday with their famous brothers and now looked forward to returning home to Ohio. Libbie had been very gracious. Most army wives shunned her because of her marriage to a half-breed, but Libbie wasn't like that. The boys left then Tom and the general joined them. Libbie did most of the talking. The Custer men were quiet, the colonel seemed introspective, and Tom acted shy. When the men excused themselves to exercise the horses, Libbie told her Tom's sweetheart, a New Jersey girl, had died of consumption last winter. "He's still in mourning," Libbie said.

"I'm very protective of him." she added. Just at that moment, outside the window, the brothers rode by at a gallop.

Libbie whispered, "It really irritates the General that Tommy's so much better a horseman than he is."

She smiled, a devilish glint in her eyes. "I have to admit, he can sit a horse. I appreciate a good looking man."

Abbey followed Tom with her eyes. Until that moment, she hadn't considered his looks. While he couldn't hold a candle to her Will, he possessed a certain magnetism, and the horse definitely knew who was boss.

＊＊

In Camelann, the day was November at its best, hot sun, crisp air, colors, all soft tans, browns, and purples against vibrant green grass. A morning on horseback was a rare treat for Summer. She cantered Rabbit along the lake road and checked on the young eagles and the swans, then rode toward the station. She felt as good as she looked.

Hal and Daniel first met Summer Rose McAllister when she was eighteen. Both soldiers wanted her; their friendship almost came to an end over this wild child dressed in ragged trousers, living alone here in Camelann, since her father and two brothers had been killed at Antietam. Within weeks, her mother too had died of grief and pneumonia. Hal took one look at the wild girl and told Daniel that dressed in style, she could stop a regiment on Pennsylvania Avenue. Today, twelve years later and the mother of four, she still could. Gorgeous in her cardinal red and black riding habit, she rode Rabbit past three Amish men unloading bags of feed from an open-bed wagon. They looked up, not just startled but with mouths agape, to see her ride the dappled gray mare into the railroad station-general store and post office. She guided Rabbit right up the three steps, passed the wooden Indian, and through the doorway.

She nudged Rabbit around the tables of dry goods and hardware up to the counter. Three women shrieked and jerked back behind the display of boxed crackers. Dexter Gideon and Matt Crew jumped to their feet so fast they spilled their checkerboard and backed around the coal stove. Rabbit, sweaty and smelling strongly of horse, eyed the candy jars and swished her thick tail, missing by inches the table of canning jars. No one spoke as Summer withdrew her Bowie knife from her sleeve and pointed to the Genoa salami.

Summer watched Martha's face contort. She knew Martha wanted to roar, but only a squeak came out. "May I help you, Mrs. Charteris?"

Summer stood in her stirrups and whacked off the salami and laid it on the counter. It was as long as a baseball bat and as round as her upper arm. No wonder Louisa had been so frightened. Now, only a string dangled from the hook.

"Yes. Wrap that up and put it on our bill. Have Lew bring it out when he delivers telegrams." She pointed the eight-inch knife at Martha. "When I was six, Mrs. Warren, who lived out on the pike—remember her?—she smacked me for throwing a snowball at her barn. When my father heard about it, he threw her in the lake—in January. You have a problem with my child or any child living at Camelann, you come to me, Mrs. Graves. Otherwise, I hope you can swim."

Behind her a woman snorted. Summer turned. "I may not be able to do the throwing, but I know plenty of strong men who would be more than happy to help me."

Using her Bowie knife, she speared two fat gumdrops from a candy jar. She daintily removed them from the blade, popped the red one into her mouth, and gave the yellow one to Rabbit. With amazing grace, the horse turned and broke nothing, then walked out the door.

Chapter 4

ON THE TRAIN

Just after crossing into Indiana, Tom Custer brought the children, Bear, and Abbey each a bottle of Venor's ginger ale. The children loved it because, although non--alcoholic, it foamed like beer. For Will, he brought a bottle of good Kentucky bourbon. When he fixed her a ginger ale, Abbey smiled and nodded to the bottle of bourbon.

Tom chuckled and said to Will, "You should have warned me, Will, or I should have guessed ...she don't look like a ginger ale kind of girl."

"She doesn't drink much or often, but she appreciates good bourbon."

Tom fixed three drinks, handed one to her and one to Will then sat opposite Will. They saluted each other, sipping their drinks in companionable silence, and watched the countryside slide by.

"We'll be detraining in a few hours, just this side of Toledo," said Tom.

"Home for the holidays?" asked Will.

Tom nodded.

He topped off the men's glasses. Whiskey seemed to oil Tom Custer's tongue. "Libbie and Ma tend to get in each other's hair. My job is keeping them separate." He let out a loud breath, and his shoulders deflated. "It's not an easy task. Both are iron-willed women." He sipped his whiskey, "and in addition to that, no one drinks. Maggie, our sister, is a teetotaler, forbids it in the house. Even her husband, Jimmy, can't drink in the house. And Autie, in a weak moment, promised Libbie he wouldn't drink, and for the most part he keeps his word." He shook his head and grinned. "Libbie's tough." He looked over to Will and lifted his glass. "I'm on leave. Why not?"

He held out a card to Will. "My address in Ohio is on the back. I'll be there until New Year's Day. Wire me if either of you need some help." He said to Will, "I've heard of Camelann and always wanted to see it." He shook his head. "I saw Summer shoot once. She's amazing."

Will grinned. "Ever see her throw a knife?" He bent and took the card. "Thanks Tom. We'll talk to Daniel and let you know. Perhaps you could come out for a couple days before the New Year. That way you could ride back with us. And Tom, thanks for your help with Emil and Alice."

Abbey sat up board straight. "What? W-what happened with the children?"

The whiskey must have loosened Will's tongue, too. He cringed a little then glanced at Tom, then his wife. "I told Bear not to trouble you." He gave a little half smile. "Tom went up on the roof and sat with them while we rode through Chicago."

Abbey froze. All color drained from her face. Finally, she stammered, "O-on the roof of the train? What were they doing up there?" She glared at Tom Custer. "And why was it you who went after them?"

Tom filled all their glasses again. "They're good kids, Mrs. Dupree. The view from up there is terrific. I just kept them from getting conked by the bridges. I enjoyed talking with them, too. It seems heights make Bear dizzy."

⚓

Daniel spread the buffalo robes on the big flat rock, the one that jutted out over the stream below the falls, just above the trout pool. Ancient hemlocks arched long lacy branches out over the water, giving them a little privacy. He'd built a fire earlier and now lit it; the smoke for a minute enveloped them then dissipated into the upper branches. He set a pot of coffee, which he'd prepared, to heat. Summer dropped his saddlebag near the fire and eased down onto the robe.

He'd met her at the main gate when she returned to Camelann. Together they rode to the falls. Over the roar of the water, he said, "I don't want her smacking our kids, but I'd love to throw her in the lake. Imagine, poor Lew, having to live with that ..."

He removed his hat and pistol then knelt beside her. Twelve years of marriage and they understood each other. He unlaced and removed her boots. She knew what he wanted; she wanted it too.

"Red is a great color for you. Your skin, your dark hair, it makes my blood run hot." His fingers inched up one leg of her culottes. Slowly.

"How was Louisa this morning?" she asked.

He unsnapped one garter, then the one in the back, and again with measured slowness rolled down her black stocking. His big hand massaged her leg; he bent his head and kissed the inside of her knee. "She appeared to be her usual exuberant self. We fixed a stack of hay below the chute and let them all jump from the loft for half-an-hour. They loved that."

Summer leaned back stretching in the dappled sunlight and rubbed the back of his neck. Chester and Rabbit grazed in the distance, the falls thundered throwing up a barely perceivable mist, which felt good on her face. His lips on her thigh felt like heaven.

He reached beneath the other wide leg of her culottes, this time with a little more urgency, and inched up, unsnapping the other garters. As he kissed the inside of this knee, he murmured, "I see this outfit is going to present a challenge."

He moved up beside her. She giggled and unhooked his belt buckle and the buttons at his waist, then reached beneath his shirt and ran her fingers through the golden down on his chest. "You have on entirely too many clothes."

He laughed and slipped out of his shirt. "Except for my boots, my clothes come off easily, but you ..." He swiveled around and presented a boot which she held as he pulled it off. They repeated the process with the other foot. Her hat, her jacket and blouse, his socks flew off. He groaned when he saw the black corset. He knelt over her, one knee on each side of her waist, his hands surprisingly dexterous unlaced her corset with speed. At last he threw the corset aside, and his hands cupped her full breasts. Her hair, now loosened in the frenzy of flying clothes, fell between them like a stage curtain.

"Good Lord, you rode Rabbit inside the store? There's probably a law against that," he said between kisses. "I wish I could have seen her expression." The culottes and trousers slid off; he rolled one blanket around them.

"Summer, you are making me crazy."

Her alto voice deepened and purred. "Shush Daniel! You talk too much. I love when you're crazy."

⚓

The whiskey energized Will, even improved his color. When Abbey's temper calmed down, he suggested the children go to the dining car with Bear for dinner. He knew the waiters would dote over them. Bear liked the dining car, and no one would bother the children with Bear in attendance. Even dressed in white people's clothing he resembled a huge lumbering grizzly. Will handed Alice some money. "Be sure to leave a tip." He had shown her earlier how to figure up the bill, and the children had often gone by themselves for breakfast or lunch but never for dinner.

Will pooh-poohed Abbey's objections. To the children, he said, "You know how to behave. Emil, wash your face, slick back your hair, tuck in your shirt, and listen to Alice." He smiled at his daughter. "You always look beautiful. I'm counting on you to keep him off the roof of the train."

Her blue eyes sparkled.

When the children left, Tom Custer signaled for a waiter, and the three of them ordered from menus, Abbey ordered lemon chicken with herbs, the men ordered roast beef.

The Baltimore and Ohio had a patent on elegance: a porter came with a little wheeled-cart that magically turned into a table; white linens, silverware, bone china, gleaming domed servers, even candles, miraculously appeared. White-gloved waiters offered glistening hot rolls held in silver tongs; they filled and refilled their crystal wineglasses. The food was delicious. The waiter said, "We have a violinist in the club car."

The whiskey and wine caught up with Will, and he fell asleep, slumped in his chair. Tom helped her get him to bed. He joked telling her about rolling plenty of his fellow officers into bed. "They've rolled me plenty of times, too."

They removed his coat, boots and belt, but left him in his clothes. She tucked the covers around him and sat on the edge of the mattress and kissed her husband goodnight then looked up to Tom Custer, who stood near the head of the berth. "He's very ill, you know. I'm taking him to Jefferson Hospital. The Medicine Men couldn't help him."

Tom nodded.

His voice came out softer than she'd ever heard it before. "Libbie mentioned to me she told you about Lucia. Asthma... TB...she was ill for a long time. It's difficult to see someone you love..."

Abbey finished his sentence. "...suffer." She winced and her breath hitched. "His color is so gray."

Tom reached down and felt Will's wrist. "His pulse is strong."

She noticed the wetness in his eyes, but didn't say anything. Instead she stood. "I hope he stays asleep." She forced a smile; her blonde curls glimmered. "Thank you, Tom Custer. I don't want the children to see him like this." They closed the curtain.

As if on cue, Bear returned with the children. A waiter with a tray of apple crisp and ice cream followed. The five of them sat around the little table and enjoyed their dessert. Alice loved the violin music, so did Bear. Emil rolled his eyes. Alice looked at her brother. "Do not lick your dish, Emil. Mother, do something ..."

Tom reached over and took Emil's dish. "Your mother is exhausted. Can you two get ready for bed by yourselves?" He swept his arm over the debris of dinner. "I'll have the waiter collect all this." He winked at Alice and pulled a harmonica from his pocket. He had played for them when they rode the roof of the train. "If you are real quick, I'll play you a lullaby."

⚎

Abbey must have dozed. She awakened, aware first of the rhythm of the train, then the clacking of the wheels. Her fingertips brushed the coarse red velvet on the chair cushion. Light from a passing town flashed by the window; the dishes, the table had all been cleared; the children and Bear were nowhere in sight. Gaslight winked from brass lamps, piano music drifted in from the dining car. Tom, still smart-looking in dark trousers and a white shirt with the collar open and the sleeves rolled up sat opposite her; his booted ankle crossed over his knee; his hand held a whiskey glass.

He set down his drink and stood. Even in civilian clothes, he looked very American, very military possessing the grace of a fit man: tall, broad-shouldered, sun--streaked hair, tanned skin, blue eyes with a charming bad boy smile. "They're asleep. I made sure they brushed their teeth. Bear's in his bunk. I've overstayed. Goodnight Mrs. Dupree. I enjoyed this evening. We detrain shortly."

She stood and extended her hand. "I'm sorry I missed the lullaby, perhaps some other time. Thank you for your help with the children and Will."

He took her hand just as the train lurched. For a moment, they came together in a silent dance. She, in her dress of loden green velvet, giggled; he smiled and twirled her around, his other arm at the small of her back. He bent her backward; his mouth came within a breath of hers. When she leaned forward and their lips brushed, just a whisper of a kiss, he spun her around and pressed her to the door. His hands stayed on her waist, but he closed the space between them. For a moment time hung breathless, passion hovered then bloomed, burst like a seedpod. Hungry, dizzy kisses, groping, greedy hands...growls, heavy breathing...

He said, his voice low, throaty, one hand touched her cheek, "I have wanted to kiss you since the first moment I saw you. Shall I stop? Tell me?"

She grabbed fistfuls of his white shirt and pulled him closer. "No, don't stop...not yet."

Thoughts of her had haunted him every night since he'd boarded the train. Now a switch flipped. His hand wound beneath her skirts and stroked the skin above her stocking, her inner thigh. She stiffened and moaned, but didn't push away. His teeth teased her earlobe and he murmured, "If you want me to stop, tell me now."

Soft mews came from deep in her throat, but no words. She knew she should stop him, but the words wouldn't come. Her hand slid to the back of his neck and she pulled him closer. They stood, clinging to each other as if a rogue wave threatened to sweep them out to sea. He moved his hand and found the magic spot between her legs, not on her flesh but on the delicate cotton fabric of her undergarment.

She folded into him, grabbed his waistband and pulled him hard against her, shaking, sucking in deep breaths. His hand remained still, tight against the soft cotton, his fingers unmoving. The angle, the pressure, the spot, all was just right. Perfect. Her body jerked; then spasms, one after another, slammed through her like storm waves pounding the beach. She quivered and rippled as if an outside force controlled her.

He had experience with plenty of women. He'd seriously pursued them since he was sixteen. In fact, an irate father's threat to blow his head off had prompted Tom's father to sign the papers permitting him to join the army at sixteen, way back in '61. Girls, enamored with cavalrymen, hung around army posts, dance halls, saloons. Easy prey, the men called them. But nothing like this gorgeous golden girl had ever before melted in his arms. Even if she wanted to stop, only a slim chance existed he might be able to do so now. Suddenly his stance shifted; her feet lifted from the floor. He was very fit. His powerful arms moved her hips onto his forearms, her legs tightened around his waist, her back pressed to the door.

"Oh God, Abbey…" With the flick of his strong fingers, he disposed of the delicate scrap of cotton. She arched her back and they came together: once, twice, three times. After that, only the moment mattered. Suddenly her body jerked, and a floodtide of warmth, soft as a blush, ebbed through her. Never had he felt anything so intimate and yet so sweet. He shuddered, hugged her hard, his hands now twined around her body, his own legs threatened to collapse. He kissed the side of her neck. His entire body softened. She clung to him and wanted nothing more than to stay right there forever.

A knock, jarring and invasive, on the outer door abruptly halted them. They pulled apart, both panting, still dazed with desire.

Boston Custer said through the door, "Tommy, Autie says for you to come now. Our stop is next."

"I'll be there in a minute." His hands curled around her back and came to rest on her shoulders. He pulled her close, again kissing her neck. "Part of me wants to apologize, to say I'm sorry, but Abbey, I am not sorry," he whispered. "How could I regret such a beautiful thing? I didn't mean for this to happen, but good God I am glad it did."

She stared at him with her eyes big and wet; her heart hammering hard enough to break bones, her fingers inched to the edge of his open collar and rested on his pounding heart. She kissed the skin there. "I didn't mean it to happen either. You must think I am…"

"…wonderful." He bent his head and kissed her, his hands cradled her face. This kiss sent sweet aftershocks to her core; her knees turned to jelly. Without his body pressing her to the door, she would have fallen and if the train hadn't screeched to a stop, she didn't know what might have happened. She only knew her body wanted him again, every fiber, every cell ached for him.

He held her cheek; his thumb brushed her lower lip. "Will Thunder Cloud is a lucky, lucky man. Godspeed, Mrs. Dupree."

As the shadows lengthened to darkness, ragged silver light from the rising moon filtered through the pines. Daniel pulled on his trousers and shirt. Summer wiggled into a sitting position with the buffalo robe around her. He added wood to the fire, fixed coffees then fetched his saddlebag from the far side of the blanket where Summer had dropped it. He returned to his spot on the robe, setting down the cups and then fixing the blanket around them, and said, "I told Mrs. Love we might be out late. She will stay."

Summer leaned against him.

"Are you cold?" he asked.

She shook her head. "I'm still catching my breath. I'm glad we don't have to rush right back. We rarely have time for…each other…for this…with the children about. Perhaps…"

He smiled, kissed the hollow of her collarbone and reached for the saddlebag. "You, my love, are insatiable. First though, I need fuel. Let's see what Mrs. Love packed."

He found pasties, golden-brown, wrapped in thick layers of newspaper and still warm, a bowl of leaf lettuce and late tomatoes, and a small tin of gingersnaps. Mrs. Love had packed crockery plates, utensils, and big linen napkins. He sliced tomatoes then fixed two servings. They ate greedily. The pasties were deli-cious with flaky crusts and a savory beef and vegetable filling; everything tasted wonderful. He set the plates aside.

He leaned against the tree; she rested her head in his lap. Golden light from the fire danced across them. He sipped cof-fee, dunking the gingersnaps and feeding every other one to her. Overhead an owl screeched and flew off. The water from the falls tumbled and rumbled lowly.

"This is just about perfect, isn't it? I wonder how Abbey and Will are?"

He shrugged. "I just know I'm the luckiest man in the world." He bent and kissed her then fed her another cookie.

She smiled up to him; her voice came out raspy. "Daniel, I am insatiable."

He set down his coffee, put the saddlebag aside. "Oh, sweet-heart, the things I do just to keep you happy." He slid deep into the covers slipping out of his shirt and trousers. Then as if emerging from the sea, he roared and rolled them together in the blanket. A few night birds flapped from the pines. The stars winked through the branches. "Never again," he whispered hoarsely, "will ginger-snaps just be gingersnaps." His voice deepened and he shifted so he lay beside her. "Every time for the rest of my life when I taste gingersnaps I will th*ink of you and tonight. I am so lucky...*"

"I found you."

⊨⊨

Still shaking, Abbey picked up Tom's glass. A little whiskey remained. She sipped it then pressed the cool glass against her cheek and sank into Will's chair. From the dark interior of the car she watched the Custer clan gather on and around the platform: soldiers, Libbie, two of her girlfriends, band members, horses, a cart full of luggage, band instruments, a carriage...

Her insides churned, her knees still felt liquid. Never before had such raw desire consumed her. Not even her first husband, Ed Kincaid, who had been a good teacher, had aroused her to such heights. When she discovered he liked men like women do, when he allowed his boyfriend to beat her and destroy her unborn child, any feelings for him curdled into hatred.

Her marriage to Will was entirely opposite: steady, strong, safe. He adored her, idolized her. He loved her ten times more than she loved him. He would protect her, die for her.

What happened tonight? Did Tom Custer even like her or she him? Was it just desire, raw lust? And she could not blame Tom Custer. He had lit the fuse, but she had certainly done nothing to stomp out the sparks. *My God, I exploded.* Another blush flashed through her body, her cheeks burned, her face... as she remembered clutching fistfuls of his shirt, arching toward him. She was no innocent. He had asked her to stop him. She did not even attempt to stop herself.

How could I do this to Will? I love him. Tears streamed down her face, the back of her throat ached. I am so sorry. It was the whiskey and the loneliness and we haven't laughed for so long. I'm so frightened, Will. You are my love, my best friend, my life. I don't want to lose you. How will I live without you? How could I melt in another man's arms? Memories of her wanton behavior, the spasms, the blush, the total abandonment rushed back. *My body betrayed me. How did such a thing happen? Will, the children could have walked out at any moment.*

Guilt swamped her, yet raw desire rolled in right behind it, threatening to drown her. Outside the window, in the gaslights flooding the platform, she spotted Tom Custer. He now wore a cream-colored, fringed doeskin jacket with a bright red scarf at the neck and a pale gray wide-brimmed hat.

A girl, definitely not his sister, perhaps one of Libbie's girl-friends, walked over to him and snatched the red scarf then playfully looped it around him, tugging him toward her. Outrage filled Abbey. Who is she? More tears washed down her face; her traitorous body ached for him. He politely turned from the girl.

Too weak to even stand, she watched the Custer Clan hug and kiss; she heard them shout and howl through the glass. The older woman who must be the Custer boys' mother, latched onto George, ignoring her other sons and Libbie. Libbie appeared nonchalant, giggling with her girlfriends. Another girl, maybe his sister, Maggie, hugged a handsome officer. Perhaps he was Jimmy Calhoun. She had heard he was part of the powerful Calhoun family who ruled the mercantile traffic in the Midwest. He'd given it all up to be part of the famous 7th Cavalry. The girl who had slid the scarf around Tom's neck tried again, but he walked away from her. Abbey felt like an interloper until Tom Custer came and stood in front of her window with his back to her, as if to block her view. *Does he even know I'm behind him?*

Suddenly he turned, his blue eyes drilled into her. Her breath ceased, her world went silent, and she felt the heat of him when he splayed his hand wide onto the outside of the window.

Compelled, drawn, magnetized as if she were merely an iron filing to his iron bar, her hand slid on the inside of the glass to his. She wanted to yank her hand free and run to the far reaches of the train, but she could not move. Her traitorous body responded with wave after wave of desire.

Oh my God! What have I become?

Chapter 5

PHILADELPHIA

Daniel and Summer waited on the platform in Morgan's Corners. She shivered a little as a wintry breeze ruffled the skirt of her soft gray suit. She pulled her Cherokee red shawl tighter and caught sight of the train in the distance, the long plume of smoke trailing behind it. Abbey had wired instructions. Daniel now spoke to Lew Graves. "Would you hold the train a minute or two longer than usual? Summer would like to see Will and Abbey, then she'll take their children home with her, and I'll continue to Philly with them." He handed Lew his ticket.

Lew glanced to the window in the station. Mrs. Graves watched from inside. "Sure can, General. Do the children have luggage?"

"Probably. We'll try to be fast about it." He too glanced at the ticket window; he refrained from sneering at Mrs. Graves. Just looking at that woman infuriated him.

He felt Summer's hand slip into his. Her concern for Will showed in her icy fingertips. He worried, too. They both tried to hide it.

"I'll miss you." He squeezed her hand. "Stay away from the gingersnaps while I'm gone." He smoothed the edge of her red wool shawl. Red—any shade-- was his favorite color; she wore it as often as possible.

She squeezed his hand again. "I'll make a huge batch ready for your return."

The train screeched into the station, the wooden platform shuddered; steam and smoke surrounded them. Lew spoke with the conductor and engineer. Both waved to Daniel; he gave a thumbs-up. Two Amish men stepped out of the car, and an older woman with a cane and a stack of luggage clogged the doorway. Finally, the conductor led them inside to the private car.

"Aunt Summer," yelled Alice. Emil jumped onto Daniel's back. Everyone hugged. Will looked winded and gray and had to sit down again.

Abbey, all red-eyed with dark circles, directed Lew to the children's trunk. Daniel stepped forward. "Here let me get this." He knew it would be difficult for Lew to lift it with one arm. Bear gathered the small luggage. He was detraining here with the children. "Kiss your parents good-bye, kiddoes. Come with me." To Abbey and Will, he said, "I'll be right back."

Summer kissed Will again and handed a basket to Abbey. "From your mother and Mrs. Love." She looped an arm around Will. "Your mother put a package of tea in there and told me to tell you to come back here and she'll treat you. She doesn't trust city doctors."

"She may be right. Give her my love." He sniffed the basket. "I smell Mrs. Love's donuts." Will chuckled. "I didn't realize I missed them so much. Thank them both."

Outside the window on the platform, she could see Mrs. Graves scolding Lew. Summer hugged her sister-in-law, then Will again.

Daniel returned, kissed his wife, and said, "The children, Owen, and Bear are already in the buggy. I'll wire you."

⊣⊟⊢

Their cousins were still in school so Emil and Alice ate lunch with Summer, threatening to talk her ears off. She found both youngsters, just seven and five years of age, precocious. Both read the newspapers. In raw brainpower they would run circles around all of their cousins. "Did you know Colonel Custer has a brother?" asked Alice. "You know, George Armstrong Custer?"

Summer nodded. "Doesn't everyone know of him? His name is always in the papers." During the war, George Armstrong Custer had been temporarily promoted, brevetted to Major General at age 23. When the war ended most wartime promotions were reevaluated. George was demoted to Lt. Colonel. Some enlisted men and close friends of George addressed him as General, but most often he was just Colonel Custer. "I think there may be more than one brother. Did you see them?"

Emil vigorously bobbed his head then gulped the last of his milk and said, "Yes, Tom—he told us to call him Tom--rode up on the roof with us--all the way through Chicago."

Summer hid a smile. She knew boys. They liked to shock their mothers and sisters, their woman folk. "How nice of him! I would have loved to ride the roof. Did you see Lake Michigan?"

Alice nodded. "Tom showed us his medals, too. He let me wear them."

Summer patted Alice's hand. "Now I remember. I read in *Harper's* that soldiers only allows their girlfriends to wear their medals." A teasing smile danced in her eyes. "Are you his girlfriend?"

Alice lowered her thick lashes; the flesh over her Indian cheekbones flushed a little. Summer took note of the girl's looks: very tall for her age, long silky black hair and huge blue eyes from her father, and from Abbey, perfect creamy skin.

"Don't be silly, Aunt Summer. I'm just seven and too little, and anyway Daddy said he hates Indians. You know we're part Indian?" She blinked. "Well, Mama isn't but Daddy, Emil, and I have Sioux blood."

Summer leaned forward and hugged the girl. "How could anyone hate you? It isn't good to hate anyone."

Alice said, "I know. Tom was nice to us, and he helped Mother a lot. You know, Daddy is ill?"

Summer's memory flashed back a decade or more to the war. She had met Tom Custer when he first became George Armstrong Custer's aide-de-camp. She'd often stood with him outside Sheridan's headquarters while the general's senior staff conferred. At the time, Summer was masquerading as Lt. Samuel Ross, a young officer under Sheridan command. To this day she doubted if Tom knew that bit of information.

Poor Tom, Summer thought, he always seemed a little clueless about what was happening. No one protected him like General Sheridan protected me. His brother gave him all the dirty work, too. She shuddered. Those days were terrible times. Terrible things happened. *I still wake from nightmares of horses squealing, of men dying on the gory battlefields.* If she allowed her mind to remember, she could still hear the cries, see the stacks of limbs, the shrouded bodies.

She turned back to Alice. "I know your Daddy's ill. That's why they've gone to Philadelphia. There's a doctor who your Aunt Tilley thinks may help him. I have doughnuts..."

Emil ate two. Alice asked, "May I take a bath? We don't have bathtubs on the reservations."

Summer stood. "What a marvelous idea. Would you like me to wash your hair? Emil, what would you like to do while your sister bathes?"

He pointed to the easel and paints in the corner of the dining room.

She studied the disheveled little boy for a moment. He needed a bath and haircut. Maybe after the painting... "Let me spread a drop cloth."

"May I take it outside?"

Great idea, she thought. "On the porch?"

Emil nodded. "I want to paint the lake. The color is unique."

"How old are you?"

"Almost six, Aunt Summer. Even my father thinks I'm older sometimes. My grandmother tells me I'm an old soul and will grow to be a great shaman."

※

Outside the Broad Street Station at Broad and Market in Philadelphia, gray skies and light sooty rain greeted them. Umbrellas bobbed along the crowded sidewalk as men and women left the buildings for home. Lamplighters quietly started their evening rounds. Daniel whistled for a cab and handled the luggage. Bear had stayed with the children. In addition to heights, he didn't like tall buildings.

The cobbled streets teemed with black carriages, but the ride to Arch Street where Tilley lived in an apartment with Dr. Emily St. Clair, was short. Both female doctors had studied in Paris and in Philadelphia and practiced medicine at the Women's Medical Hospital, which stood right across the street from their apartment.

Mrs. Violet Montour, statuesque with an imposing bosom and silver hair, their housekeeper and duenna, answered the door. Abbey had met her a year or so ago. No men in either girl's family approved of these young ladies living alone in the city. Aside from criminals and hoodlum lurking in alleys, unmarried, respectable young women just did not live alone, so Tilley and Will's father and Emily's parents insisted on Violet Montour, a widow and distant Dupree relative, coming to Philadelphia from Toronto, to watch over the girls. Everyone except the young female doctors thought her a godsend.

Now, Tilley, her ink black hair swept back in a braided knot, blue eyes flashing, burst into the hallway behind them. "Sorry about this weather. It's grim. Em will be a while. She's delivering a baby." She handed her umbrella, cape, and doctor's bag to

Mrs. Montour and hugged Will then Abbey then Daniel who was managing the luggage.

The confusion in the small vestibule verged on chaos. While Mrs. Montour directed Daniel and the luggage to the proper room, saw to coats and umbrellas, and escorted Will to a comfortable chair by the gas fireplace. Tilley whispered to Abby, "She is the bane of my existence. I'm studying urology at Jefferson with Dr. Gross' son—an honor in itself-- but don't mention a word to my brother." She giggled. "Will's almost as big a prude as she is." She rolled her eyes. "If either knew I inserted a tube into a real living, breathing man's penis this morning, and fished out a stone... why my brother would have a conniption." She looked over her shoulder to Mrs. Montour. "And she guards me as if I were still a virgin. Don't tell Will that either."

Daniel returned, hurriedly said goodbyes to Will and Abbey. He was staying at a guesthouse down the street because the apartment was small, and he had arranged dinner with a potential client. "I'll see you all at breakfast. Eight o'clock, Tilley?"

She nodded then walked him to the door. A powerful gust of wind blew leaves into the hallway. Mrs. Montour quickly instructed a maid to sweep them up.

Abbey and Tilley walked arm-in-arm into the cozy living room. Tilley's breezy and brazen words somehow improved Abbey's spirits. She went to Will and lifted his feet to an otto-man and tucked an afghan around his legs. The walk in the station and the cab ride had been obviously exhausting for him. The gas fireplace sent waves of warmth into the room, but he still shivered. She asked, "Would you like some tea?"

He reached up and took her hand and winked. "Would you ask if they have any whiskey?"

Tilley thought whiskey an excellent idea. As she scurried off following Mrs. Montour, she said, "I know Elliott prescribes whiskey quite often."

While Abbey waited for their hostess to return, Will held her hand; his touch brought comfort. However, the horrid guilt still haunted her. *How could I? ...* Not whitewashing her actions, she knew part of the reason had to be the lack of intimacy between her and Will. She wondered if they would or if they could ever be husband and wife again? Their recent attempts had been wretched failures. They both felt responsible. The spark ignited easily enough but they couldn't sustain a flame. *What are we doing wrong? Is this what happens after years of marriage? It certainly doesn't seem to bother my brother and Summer Rose. The fire between them, just in those few minutes I saw them together, seemed electric. Why is this happening to us now? How do you ask a doctor about such a thing? Am I just being selfish? Is it even important? Yes, it is. I know Will misses it too.* A little voice in her head whispered, *"Don't lie to yourself, Abbey Dupree, you've never ever experienced anything like what you experienced with Tom Custer.*

Get a grip on yourself, Abigail. You have two children, a house you love, a school you built. You're married to Will. Look at the good in your life. She studied Tillie's cozy sitting room, done in pink, blue, and white chintz, flowers and stripes covering dainty furniture and voluminous drapes. Gas lights with pink crystal shades threw out ambient light. She tried to imagine such a room in the Indian Territory and her husband with his Indian cheekbones and dark skin looked so out of place. For a moment a picture of Will Thunder Cloud, bare-chested on horseback, the wind blowing his hair, his rifle strapped to his back, a tomahawk at his belt, the plains and the buffalo in the background, loomed in her mind. He had been the handsomest man she'd ever known.

The rain picked up momentum, pinging against the windowpanes. Her mind ran wild. Tom Custer's devilish smile flashed in her brain, his hand cupping her chin. *He is nice looking but can't hold a candle to Will, but something about him ... Is it raining in Toledo*, she wondered? *Is he inside or out? I wish I could remember his voice. Is he reading or eating or playing his harmonica?* He told her he played the piano, too. He had even written a couple songs. She smiled. *I know he's not drinking. He doesn't drink around his family.* She shook herself. *You must quit these daydreams Abigail. You are going to make yourself crazy.*

Tom Custer leaned against the bar in the Bowling Green, Ohio Hotel just south of Toledo. The Custer family home farm where another brother, Nevin, lived was near Tontogany, an even smaller village than Bowling Green. He had ridden to Bowling Green to escape his family. Autie had followed him. Tom ordered a shot and a beer; Armstrong frowned and asked for a ginger ale. Tom could tell that tonight Armstrong would have liked a drink, but Tom also knew Autie would not return home smelling of booze and incur Libbie's wrath.

"What in the devil is wrong with you, Tommy?" asked George Custer. His voice shifted to a high pitch when angry.

It was close to shrill now. "Ma's in bed sick with a headache. Libbie won't speak to me. You cannot mention that Indian girl's name around Mother or Libbie. Great Scot," George also made a sincere effort to not use profanity, "especially don't ever say it with Ma and Libbie in the same room. And did you have to call Monaseetah, a princess?"

Many people considered Monaseetah a princess. Daughter of the Cheyenne chief, Little Rock, a member of Black Kettle's tribe, she certainly appeared beautiful enough and quick-thinking enough to be a princess. When the 7th Cavalry killed her father and brother, she quickly divorced her husband, Indian style, by shooting him in both kneecaps and arranged an immediate marriage with Yellow Hair.

Becoming the second wife of the colonel improved her status, but the supposed marriage gave fodder to George's wife and to his enemies. Major Marcus Reno and Captain Frederick Benteen, petty rivals of the Custers since the war, spread hateful rumors that both brothers slept with the Indian girl and while carousing with her were derelict in looking for Captain Elliott's troop who became lost in a snowstorm. While the rumors regarding Monaseetah caused domestic havoc for years, the charges of dereliction of duty brought on an official inquiry under United States Code Title 10,892, Article 92 and haunted him like a bad dream for years.

Now, standing at the bar in the Bowling Green Hotel, Tom rolled his fist in a wet spot on the mahogany surface. The Custers were fighters. At the sound of gunfire, they grabbed their rifles, jumped on their horses, and raced toward it. They rallied round any family member attacked. However, they fought fiercely among themselves. At the moment Tom's fist longed to punch Autie, but knowing Autie would probably court martial him prevented any altercation.

"You're the one who called her an aristocrat, one of the nobility. Do Indians even have an aristocracy? Or nobility? I couldn't remember those words so I called her a princess. She thinks she's a princess. She puts on airs like one. Anyway, Libbie knows Monaseetah is back in the picture. She told me she didn't care where you sleep as long as it wasn't anywhere near her." He shot a scowl at his brother. "Don't go blaming me if Libbie's upset. You're doing just fine all by yourself."

George removed the toothpick from between his teeth. His chest swelled. "Watch your mouth, Boy. I'll knock out a couple of your pearly whites." Both men prided themselves on their straight bright teeth. "Libbie might know about my philandering, but that doesn't mean she wants anyone else to know she knows, especially not Ma. And keep your ugly face out of Libbie and my business. That's her pride talking, Tommy. Don't you know anything about women?"

A barman brought their drinks. George frowned as Tom plunged the whiskey shot glass and all, into the beer mug and drank the boilermaker as it foamed. He shook his head in disapproval, but refrained from lecturing his younger brother on the evils of alcohol. Tommy had other sins to address.

"You still mooning over that blonde on the train? Good grief, she'll burn you, Boy. She's married to a half-breed. Her kids look Injun. In case you've forgotten, we're Indian fighters. We kill Indians. And her brother is Daniel Charteris. Remember him at Wilson's Creek? You don't want to mess with him. You're just asking for trouble."

George took a long pull of his ginger ale. **Garry Owen**, an ancient Irish ditty and now the 7th Cavalry's fight song, played on the piano. George Custer paused and took a deep breath. His voice softened. "Good Lord God Almighty, Tommy, I'm the last person who should be lecturing you on women, but mark my words that blonde is dangerous."

George took another swig of his ginger ale. "A girl who looks like she does…and built like she is… could have anybody. Something's not right with her being married to a half-breed." He shook his head. "What a waste."

They didn't speak for a few minutes, and then Autie leaned forward and put a hand on Tom's shoulder. "I'm really sorry about Lulie. Tuberculosis is such an ugly disease; takes them way too young. You do need a girl to settle down with."

Tom's face softened. They hadn't spoken of Lulie's death. **Garry Owen** repeated, a few men sang the lyrics. George's demeanor softened. He had an inordinate fondness for that song and for his family. "Want me to hit you upside the head?" He finished his drink and started to leave. "Do any of Libbie's girl-friends appeal to you? That Nettie is a doll."

"Nope."

"You didn't sleep with her, did you?"

"Go home, Autie. I'm a big boy. I can take care of myself."

"I've noticed," said Autie sarcastically. "How many sweet young things in northwestern Ohio named their baby boys Thomas?"

Tom held up both hands, palm out. "Whoa! Big brother! I can't stop the girls from wanting to snag me. I'm quite a catch. The famous Custer's brother and, in my own right, the winner of the Medal of Honor twice!" He took another long drink of beer. "Christ, Autie, I don't even know some of their names and wouldn't want to. Dad told me just to ignore them."

"Well, ignore the blonde. She is trouble."

Tom took another sip of his beer. "Well, Autie, don't we Custer boys look for trouble?"

<hr>

The rattling of the drinks cart snapped Abbey back to the present.

"We're supposed to be getting a nor'easter," said Mrs. Montour as she parked the cart bearing several crystal glasses, china cups, a tea service, bottles of sherry, whiskey, and wine, and a crystal bowl of ice. She looked at Will. She'd known him as a boy in Toronto when he'd visited his father, and had always liked him. His gray complexion and emaciation concerned her now. She remembered him as a handsome, robust youngster, but not now. "That's three days of storms. Let us pray it's rain not snow."

Tilley followed with a tray of pâté on toast points, soft cheeses on crackers, and finger sandwiches. Little radish roses decorated the platter. She glanced at Will who still dozed. "I invited Elliott, Dr. Elliott Cutter, for tea. He's a friend of Izzy's." Israel Hagan was Tilley's current boyfriend. Mrs. Montour abruptly left the room.

Color rose in Tilley's cheeks. She smiled but her tone iced. "Mrs. Montour tolerates only Canadians and some Americans. Elliott and Izzy are Scottish. They studied in Edinburgh and Austria. Both are gifted doctors. I would like Elliott to examine my brother."

Abbey wished her brother was still with them. The few hours on the train from Camelann to Philadelphia when Daniel had been with them were the only hours she'd felt safe since ... since Will became ill. Good God, please help me. *Fear has its teeth in me. How can I live without Will?*

A snippy voice inside her head, one that sounded a lot like her mother, said. *"You seemed to do fine outside Toledo!"*

Abbey's own voice spoke inside her head. *What is happening to me? I can't get him out of my mind. I'm daydreaming about him...Good Lord, I let him...what would Daniel think? Danny who would never dream of looking at another woman? And Will? He's the best man in the world.*

She stood and fixed her husband a glass of whiskey; she decided not to make one for herself. Liquor made her say and do stupid things. Will smiled and straightened up as she handed it to him. To Tilley, she asked. "Where may I freshen up?"

"Come with me." She led Abbey through the apartment to a large bedroom at the rear where a maid unpacked their trunk. Tilley stopped and hugged Abbey. "You look exhausted darling. You've come halfway across the continent." She motioned toward the bathroom. "I hear the doorbell. Take your time."

Chapter 6

THE CAMELANN NINE

Summer arranged the children around the dining room table. Boys outnumbered girls, six to three. Summer had invited Hal and Fanny St. Clair and their two boys, Hank and Charlie, to join them. Two Duprees, four St. Clairs, and six Charteris made twelve, nine children, three adults.

"Aren't you glad you added this big dining room?" asked Hal as he pulled out a chair for Fanny and put Charlie beside Johnnie, Summer's youngest boy. Last year she and Daniel had added a new kitchen and dining room with six bedrooms above, and upstairs and downstairs bathrooms to their cottage. No one called it a cottage anymore.

Summer nodded. "After the bathrooms, it is my favorite room. I must tell you though; hot and cold running water, flush toilets, and a septic system have changed my life. Thank you Hal, for introducing us to modern plumbing and sanitation."

"I can't take credit for it or I would," he said. "The French beat us on this one. Patents are pending on septic systems all over the world."

Emil's big innocent blue eyes looked up to his aunt. He appeared presentable tonight: bathed, trimmed hair, and wearing clean clothes. It had been a battle. He'd talked nonstop through the ordeal, and it was difficult to believe he was just five years old. After choking on a grape he told her not to worry. "It went down my esophagus not my trachea."

Now he asked, "You have two bedrooms downstairs and six upstairs. That makes eight. Why do you need so many?"

Summer frowned. "You count very well, Emil." She ticked off on her fingers. "We already have five children, Mac, Gus, Johnnie, Louisa, and Lilly, and we like to have room for guest, like you and Alice."

Hal, Daniel's law partner and best friend, said, "Knowing Daniel, you'll probably have at least six more kids."

Summer shot him a look and passed the rolls. She had suffered two miscarriages after Lilly was born; a heartache she didn't share. "Bite your tongue, Hal St. Clair. Fortunately, we both adore children." In an attempt to change the subject, she prompted Emil, "Tell your cousins about the train trip."

Emil nodded as he speared a slice of carrot. Mrs. Love had prepared creamed chicken with vegetables over egg noodles, which the children managed well. He held up the carrot slice and examined it. "A whole bunch of Custers were on the train. Tom, Autie's brother, spent a lot of time with us."

"Who is Autie?" asked Louisa. She sat between Alice and Lilly. Tonight the three girls dressed similarly: white ruffled pinafores over dark-colored wool dress with dark stockings. Although Alice and Lilly were only months apart in age, Alice's long legs made her appear much older. Lilly, too, was the baby of the family and liked that position. *Perhaps some time around Alice will be good for Lilly,* thought Summer.

Hank at twelve was the oldest cousin and quite a reader, answered. "Autie is George Armstrong Custer's nickname. All his friends call him Autie. It's short for Armstrong."

Summer said, "Tom Custer rode on the roof of the train with Alice and Emil, and he allowed Alice to wear his medals."

Petite, with ginger-colored hair, Hal's wife, Fanny lifted her perfectly plucked eyebrows. "Why, Miss Alice, it sounds like he's sweet on you?"

Alice blushed.

Hal said, "During the war, Tom didn't have an easy time of it. Just a kid when he came out to the Shenandoah to serve as Armstrong's aide-de-camp." Hal leaned over and wiped Charlie's mouth. "Armstrong gave Tom all the dirty work."

"What kind of dirty work?" asked Mac, Summer's oldest twin, blond, green-eyed, the spitting image of Daniel. Gussie, the other twin had Summer's dark coloring.

Summer knew a little about the dirty work. She'd been in the Shenandoah Campaign with them. General Grant decided on a scorched earth policy to end the war. He ordered the Shenandoah burnt, the livestock killed. "The Shenandoah can no longer be the breadbasket of the Confederacy."

She'd heard rumors of Tom killing the horses and burning barns. She did not want it discussed at her dinner table. "That's a question for your father, boys."

Hank had no intention of not impressing his cousins with juicy tidbits of Custer lore, said, "Tom Custer captured Rains-In-His-Face, a murderer, and embarrassed him in front of his friends. Rain vowed to kill Tom Custer, cut out his heart, and eat it."

Lilly, with her mop of dark curls, was hands down the drama princess and screaming champion of the valley, maybe even all of Pennsylvania. Now she screeched. "Eat his heart?" Her bright blue eyes were huge and her little hands crisscrossed her chest.

Summer Rose's diplomatic skills stretched. This is exactly what she wanted to avoid. Lilly, her youngest child, acted three rather than six. "Sit up straight, Lilly. I'm not sure that's true."

She set her napkin beside her plate. "Tom Custer cannot be all bad. I read where even George said Tom should be the Colonel of the 7th Cavalry instead of him, and the young man was awarded the Medal of Honor twice. Hal, what did he do to win the medals?" She regretted her words the minute they flew off her tongue. If it were bloody and gory the boys would talk of nothing else.

Fanny helped her out. "I knew Libbie, George's wife, quite well when we lived in Washington. Oh! Such beautiful clothes and gracious manners, her father was a judge in Michigan, very wealthy, and he doted on her. He had no time for George, though."

Hal groaned. "Not many people can tolerate George. He's arrogant, pompous, and he gets a lot of bad press and someone may shoot him in the back, but General Custer knows his military tactics, and he's one of the few officers who lead in front of his men. Most generals sit on a horse and watch from the rear, safe from any flying bullets. I'd like either Custer with me in battle." Hal looked at Alice; the little girl was about to burst into tears.

Hal, who would rather shoot himself in the foot than cause a girl to cry, said as he walked round the table and knelt beside her chair. "What's wrong, honey?"

The tears came. "I hope no one hurts Tom. He was so kind and he helped Mother so much. Can we not talk about this anymore?"

Hal brought her back to sit on his knee. He pulled peppermints from his pocket for all the children. "I will tell you miss, Tom Custer is one of the finest horsemen, I've ever encountered. I watched him jump his horse across a nineteen foot wide stream."

Summer tapped a spoon on her water glass. "Children, carry the dishes to the kitchen, scrape the plates, and stack them. Do not allow the dogs to lick the plates. We don't do that here. I heard a rumor the dessert is apple pie with whipped cream or Devil's Food Cake."

※

Abbey eyed the big bathtub and promised herself she'd take a long soak before bedtime. It had been at least a year since she'd seen a big tub, let alone stepped into one. A copper washtub had served her bathing needs in Pine Ridge. Life in Indian Territory didn't allow many luxuries.

Quickly, she washed her face and hands, sprinkled some talc under her arms, and put on a fresh, only slightly wrinkled, shirt. She unpinned her golden hair, brushed it then pulled it back and tied a wide black ribbon around it to lift it away from her face and off her neck, the way Will liked it. A touch of face powder, a dab of rouge, didn't do much to erase the tiredness. "However, at least I smell a little better."

Tilley introduced her to Israel Hagan—Izzy—her current boyfriend, a serious young man with dark hair and darker circles beneath smoldering gray eyes. Another older, barrel-chested man bent over her husband. He listened with a stethoscope to Will's chest. Between forty-five and fifty-five, with a full head of fiery red hair, tamed by streaks of gray, his large straight teeth flashed a smile then he turned back to Will. Abbey liked him immediately. She took a seat and waited.

Finally, he removed the earpieces and took Abbey's hand. "I'm Elliott Todd Cutter." I believe I can help your husband." He smiled disarmingly, his voice soft and warm, his eyes crinkled at the corners. "I know Cutter isn't the best name for a doctor." He grinned to Will then back to her, showing his big white teeth. "My students call me *Et Cetera* after my initials ETC." He paused and smiled again, "or better yet, just call me Elliott. I believe we'll become good friends."

He looked to Will. "As you all suspected you are ill, Mr. Dupree. Your heart is not working quite right. I'd like you to come and see me at Jefferson Hospital in the morning. We cannot cure your heart, but perhaps some medicine will improve your quality of life."

He nodded to Will's drink. "Whiskey in moderation is good. He held up two fingers. "Two ounces of whiskey in the evening and one in the morning." He shook his big head. "No more. You aren't one of those Indians, who cannot drink alcohol, are you?"

Both Abbey and Will shook their heads. They knew of such men, but Will wasn't one of them.

He handed Will a pill. "Digitalis. It's made from foxglove. My colleagues in Edinburgh developed it in pill form." He smiled. "We are not sure how it works, but it does work."

He held out a small envelope to Abbey. "One in the morning and one with dinner." He didn't release the envelope when Abbey went to take it. "Mrs. Dupree, you look exhausted. May I fix you a sherry?"

"Yes please, Elliott." She motioned to her husband. "And we are Will and Abbey." *One glass of wine won't hurt.* She took a seat on the big round ottoman beside Will's feet, leaning against his leg, happy to have some hope. Tilley and Israel sat on the sofa speaking in soft voices. Elliott fixed himself a whiskey on ice, her sherry then a plate of appetizers.

Dr. Cutter handed Abbey her wine and placed the plate on the ottoman. Will went to move his legs, but the doctor held up his hand. He leaned toward them. "That's for the three of us," he motioned with his hands, "We are a team. I find holding a drink and a plate, and talking at the same time difficult." He smiled. "The heart is a pump." He moved his hand, squeezing and releasing his fist several times. "Your heart is tired, Will. It finds it difficult to do more than one thing at a time, too. Keeping your brain, your lungs, your digestive track working and doing much else is a strain for this amazing organ. I find the heart seems to be very intelligent; when threatened it slows down and only does what is absolutely necessary to just keeps you alive."

Dr. Elliott Cutter took a toast point and a sip of his drink. "Tonight. Relax. You'll find the little pill will give you energy."

⚛

"Monaseetah, that Indian girl? You've seen her again?" asked Mrs. Custer to her son, George. She'd cornered him in the stable. "She has a son?"

"Ma...don't start."

Her voice smoldered with sarcasm. George hated it when Ma's tongue came out of the sheath. Rapier sharp, her words aimed for the jugular. "Tell me. Is Libbie really barren or just cold?"

George didn't respond.

Mrs. Custer blinked. "I knew that girl had ice water in her veins the minute I laid eyes on her. Guess it doesn't matter. I heard this Monaseetah had a yellow child. They say the squaw's beautiful, and they say you married her, and some say her baby is yours and others say Tom fathered him." Her voice cracked like a whip. "Whose is it?"

George's voice slid up an octave. "Ma, quit reading those scandal sheets. None of it is true."

"I didn't read that in any newspaper."

"Who? Did Bos tell you? I'll kill him."

"Don't you go hurting Boston. His candle doesn't burn too bright, but he doesn't lie."

George's voice was real high now. "Ma, why are you so angry with me? I can't stand it."

"You know I'd never reject any child, but I'd prefer to not have a yellow grandchild. I want a nice white baby." She reached up and touched his hair. "One, with nice blond curls. You and Tommy were such darling little tow heads, white blond, and in the summer you both were brown as walnuts."

Her expression changed. "I told you that Libbie Bacon would be trouble, too high and mighty for the likes of us. If she won't give you a baby, find some girl who will. I don't care if it's legitimate, just white and blond."

"Don't go blaming Libbie," said George. "She's the best thing that ever happened to me. Or Tommy. All kinds of lies float around about Tommy and me. None of them are true."

Mrs. Custer hugged her son. "You've always been my favorite, Autie. I can't help it. I just love you so much."

⚞⚟

Mrs. Montour walked into the living room bearing a silver tray with the glass of tepid lemon water on it. "As you requested, Dr. Cutter," said Mrs. Montour with a wide smile.

"Oh, yes. Thank you, Violet." He took Will's glass and poured half of the lemon mixture into the whiskey. "It's not necessary, but best if you dilute his drinks with lemon water. I'll write that down for you."

Abbey shook her head and squeezed Will's ankle. "I'll remember."

Chapter 7

PILLOW TALK

Will walked into Tilley's guest room and stood gawking for a minute. He wasn't used to such opulence. Blue and white wallpaper, carved white woodwork, cornflower blue silk drapes, and a matching comforter under a white lace counterpane on the huge bed greeted him. Dutch tiles surrounded the fireplace where a cozy fire burned. "Wow! This is nice." He noticed too the bed covers were turned down, and their night clothes—Abbey had made him two nightshirts for the trip—one now neatly folded sat on a pillow. Life in the Indian Territory didn't offer such touches.

Abbey quickly started to fill the tub, sprinkled in bath salts then helped Will remove his boots and socks. He loosened her stays then cocked an ear toward the bathroom. "You'd better check the tub. I can manage."

She grabbed her nightgown and robe and stepped into the bathroom. The scent of jasmine enveloped her; bubbles rose in the tub. With abandonment, she tossed her clothes in a corner and stepped into the tub. The soft warm water felt almost as good as it smelled. A faint tap sounded at the door and Will peeked around it. "I'm praying you are not decent. Want your back washed?"

A smile and tears both came unbidden. She slid to one side. He dropped his towel and climbed in beside her. The tub nearly overflowed.

"I like how you fixed your hair." He smiled shyly. "Nothing may come of this, but let's just enjoy this big lovely tub."

※

They awoke to a harsh rain slashing against the transom. Distant thunder rumbled over the city with the only light coming from the streetlamps. "It sounds like an all day rain," said Abbey.

"I've always loved the sound and smell of rain." He reached over and pulled her close. "You still smell of jasmine. Last night was perfect. Thank you."

She snuggled against him, skin on skin. "How did we manage success? Do you think it was the pill? Digitalis, I think."

He shrugged. "Maybe. No children, the rain. I liked the doctor. I wanted to call him Dr. Etcetera. I relaxed. The warm bath helped. I like how he explained what's happening with my body. I haven't been happy with what was not happening between us. I guess I have hope now. I liked too how your body was all silky, smelling of jasmine, and you, all soft and willing. You are wonderful. I love you, Abbey Yellow Bird. You deserve more than a broken down half-breed."

"You certainly weren't broken down last night." Waves of guilt swamped her. She didn't want to cry so she added. "I think it was the lemon juice."

He felt her smile. "Camelann has a greenhouse and lemons already." His arm lay across her waist. "What happens between us is important. For a Frenchman or for that matter for an Indian man to lose his ability to please a woman, especially a woman like you, is to ...well, he becomes an old man."

His fingers played with her hair. "What would you think of moving to Camelann? Building a house there? I'd be close to these doctors. I'd like to spend more time with my mother, Splashing Rabbit, and your family. Our students on the reservation can take over the school there. We might have to go back for a month or so to get them started, and, now with the train we could visit a couple times a year to check out your school." Abbey and Mary Hathaway had designed the school, and the curriculum. "You could teach here, and Daniel has hinted he'd like my help. It would be safer, too. No bloodthirsty Cavalry and renegade Indians creating havoc. You have to admit, Camelann is a beautiful place for children."

A shaft of lightening lit the room followed by an earth-cracking clap of thunder. She rolled tight against his side. "I thought you never wanted to leave your long hills or the real mountains? You didn't want to become civilized."

He motioned around the room. "I don't need all these trappings, but you have to admit the bathtub is nice. And if I do die, I'd like you and the children here with Daniel and Summer. You, my gorgeous wife, need someone to protect you." He reached over and touched her breast. "I see how men look at you. They all want you. Tom Custer was good to protect you on the train." He smiled. "However, I caught him watching you, too."

Another shaft of lightening lit the room. "No talk of dying or someone to protect me. We'll move to Camelann and have more babies. Can we do that? I'll teach; you can help with the horses." The thought vaulted through her mind that she could be pregnant with another man's child right now. *Good God, please, please help me.* Half of her wanted Tom's child, the other half thought she'd lost her mind. *Such a child would never pass muster as part Indian.*

※

Five hundred miles west of Philly, Tom Custer opened his eyes. A streetlamp illuminated a whiskey flask and a couple of glasses on a hotel dresser, his jacket hung on one bedpost, a woman's stocking hung on another. He turned his head and saw the mass of red hair on the pillow beside him. He groaned. Pieces of the previous evening roared back into memory---another night in the Bowling Green Hotel. He grabbed his clothes and ran to the bathroom. He brushed his teeth—all the Custers, vain about their white, straight teeth, carried a toothbrush and powder with them. Everywhere. He made plenty of noise.

He heard movement in the adjoining room and gave the woman enough time. Then he stepped into the still dark room. He couldn't remember exactly what happened but he noticed dollar bills on the dresser. He'd paid her last night so now he held her coat—what was her name? He kissed her forehead, and escorted her to the door, tucking the money into her hand. "Goodnight, sweet girl. Thank you." As the lock clicked he fell facedown onto the bed and stuck his head under the pillow.

Holy Mother of God! How many boilermakers did I drink? I've got to stop this!

Good Lord, Autie, you just don't quit with the lectures, do you? "Loose women, they'll kill you, Tommy," *he said. On and on, he harped.* "Keep Ma and Libbie from fighting and do not let Boston run off at the mouth."

How on earth, am I to do that? Then he again yells about how I need to make sure Ma and Libbie don't claw out each others' eyes. Christ, he went on and on about how to kill Indians efficiently. He doesn't like the Gatling Guns. "It wastes ammunition. If you run across a whole mess of 'em," *he said,* "and have time to pitch in and set it up, go ahead, but our men should all be good enough marksmen to just pick the buggers off."

"Now, horses, Tommy, if at all possible, do not let the horses see the guns if you have to kill them. Remember down on the Washita when we had to put down eight hundred of them? And the squaws and children tried to save them. In the snow..."

Tom thought of Alice and Emil, they could well be the children in the camps...their blood in the snow. He shuddered. *Not her beautiful bright children.*

I told him I didn't want to do any of it anymore. I'll do all the paperwork, I'll be quartermaster, but I'm done with the killing. If someone's shooting at us, I'll protect the men. I'm not that stupid, but I'm done. Tom punched his pillow again and gave a half laugh, half groan. *That sure didn't sit well. He went on a tirade about how dangerous women were.* "Stay away from the real pretty ones, *Tommy, the ones with the big tits. They'll make you crazy. Look for plain girls, dark little mice."*

Tom shook his head and spoke aloud. *"I made the mistake of saying Libbie certainly wasn't any little dark mouse."*

He screamed at me. "And look at the trouble I have keeping her happy." He punched me hard.

Tom clenched and unclenched his fists. *Christ, I came close to punching him. I should have, but no, I drank a bucketful of boilermakers instead and brought the redhead up here. He punched his pillow again and sat up. I am sick to death of him preaching to me. Ma, you're going to be madder than hell, but I can't do this anymore. Taking care of Autie is like babysitting a box of rattlers. I'm not sixteen. I'm thirty. I'm sick of the killing and I think I'm in love? I have a reason to live.*

He rolled over and stared out at the lightening sky. *I know she's trouble, Autie, more than you can imagine. She's married to a decent man, too. Can't believe he's half Indian? Isn't that a cracker? I'd be ashamed if she knew the things I've done, but I've never met anyone like her. I cannot quit thinking about her. I want to do something to make her proud of me. I want her to love me. And I want to protect her. What if she was lost and ended up in one of the tent towns popping up along the railroads? They must be a preview of hell: not a blade of grass or a tree within miles, ankle deep dust, and full of the scum of the earth, gambling joints, tent stills, all lined up along the tracks, tent whorehouses, not a church or school in sight. Deserters like her first husband, Kincaid, are hiding up there or in the caves along the western Yellowstone.*

In his mind, he again held her face, felt her spasm and quiver. *Oh Ma, you always worry about Autie. I deserve a life too. He* punched his pillow again and was surprised to find it wet. *How in the hell did that happen?*

⚎

His older brother didn't sleep much either, not with Libbie beating him with the pillow until feathers flew, then she threw his pillow and a blanket into the hall. She screamed at him, not caring if the whole house woke up. "Don't plan on coming back here until you send Her Highness and her yellow bastard back to Texas. Send Tom. He's good at cleaning up your messes."

⚎

Daniel slept well at the guesthouse. His dinner with Alan Durant, an inventor, had been a resounding success. The young man had dozens of sketches of innovative devices from an improved axle on a three-wheeled cycle to a corn-picking machine. All were patentable and the inventor wanted the law firm of St. Clair and Charteris to file them in the Patent Office.

He awoke to a steady rain and the rumble of thunder with his mind brimming with ideas. He bought an umbrella at a street vendor's stand, took a long stroll around the city, and treated himself to a shave and a haircut, then walked to Tilley's apartment. Of course, he was early because he always got up with the crows. However, Mrs. Montour spotted him from the kitchen window, quietly fetched him then steered him into the cozy sitting room. All starched and corseted, the housekeeper took his coat and umbrella to the kitchen to dry and brought him coffee and the papers. Her efficiency impressed him.

Dr. Emily St. Clair, Hal's little sister, rushed into the room and kissed him hello. "Nice haircut, Uncle Danny. You smell great. I am running to check on a baby about to pop into the world. Don't you love it? Little Emily is now a doctor. I will be up at Jefferson later today. I hope to see you there." She dashed out the door.

Daniel shook his head. Way back before he met Summer, he'd considered asking Emily to a school dance, and now she was calling him Uncle Danny! At times he felt ancient.

He had just resumed reading when a courier arrived with a message for Tilley. Mrs. Montour fetched her, and Tilley came into the hall in a robe, read the message, scribbled a return note, waved to him then ran back to her room. Will and Abbey wandered into the sitting room, holding hands and looking happier than they did last night.

Mrs. Montour announced. "Breakfast is served."

※

Summer awakened with Emil's foot in her stomach. Lilly was tucked under her arm with Johnnie and Alice asleep on Daniel's pillow. Thunder and lightning had brought them to her bed, but the storms had passed. She straightened them all and made sure they were snug under the quilt, and wiggled deeper into the covers hoping to dream again of gingersnaps and Daniel, at least until the sun came up. However, a tap sounded on the hall door. The twins with Louisa, Hank, and Charlie surrounded the foot of the bed. All were combed and dressed and smelling of toothpowder. Mac spoke. "Hank and Charlie want to see the eagles' nest. It's important we get there before dawn. Can we go with them?"

Summer sat up clutching a pillow to her chest. "First, Mac, it's *may* we go, not *can* we go." They looked so serious and young, she decided to forego the grammar lecture; it was also too early. "Yes, you may, but first eat something. Don't make a mess and wear jackets. Leave a note for Mrs. Love."

Johnnie and Emil climbed out of bed to join the gang. Alice threw back the covers. "Give me a minute to get dressed. I'd better make sure an eagle doesn't carry him off."

Summer watched them file out of the room. They looked so young. Except for Hank, Hal and Fanny's oldest son, they'd all been born after the war. She pulled Lilly with her and stood.

"Wait for us."

Chapter 8

OPINIONS

Camelann didn't have a hospital. Dr. Ray Stone, who served in the war with Daniel and Hal and who had close ties with the Charteris and St. Clair families, was the resident physician. He treated patients in their homes, and family members cared for the ill. Ray also liked to fish whenever possible, and he lectured at both the medical schools of Thomas Jefferson University and the University of Pennsylvania so he often was not available. At such times, Summer Rose or Wakanda took charge. Summer traveled to the home; Wakanda treated his patients and her Indian children from the entrance to her tipi.

Jefferson Hospital sprawled over a city block. The masses, often immigrants who left their families in Europe, the orient, or Africa, when ill flocked to the hospital and were cared for by strangers. Daniel had visited army hospitals during the war so the size of the hospital didn't surprise him. The cleanliness did. Every surface gleamed, the entire hospital smelled of disinfectant and chlorine. A sign in the lavatory read: **WASH YOUR HANDS. CLEANLINESS IS NEXT TO GODLINESS.**

Toward the end of the war and shortly afterwards Army doctors on both sides learned the value of such a simple thing as hand washing and saved the lives of countless soldiers and new mothers. The obvious results ushered in the sanitary age and dramatically changed medicine.

One particular incident buzzed around hospitals. At the end of the war, the Confederate surgeons unable to acquire basic supplies innovated. In lieu of thread for sutures, the surgeons used the long hair from horsetails and manes, boiling it, not to clean it but to soften it. The results were astonishing. Cleanliness became the new manifesto.

Emily and Tilley waited with Abbey outside Elliott Cutter's office. Will had allowed only Daniel to accompany him. "I don't care if you are a doctor, Tilley. I do not want women poking me."

Abbey ignored his prejudice. She had recognized Indians were no better than whites in their prejudices and generalizations. "Are the appointments always this long?" asked Abbey.

Tilley shrugged. "Elliott's meticulous."

Just then the door opened and Elliott motioned them to come inside. His assistant, a young man with severe acne scars, brought chairs for everyone. Will reclined under a sheet on a narrow examining table. Abbey took the chair closest to him.

Once everyone was seated, Dr. Cutter held up a fistful of papers. He handed one to Abbey. "I am suggesting many, many changes to your way of life. Here is a sensible diet. I follow this myself." He looked around the small room. "You will all benefit from it. Only three eggs per week, limit your salt, and each morning ingest a teaspoonful of apple cider vinegar and in the evening take a spoonful of olive oil. Please drink the three whiskeys with the lemon every day, and eat calves liver once a week. I gave Will pills: the small ones as needed for pain and the large one every morning. I have spoken extensively about changing Will's habits. Come back next Thursday."

Daniel interrupted. "Our national day of Thanksgiving is next Thursday. Tilley, Emily, and your friend, Israel, will be joining us at Camelann for a couple days. Tilley tells me your family is in Scotland. Please join us? We're making it both a day of thanksgiving and remembrance of those who gave their lives in the war. The trains make travel easy."

⚌

At exactly eleven o'clock on Thanksgiving morning, a large party consisting of Will, Abbey, Tilley, Izzy, Elliott, and Mrs. Montour-detrained at Morgan's Corner. That morning, Summer instructed Lobo to hitch the enormous black Percherons, Romeo and Juliette, to the big red, yellow-wheeled wagon which possessed benches and sidewalls. Earlier Summer and the children had festooned it with bells, cornstalks, Indian corn, and ropes of dried flowers, for the guests and their luggage. She wore her bright cardinal red riding habit and hugged, kissed, introduced herself, if necessary, and shook hands with everyone. She and Daniel rode Rabbit and Chester, leading the party to the top of Forty Foot Falls where a huge bonfire waited with Hal and Fanny, Wakanda, and the children, Indian and white, and a chuck wagon loaded with two drums of hot cider, one with a bite and one without, and Mrs. Love's famous apple cider donuts. Daniel lit a match; the fire swooshed to life. Everyone cheered.

When settled and served, Abbey walked over and hugged Summer. "Thank you for caring for the children. I don't think they missed me at all. And thanks for this warm welcome. You are so creative, the horses, the bells, and all this. She gestured to the chuck wagon. Look at the children. They love it." Abbey sighed. In a soft voice, she said, "Look at my Will. Doesn't he look happy?"

Summer hugged her sister-in-law. "You look happy, too."

Abbey nodded to Dr. Cutter who stood with Will at the top of the falls overlooking the fields and forests of Camelann. "I am. Elliott's kindnesses and attention have been monumental. He stops by the apartment every morning to supervise Will's medicine, to listen to his chest, and to accompany Will on a short walk." She lifted the cup of hard cider to her lips allowing the steam to warm her cheeks, then she took a big swallow. "And he comes by every afternoon for tea and repeats the ministrations and the walk. Each walk is a touch longer. Will's stamina has improved already."

Abbey hugged Summer again. "We have such hope. How have you been?"

Summer blinked and lowered her voice. "I think I'm expecting another child." She joined her hands in front of her stomach. "I have all the signs and soon I'll be big as a house."

Abbey squeezed her hand. Thoughts of a possible child growing inside her belly sent waves of fear and guilt through her. She hid the emotions well. "Are you happy?"

"I am happy, a little nervous. Daniel will be thrilled. He wants a houseful of children, and ... Don't mention this to anyone. Daniel should know first, don't you think?"

They linked arms and walked over to the group around Elliott and Will. Elliott stepped aside. "Mrs. Charteris." He motioned to the fire, the chuck wagon, and the view. "What a welcome!"

"Please, it's Summer. We aren't formal here. Are you enjoying the donuts?"

Dr. Elliott Cutter, tall and heavy boned, nonetheless appeared slim. He snapped his braces. "Yes." He touched Abbey's arm and held up a finger. "Allow our Willie one donut." He waved the finger. "He must watch his diet. Plain, simple food."

Abbey took Will's hand, pressing it to her cheek then kissing it. "Tell them about the medicine."

Dr. Cutter loved an enthusiastic audience, especially one of attractive women. "There are two medicines. They've been in use in Europe for some time. Nitroglycerin, made of the same elements that makes bombs go BOOM, and another derived from foxglove. You know the flower? From foxglove we distill Digitalis. It's actually an ancient folk herbal remedy. Welsh legends tell of how the wee folk, fairies gave it to us." Elliott's face grew smooth but his eyes twinkled. "Fairies, you know, lurk in foxglove, they hide in its bell-like blossoms."

He grew serious and continued, "The amounts of Digitalis must be monitored. Foxglove grows in Europe, the British Isles, Asia, even here. Elsewhere it's called 'bloody fingers, lambs-tongue, fairy-folk-fingers. It relaxes the blood vessels; the heart does not work so hard." He smiled at his patient. "We are going to improve our Willie's diet and strengthen him in the proper manner."

Summer took Will's arm and clasped his hand, noticing for the first time the tattoo of a lightning strike on his wrist. She didn't make a fuss about it but planned to ask Will or Abbey about it later. "When we first met Will, he was one of the healthiest and strongest men I've ever known." She grinned devilishly at her brother-in-law and Abbey. "Also, one of the handsomest. I have some photographs at the house. I'll show you." She elbowed her brother-in-law and grinned at Dr. Cutter. "Is he allowed seconds on the cider? It is a holiday." She hollered to everyone. "Last call for the cider."

Elliott stepped up beside her. "Of course he can have another cup of cider. I'll have a second also. Now tell me Summer, how on earth has your husband acquired so much land?"

She looked away, returning her attention to Dr. Cutter. She stuttered a little. "Is-isn't that the true wonder of America? My father emigrated from Scotland. Widowed, with five sons and a little gold, he acquired about a thousand acres, which included the lake and falls before he met my mother. Shortly after they married, his two youngest sons died of yellow fever. Immediately, he and my mother moved here with his three remaining sons. I was born and grew up here. My first memories were of living in a one room cabin."

Daniel took over the telling. "So with a Scottish laird for a father, a Philadelphia debutante for a mother, and three wild brothers who tossed trees—they are called cabers—around for sport, my Summer Rose flourished." His big hand rested on her shoulder. "Her parents provided a classic education, and in addition, her mother taught her French, the piano, style, and proper decorum. Her father and brothers taught her to track, shoot, throw a knife, climb trees, swim, and ride horses." He kissed her cheek. "My girl can blow out the eye of a buck at nine hundred yards."

Summer grimaced and blushed. "Just how every girl wants to be known, right? I guess I was what you might call a tomboy. I do know I was angry as a wet cat that I couldn't toss cabers, too."

Her voice thickened; her expression changed. "At Antietam, my father and my two oldest brothers died." She placed a hand over her heart. Her breath caught, and her voice hitched. She gestured toward the south ridge. "It's been thirteen years. You'd think I'd be okay," she brushed away a tear, "but I'm not." She had everyone's attention now. "Maryland is on the other side of the mountains, not far as the crow flies. Lee was poised to invade our homeland. They died stopping him."

She swallowed and recovered her composure. "Jack, my remaining brother, didn't want the land so Daniel and Hal bought it. The story is more involved but essentially after Daniel and I married, Hal and Daniel purchased adjoining farms as they came up for sale during the war, gradually increasing the acreage to twelve thousand acres. Most of the tillable land is now leased by veterans, men who served with Daniel and Hal."

"Quite a tale," said Dr. Cutter. "Willie speaks of tracts of thousands and thousands of square miles out west. I cannot imagine." The size of America and Will's Indian background fascinated Dr. Cutter. He motioned with his hands. "Tumbleweeds as big as shoats rolling over the prairie, can you imagine? Before I return to

Scotland, I hope to ride the train across your country. What is it? A week to travel from New York to San Francisco?"

Summer clapped her hands then swept her arm to the big red wagon with the yellow wheels. "Everyone into the wagon please. Next stop is our house where we will see you to your rooms and allow you to rest for a few minutes then we're off to the Indian School for Thanksgiving Dinner." She looked down. Emil with his shirt hanging loose and his dark hair a wild tangle slid his hand into hers. She leaned down and whispered to him. "Now, do you understand why I need eight bedrooms?"

His big blue eyes looked up and he winked. "I think you need a hotel."

⚜

After prayers and an abundant Thanksgiving Dinner, Daniel sold a horse to each doctor, which pleased everyone involved. Daniel promised delivery in the spring. On Saturday morning, Summer transported the majority of the guests to the train station in the big farm wagon. Daniel drove Will and Dr. Cutter in the more comfortable and enclosed buggy. Will brought up the idea of him and Abbey turning the Pine Ridge School in the Dakota Territory on the reservation over to the Indian teachers, and permanently moving to Camelann. "We would need to return to the Pine Ridge School for a few weeks to start them on the right track."

Elliott and Daniel applauded the idea. Elliott spoke. "However, Willie such a distance right now would not be good for you, perhaps in the spring. Would Abbey go by herself?"

Will and Daniel looked at each other and shook their heads. Will said, "She would, but a woman alone on the train would be dangerous. And a woman like Abbey alone is never a good idea. Tom Custer did offer to accompany us on the return trip. He'd be the perfect escort. He's perceptive."

Daniel interjected. "I always liked Tom. He handled himself well in the Shenandoah. I think he's a good choice. Do you have an address for him?"

Will handed Daniel Tom's card.

"I'll get in touch with him."

"Is the West really so wild?" asked Elliott.

Nine children on seven ponies—the Camelann Nine as they called themselves-- surrounded the buggy. Some wore feathers, some cowboy hats, all whooped and waved.

Will chuckled and pointed out his children to Elliott. "Emil wears the full Indian headdress; Alice has a headband and a buckskin dress. There is your Wild West, Elliott. Except out west it's real. Camelann is a safe place." He waved to Alice and Emil. He was proud to see they were the best riders in the bunch.

"To answer your question, can you trust any red-blooded soldier around Abbey? Half of the enlisted men can barely speak English, many are petty criminals. They only joined the army to escape jail and are looking for a chance to desert. The officers are a little better but they're all starved to see a white woman. Tom was wise on the trip out here. And to be candid, Abbey's reputation is compromised enough now by just being married to me. Why would a respectable white woman marry a heathen? I'm not a heathen but people assume I am. We'd need at least another woman to travel with Tom and her. Could Summer go with her?"

Daniel took a deep breath. He suspected his wife's pregnancy and waited for her announcement. Instead of telling these men, he said, "Summer would no doubt jump at the chance for such an adventure. But you are not leaving me with all these children? They might kill each other." He shook his head. "Or me."

Elliott grinned. The big red-painted farm wagon with the yellow wheels pulled up to the station. The Indians and cowboys surrounded it. Summer and Abbey both stood with their hands raised, playing along with the children. Abbey wore a fitted dark green coat, and Summer wore what she often wore around the farm: Indian trousers and a jacket, both fringed and made of walnut-colored buckskin. Both women looked stunning.

Dr. Cutter opened the carriage door and stepped down. "I don't want to hear either of you complaining again. You are paying the price for marrying exquisite women. If you need a chaperone, consider Mrs. Montour. She and Tilley are at each other's jugulars. They could use a hiatus from each other. Mrs. Montour would make an excellent chaperone with Abbey and this Custer fellow. He's really George Armstrong Custer's brother? I hope to meet him." America's Wild West fascinated Dr. Cutter. "Do you know Wild Bill Hickok?"

Will said, "Yes, we do; we know Wild Bill, Annie Oakley, and Buffalo Bill Cody." He grinned. I can introduce you to Sitting Bull, Crazy Horse and some of my relatives." His face grew serious. "Do you think Mrs. Montour would go along with it? They'd be gone about a month and it's winter?" asked Will.

Daniel said, "I think so. I noticed the tension between Tilley and Violet. She impressed me as one iron-willed lady. And she's Canadian so the weather shouldn't intimidate her. Let me ask her." He grinned. "She likes me."

⊰⊱

While Will wasn't racing through the streets of Philadelphia, he continued to improve under Dr. Cutter's attention. A close friendship grew between the two men. After their morning constitutional, Abbey or Mrs. Montour fixed them a simple breakfast of oatmeal, fruit, and tea. Daniel, on his next trip to Philadelphia, spoke with Tilley and Mrs. Montour, separately, about Violet accompanying Abbey to Indian Territory. Both women privately agreed; a vacation from each other was just the right move for both.

Tom Custer received Daniel's telegram the same day he learned Autie and Libbie had made arrangements to spend New Year's in New York. The possibility existed that Armstrong would be called to Washington to testify before Congress regarding one of many scandals threatening to topple President Grant's administration.

George Armstrong Custer eagerly wanted to testify. Secretary of War William Belknap's second wife, Carrie, secured a lucrative army post tradership at Fort Sill for a Mr. John Evans. Reportedly Mrs. Belknap received $6,000 per year for this service, and after her death in 1870 her husband continued to receive the payment from Mr. Evans. Many government agencies, which affected not only Armstrong's troops but also the Indian and their allotments, were rife with fraud.

Tom and Autie both knew Secretary of War Belknap's fingers were thick in this mess.

Last summer Autie complained to General Phil Sheridan who acknowledged his own frustration, but advised Armstrong to stay clear of the scandal.

"Whatever you do, do not make President Grant, his administration, or anyone close to him look bad. Ulysses is ass-deep in scandals. Never forget, Armstrong, all promotions and postings cross his desk. Even you could find yourself posted on the Canadian border, far from your beloved 7th. Need I say more?"

⁂

Tom wired acceptance to Daniel, spoke with his parents, and made travel arrangements for himself and his new blood bay thoroughbred, Toledo, to arrive in Camelann on Sunday at dusk, the day after Christmas.

⁂

Abbey and Will spent a magical few days before Christmas with the children at Camelann. Dr. Cutter visited, also. The weather remained unseasonably mild. In addition to Will's daily constitutionals, the three of them took easy horseback rides exploring Camelann. The children, adorned in feathers and cowboy hats, captured and rescued them several times.

Evenings consisted of cards and conversations, music, and parlor games. Dr. Cutter and Reverend Tuttle discovered a mutual love of all things Scottish including good whiskey and Bobby Burns' poetry.

On the Sunday after Christmas, as Will and Abbey left vespers, she looked to the stone bridge as she always did. They planned to take the carriage over to the ground where their new house was to be built. She spotted the beautiful blood bay and an army officer riding over the high arch into Camelann. The men each thought the other told her the plans. They had not. When she recognized the rider, she fainted.

Through a haze she became aware of Tom taking control just as he had done at the railroad station in Pine Ridge. The weeks of Dr. Cutter's ministrations, the quiet, relaxing honeymoon-like atmosphere in Tilley's peaceful apartment (no children, no stress) had mended the scars in their marriage. Now as she regained consciousness, she heard Tom Custer's rumbling voice, and like a rock dropping on her heart, the guilt and desire roared back onto Abbey.

"Excuse me. Step aside, please. Give her some air." He winked at Alice and squeezed Emil's arm and whispered. "I think she just fainted. She'll be okay. Alice, fetch your mother a cup of water from the pump. Emil, please hitch Toledo. That's a good boy."

His army great coat came with a removable cape. Swinging it free from his shoulders, he tucked it around her. Will knelt beside him; they shook hands. He gestured toward a lone carriage parked in front of the chapel. "Is that your carriage?"

Will nodded, his hand caressed her cheek. Tom felt the passion, saw it in Will's face, the movement of his hands. Her husband's raw emotion choked him. This man loved her every bit as much as he did. And for a fleeting second he sensed they both knew it, but something broke the moment and it was lost.

She took the water from Alice, sipped a little, smiled at the people gathered about her, and started to sit up. Will took her arm and together, he and Tom helped her to stand. Tom steered Will to her far side, while Dr. Cutter, mumbling, "I'm her doctor," took Tom's place.

He smiled at Tom, who held the door as Abbey settled inside the carriage, and asked, "So you're the famous Custer?"

Tom's twinkling eyes flashed to Abbey's pale face and his voice softened. He realized no one had told her the plans. "No, I'm the other Custer. Her brother hired me to escort Mrs. Dupree and another woman to the reservation. And you are, Sir?"

"I'm Elliott Todd Cutter, Willie's doctor," said Elliott, his brogue announcing his Scottish roots. Abbey's face turned milk-white. She would have fainted again except Dr. Cutter's strong fingers cracked a tiny glass vial of ammonia he had taken to carrying in case Will grew lightheaded. He held it under her nose.

She jerked upright and choked, tears running down her face.

Elliott chuckled. "See, the ammonia works. I know it seems a little cruel, but it certainly gets the ticker ticking. You might be wise Major Custer to carry some of these capsules with you." He held up a long mesh-covered glass vial, the mesh cleverly in place to catch the broken glass. "It's very thin glass; I'll make sure you have some."

⚜

She had always been able to talk with Summer. Not now. How could she admit such a blatant sin? She considered speaking to Reverend Tuttle, but he was married to her mother. That wouldn't do! Flora would never let it rest. Daniel? She couldn't bear to look so heartless in Daniel's eyes. Will was fighting for his life. The selfishness of her actions twisted and tightened around her chest, cutting into her as if it were barbed wire. *How can I be so selfish?* However, nothing stopped her irreverent thoughts.

Chapter 9

A DANGEROUS JOURNEY

As Summer stacked clean, wet dishes in the wooden rack, she said to Tom Custer. "You don't look much older than you did during the war."

Tom picked up a dishtowel and grinned. He had stayed here in Camelann while Abbey and Will returned to Philadelphia so she could pack her trunk. They planned to depart from Morgan's Corner on the 6:03 morning train to Pittsburgh on Wednesday. "Don't flatter me, Summer. I was a *wet-behind-the-ears-dumb-kid* then.

"I'm not now. Libbie took me under her wing and hammered proper manners into me. She graduated from a girls' school in Michigan. She ordered all the books on her reading list. I read everything from Beowulf to Sir Walter Scott and Dickens, all of Shakespeare, the American authors, too. My brother gave me every government pamphlet on military protocol he could find. They both tested me. I was always good at math. Autie hired an artillery officer to teach me trigonometry. The war took the boy out of me."

He shook his head. "And Armstrong cut me no slack because we were related. If a message needed to be delivered in the middle of the night, through a blinding snowstorm into enemy territory, it was me who delivered it." He puffed out his cheeks. "I had chubby chipmunk cheeks then." He chuckled. "And freckles not …." He touched the scar from a rebel bullet on his cheek. "Remember?"

She nodded. A picture of him as a teenager came to mind, and she had to admit, too, his manners were impeccable now. She'd finally told him to quit standing every time she came into the room. "How is Libbie?"

"Very much the same. She's my heroine. How she puts up with my brother, I do not know. She is still trying to civilize him." He grinned. "I told her that won't happen."

Summer watched the young man: handsome, tall, lean, and extremely fit, he oozed charm. The children, even the dogs idolized him. Dressed now in civilian clothes, wool trousers and a heavy hand-knit sweater of navy blue wool, he appeared relaxed, and especially in the presence of women, he lost his warrior countenance. She asked, "When do you need to be back?"

"Libbie and Autie are visiting in New York for a fortnight. They may extend his leave. Then I suppose it's back to Ft. Lincoln if they can make it."

"Will they expect you there?"

Tom moved the stack of clean and dried plates to the cupboard. "You've never been to Bismarck in February, have you? I will be content to miss winter at Ft. Lincoln. Most days are spent checking to see if the guards aren't frozen stiff. The temperatures plummet to twenty below, sometimes forty below."

Daniel stepped into the kitchen at the tail end of the conversation. "I wired General Sheridan and asked him to put Tom on escort duty."

Summer said, "Little Phil's always had a soft spot for Abbey, even after he married Irene Rucker." She looked to Tom. "Have you met Little Phil's wife?"

Tom nodded, smiled, and shook his head. "We did. Autie and I met Irene last summer. She's pretty, a tiny thing, the daughter of an army officer so she knows the drill, so to speak. He adores her, and acts like he's fifteen."

Daniel placed an arm around his wife. "Will you excuse our guest from kitchen duty? I want to move that lumber into the barn. Would you mind, Tom?"

She glanced at his sweater. "It's not so warm today; you might want your jacket and gloves." She paused for a moment, studying his forearm. "Is that a tattoo, Tom?"

His cheeks flushed a little. "Just my initials." He pulled down his sleeve. "An old Indian did it at Ft. Sill. One of my poorer decisions."

Daniel mumbled. "A lot of soldiers get them. You'd better grab a jacket, Tom. She's the boss around here."

⧏⧐

They spent an easy hour moving a stack of long chestnut boards into the barn. When finished, they stood at the pasture fence. Daniel pointed out Scout and Shortcake, both sturdy buckskins. "I'm sending those two with you for the ladies. That is certainly a beautiful horse you have."

Tom leaned against a post. "My dad's a blacksmith. He knows horses. He taught me. I've always loved horses and dogs, too."

Chester trotted up for a treat. Daniel asked. "Ever consider resigning your commission?"

"At least once a day." He pulled a sugar cube from his pocket and gave it to Chester. "I remember him from the war. He's still handsome."

Daniel nodded. "He's living the good life now, managing all his ladies." He rubbed Chester's neck. "This area is growing. We need a sheriff. I could help you slide into that spot. Would you be interested?"

"Me? Here?"

Daniel nodded. "Will and Abbey are moving back here. They plan to build a house fronting the lake. It's a nice place for a family. Any marriage plans?"

Tom shook his head. A picture of Autie running around spluttering like a rooster with his head cut off came to mind. *It might,* he thought, *be worth it just to see him like that.* He shook his head then looked to Daniel. "Why me?"

"I watched you handle that crowd around Abbey when you rode up, when she fainted. You stayed calm but in control, reassured her children and Will. Everyone listened to you. We've had some incidents with the Klan here, and there are illegal stills up in the mountains. I remember they assigned you to exactly that kind of duty after the war in South Carolina, wasn't it?"

He nodded again. "I heard the Klan moved north."

"Yes. They have a stronghold in York. We also have our share of criminals. It's a beautiful spot. I want to protect it."

"It is gorgeous country. It's tempting. May I think about it?"

Daniel nodded. "Let me know when you return with the ladies. You have no idea how much better I'll feel with my sister here rather than in Indian country.

"How do I put this? You'll have your hands full, Tom. She's a lot of woman, and she draws a great deal of attention from the wrong sort. She's not a flirt, but trouble seems to follow her. And she faints, not all the time, but often enough...damndest thing. If she's startled or frightened she just keels over like a grounded sailboat."

Tom took the train into Philadelphia early on the 28th and escorted Abbey and Violet—he insisted on first names—to Camelann the same day. "We're going to be spending a great deal of time together. Let's not be formal."

He intended to talk to Abbey by herself and assure her he would not pounce on her. Although he admitted to himself he was in love with her, he knew she was married. She was not the type of woman to cheat on her husband. He'd encountered plenty of them. He knew, too, that what happened between them was different, actually special, and to want Will dead just so he could marry his wife, was the devil's work. He felt less than human. Abbey and the children would be devastated. Autie told him he didn't understand women, but he understood Abbey. He told himself what he wanted was just to be around her, get to know her, and most of all he wanted to protect her and her children.

However, he never had a chance to talk to her. Every time he almost managed to speak privately to her, Vi or Summer or one of the children came along. And the more he simply watched her, the more he realized how much he loved her. She was the girl he wanted for the long race. He could wait, make sure she was safe. So he stayed his distance and kept busy playing checkers with Alice and Louisa and showing the boys magic tricks. He helped Daniel groom the three horses to perfection, carried the trunks to the wagon.

Daniel finalized the arrangements. Through his connections with the Pennsylvania Railroad, he reserved a private railcar; one J. Marshall Heath had built for his private use. Every oil tycoon wanted a fancy, individualized boxcar, and since rock oil had been discovered in western Pennsylvania, millionaires mushroomed. They parked these luxurious boxcars on sidings and without dirtying their boots the tycoons and their guests could shoot buffalo and antelope from inside the fancy railcars, taking home trophy heads to decorate their Newport or Long Island estates. Not long after the car was finished, Mr. Heath upgraded to a larger boxcar, and not one to waste a dime, rented out the smaller one.

This car, fitted with mahogany paneling, a marble-topped bar, red silk drapes, leather furniture, and oriental rugs, possessed several sleeping berths, a bathroom, and a large sitting area. At the end of the car, accessed by a locked door, were horse stalls.

An hour before dawn, goodbyes were said at the house. Summer stayed home with Alice and Emil, not so much to avoid hysterics, but rather in fear that Alice and Emil would attempt to stow away on the train. Both were so enamored with Tom, they wanted to ride back to the reservation with him.

They arrived early to the station. Daniel drove the wagon with their trunks and the ladies while Tom, on Toledo, led the other two horses. Lew and Martha Graves right away recognized Tom from newspaper pictures. She embarrassingly gushed over him like a love-struck teenager. When the 6:03 to Pittsburgh arrived Abbey and Vi struggled to help Lew with their trunks and hand luggage while Martha led the men and horses down the tracks to where the horses would board. Martha Graves hovered over them telling them to hurry. Toledo balked and refused to board until Tom settled him. She went to touch the horse's bridle, but Tom grabbed her hand. Finally, the horse calmed, and Tom muttered something about shooting the nag. "And I'm not talking about the horse."

"I know how you feel," said Daniel.

⚞⚟

As the sun dawned in a mackerel sky, the train chugged westward over the snow-dusted Alleghany Mountains. Once settled, the three of them walked to the dining car where they ordered omelets. They waited, reading the papers like the other passengers. Abbey recalled riding the trains west with Ed, her first husband, almost a decade ago. It had been her honeymoon which led to the worst year of her life. She boarded that train a naïve bride and over the next few months became more grown-up than she ever desired. This car, except for the clatter of cutlery and china was quiet, and it remained so through breakfast.

Violet stood suddenly. "Excuse me, I'm going back to the car." Tom stood and watched her move through the tables then he motioned for their waiter to refill their coffee cups. He sat down and looked across to Abbey. This first instant alone felt both exhilarating and awkward. She did look fresh and lovely in a taupe wool skirt with matching cardigan and a pink ruffled cotton blouse. He also noticed every man in the dining car stole peeks at her when they thought no one was looking. He again reminded himself of his vow to not touch her.

She watched the coffee swirl into the cup. The entire time she'd been in Philadelphia she asked herself, over and over: *How did I allow him to … It was nothing, it meant nothing; it was only a drunken moment. He probably doesn't even remember it. She smiled to the server when he offered cream.*

Who am I trying to convince? He hasn't forgotten anymore than I have. A shudder of pleasure raced through her and she felt her cheeks flush. How could I forget?

When the waiter left, she looked over to Tom. Out of uniform, he looked ruggedly fashionable in a tan corduroy jacket and British brown riding boots that matched the leather buttons on his coat. He busied himself with folding the paper. *He must be as uneasy as I am.*

He certainly looked as uncomfortable as she felt. To ease the tension, she said, "It is strange to see you out of uniform." She could see the bulge of a pistol under his left shoulder. "I brought several novels. What do you plan to do for entertainment?"

The minute the question slipped off her tongue, she regretted it. However, he didn't take it the wrong way. Ever since yesterday when he turned up at Tilley's apartment, she sensed how he wanted to make her comfortable.

"Summer gave me *A Tale of Two Cities*." He smiled his engaging little boy grin, "and if you ladies stay away from the faro tables and out of the bar, I may read, too."

She appreciated his attempt at a joke.

His face grew serious as he looked down at Abbey's coffee cup and nodded to her newspaper. "Finish your coffee and stay here for ten minutes. I'd like to do a quick reconnoiter of the train."

Abbey watched him exit the dining car; she expelled a long sigh.

She resumed reading and was so deep into Wilkie Collins' romantic tale in *Harper's Bazaar*, when she felt the chair beside her move. For a moment she thought Violet had returned, but then the edge of her vision caught the gleam of a West Point ring as a voice from her past said, "Do you remember our honeymoon on the train, Sunshine?"

She raised her eyes, felt as if she'd been kicked in the stomach, and her world turned black. Her limp body slid under the table, pulling the tablecloth and dishes on top of her. By the time Tom returned two waiters hovered over her. Pieces of broken crockery stuck in her hair.

Chapter 10

HEROES

Louisa and Hank organized the winter picnic and the ride around the lake adventure. Violet, Tom, and Abbey had just left that morning. The children approached Summer and Daniel as they sat in the dining room enjoying a second cup of coffee and reading the papers. Summer and Daniel heard the other children twittering on the porch and suspected some mischief was in the making.

Louisa attempted to sound very adult. "The cousins, Hank, and I have been thinking we're bound to get a foot of snow soon. We could be frozen indoors for a month. May we, all the cousins, pack a lunch, and ride all the way around the lake? By ourselves?"

Daniel smiled at his half-sister and Hank. They were good looking kids. Hank inherited Fanny's ginger-colored hair, which on Hank stood on end like the bristles of a hairbrush, and Hal's ice blue eyes. Summer told him Louisa, except for her dark hair, looked like a miniature of him.

He asked, "All nine?"

Louisa and Hank both nodded. "Yes, all nine. Lilly and Charlie would never forgive us if we left them home." He added, "and my mother insists I take Charlie." Neither his face nor his tone seemed happy.

Louisa nudged him with her shoulder. "Charlie's a sweetheart. I'll watch him, and he entertains Lilly."

"Do you want the pony cart?" asked Daniel.

"Absolutely not," said Hank. He knew he'd get stuck driving it. Even the little kids hated it. The wicker scratched; it bounced everyone around. "We'd have to stay on the road if we took the pony cart. Lilly and Charlie can ride behind Louisa and me. I already asked my parents. It's okay with them if it's okay with you."

"All right. Hank saddle seven ponies. Ask Mac and Gus to help. Louisa, see to lunch. Ask Alice to assist, and Mrs. Love will help too, just to get you all out her hair for the day. Pack healthy stuff not all cookies and candy. Summer will supervise clothing; I'll inspect the ponies and the lunch." Daniel was a stickler regarding nutritional food.

He kept several rifles and two shotguns on a rack beside the dining room fireplace. He chose the .22 rifle, checked the chamber, and handed it to Hank. Then he reached into one of the ammo chests and handed Louisa a box of bullets. "Put those in your bag. I want the rifle and the ammunition separate. Fire three shots in quick succession if in danger. Wait fifteen minutes and fire three more, then one shot every five minutes until we are there. I'll give Mac my watch. Under no circumstances are you to use the rifle for anything but a call for help. You all know the *Boy Who Cried Wolf Story.*"

He looked over to his wife who looked a little pale. "When did you first carry a gun?"

"I was nine."

"So was I. The oldest four all know how to handle the .22."

⚜

Tom knelt beside her. A tiny stream of blood trickled from her hairline near her left temple. He removed a piece of broken crockery from her hair. He had vowed to himself when he returned Daniel's first telegram, not to touch her, especially not to hold her. The minute he saw her again he knew what he felt for her was a lot more than just lust. Pictures of her children, her husband flashed in his head. What a mess of emotions grabbed at him. *God, help us.*

Now, he lifted her, clutching her so tight to his chest; he felt the wild thumps of his own heart harmonize with the sweet tap-tap of hers. For a second she opened her eyes, looked at him, and sighed with such contentment, a lump rose in his throat.

He glanced at the other diners, who were all staring at them. "What happened?"

A balding man in a brown suit with a chalk pinstripe said, "A rough looking character sat down beside her." He looked around at the other passengers. "He only had one arm and he wore an eye patch. He ran off when she fell."

"He waved a gun," said a middle-aged woman. "He must have said something to her. She just went limp and slid under the table."

Tom gestured with his head to the smaller waiter. "Open the doors for us, please."

Once inside their car with the waiter waved off and Violet nowhere in sight, he slowly crumbled onto the sofa with her still cradled in his arms. He kissed her forehead, her eyelids then rested his cheek against hers. *So much for my resolutions!*

All the lectures about remaining objective, of not falling in love with her went poof out the door. And when her eyes opened he felt like Prince Charming. Nothing ever felt better.

"What happened?" he whispered.

At that moment Violet came out of the bathroom, her skin the color of moldy clay, and the waiter barged through the door with a tray bearing a coffee service and cups.

Who ordered that? In the confusion Tom managed to stand and situate Abbey on one end of the long leather sofa with pillows beneath her shoulders and a blanket draped around her legs. His voice snapped. "Vi, come, sit down. You look about to faint."

He nodded to the server to place the tray on the bar and pulled a footstool beside Abbey. Violet ran back into the bathroom. Tom wonder if dealing with Crazy Horse or his family might be easier.

He sat down on the footstool and looked to the young waiter. "It's Joseph, isn't it? Thank you for the coffee. Did you see anything?"

Small, dark, gypsy-eyed Joseph shook his head and looked at Abbey as if he'd never before seen a pretty girl. He dampened a linen napkin at the sink and gave it to Tom as she showed some life. "Oh, Miss, you gave us such a scare. I only heard the crash of the dishes. A man with an eye patch rushed past me." He motioned to Tom. "Be careful. There are shards of china still in her beautiful hair."

Tom dabbed at the small cut on her forehead, and noticed the patch of blood on the front of his own shirt. It was her blood.

Abbey quivered. In a timid voice, she whispered. "It was Ed, my first husband."

"Ed Kincaid?"

Abbey still whispering, said, "I hoped he was dead." With her face toward Tom, she glanced at the waiter then turned back to Tom and rolled her eyes toward the door.

Tom understood. "Joseph, would you check to see if any of the staff saw him? Perhaps post officials at all the exits. How soon is it until the next stop?"

Joseph pulled out his watch. "Five minutes to Bedford. I'll alert the conductor."

When he left, Tom asked, "Abbey, are you sure?"

Abbey sat up and frowned at the bloodstains on his shirt; her legs stretched out on the sofa. "He asked if I remembered our honeymoon on the train. Who else would know such a thing? I just saw his face for a second before I blacked out. Even with one arm and the eye patch, I knew it was Ed. I will never forget him. God forgive me, I hate him. How did he know I was on the train? Thank heavens you were here."

Tears started again.

He handed her the damp cloth. "Perhaps it was just a coincidence."

She wiped her face and calmed down. "I don't know if I can take much more. Will is sick, probably dying. Ed showing up..." She wrapped her arms around herself and shook. Her big eyes looked up to him and inside her head she added, *'and you.'*

He'd already broken his vow not to touch her. His hands lingered on her shoulders. "Abbey, I'm here to protect you, not cause you more grief." He was about to embrace her again, to pull her tight to his chest, when Violet came out of the bathroom. Now, her color looked normal.

"I apologize. I suddenly became ill, felt as if poisoned. What happened?"

They all turned to the rear half of the car at the sounds coming through the connecting door, the horses squealed and screamed. The car rocked.

Tom jerked to his feet and rushed to the connecting door, his Smith and Wesson in his hand. Both Violet and Abbey stood. For a moment, he fumbled with the lock then slipped inside the stall section of the boxcar. Two shots rang out. He returned to the luxurious side of the car. "Violet, are you able to fetch the conductor, a porter, anyone official?"

Violet moved as if to find a porter, but Abbey held onto her arm and asked, "What happened?"

Tom moved toward the women. "Someone slit the throat of one of the horses. I had to put it down."

"Scout?" asked Abbey. Her voice was barely discernible. Scout had been her horse for the past few years.

He reached her. "I'm afraid so." The train screeched into Bedford.

She fainted again, this time collapsing onto the sofa. He scooped her into his arms, then his lap as he sat down. "Vi, can you...?"

She efficiently fetched a conductor.

Within minutes the car filled with officials. Tom didn't even try to hide his concern for Abbey. She didn't awaken. Chaos ruled. Violet remembered the ammonia vials and came over to the sofa. "Turn her over Tom. If we loosen her stays it might alleviate these fainting spells."

He looked puzzled, but did as requested. Violet stood blocking the view with her widespread skirts while he unbuttoned her skirt and pulled out her shirttail, and loosening the laces. "Good Lord, Vi, don't let her wear them that tight again. No wonder she faints. If she insists tell me. I'll cut the damn things."

Violet switched places with Tom. "We're a good team, young man. "Go find those vials Dr. Cutter gave you."

⚏⚏

Although gray and damp, the air felt spring-like, a tease before winter blasted into Pennsylvania. The Camelann Nine—Emil came up with the name--took the long way around the falls with a stop at Eagle Alley, a thirty or forty-acre ravine full of every size rock from pebbles to house-sized boulders. Summer told guests that God must have emptied baskets full of rocks, and allowed them to tumble down the hill. The men who fought at Gettysburg said it reminded them of Devil's Den.

An enormous bald eagles' nest, at least twelve feet long, stretched along the tops of the rocky cliffs. "Stay away from there." Hank warned the others. They counted five eagles.

When Daniel had shown Tom around Camelann just the day before, they had checked out the rocky trails for half-awake bears or other predators and found nothing untoward. Now, Alice and Louisa held the reins of all the horses and watched the little ones while the boys climbed and leapt through the rocks, splashed in Little Whipping Run and Hunting Owl Creek. Even if the snakes were hibernating, they wanted no part of waking one up.

After an hour exploring Eagle Alley, the Camelann Nine wove their way through rough thick woods and rocks toward a clearing atop Switch Back Falls. Louisa tied yellow hand-kerchiefs on long sticks and gave one to Lilly and the other to Charlie. They held them aloft and waved them. When they reached the clearing, Hank and Louisa planted the pretend flags in the clearing and spread blankets.

Forty-Foot Falls made more noise with its dramatic wedding veil drop, but Switch Back Falls fascinated the children. Shallow on some switchbacks, deep on others, Whipping Creek zigzagged through impassible thickets of briars, roaring over some boulders, splashing over others. Local legend told of caves, part of the Underground Railroad, somewhere near Switch Back Falls. The Mason-Dixon Line, the border between Pennsylvania and Maryland, the line separating North and South was just on the far side of the mountains. However, the stories meant little to this crew. All but Hank had been born after the war.

Hank had spent a lot of time fishing, hunting, and camping with his father and grandfather. Now, he put to use what he'd learned. He dismounted and laced a clothesline-weight rope he'd brought for this purpose around several aspen trees to make a corral of sorts for their horses. He unloaded the picnic hamper and placed the bottles of ginger ale and root beer in the icy spring. And he took charge of Charlie and Lilly while Louisa and Alice fixed lunch.

The small spring fed into a brook which eventually dropped into Whipping Creek. The girls and Hank watched Lilly and Charlie, who were determined to follow the dogs. When Emil, Mac, Gus, and Johnnie took off with Owen and Mayo, Lilly sat in the middle of the picnic blanket crying. Hank picked her up and entertained both toddlers with the magic tricks Tom Custer had taught him. The girls set out tin plates, the hamper of sandwiches, two jars of pickles, a tin of pretzels, and apples. "I have Fry's Chocolate Cream bars and cookies for dessert," said Louisa.

<hr />

As Violet tucked covers around Abbey, who continued to sleep, Tom fetched a cool cloth for her forehead, then more blankets, and from his valise he retrieved a few ammonia capsules. He smiled at Violet. "We do make a good team. I forgot about these." He handed her two capsules and stuck two in his pocket.

She nodded. With railroad officials, local police, a cleanup crew, and gawkers going in and out, the doors were left open and the interior temperature of the car plummeted. Violet huddled under blankets with her charge. Tom took the other horses out for exercise and away from the odor of death. The strong smell of blood and horse permeated the car.

Here in Bedford in the picturesque Alleghany Mountains, snow fell, covering the roads and railroad yards and created a Christmas card setting, but in reality it provided slush and ice slowing all their efforts. Procuring a flatbed farm wagon, moving the cumbersome carcass, scrubbing out the stalls, and searching the train for the one-armed man with the eye patch, or anyone else suspicious, took hours. When the horses returned to their stalls now spread thickly with sweet smelling straw, Tom slipped feedbags over their heads. Passengers and the railroad crew walked around the outside of the car, asking questions. Tom, in turn, asked if they'd seen the man with the eye patch. A few remembered him at the faro table, but he was not on the train now. Abbey, bundled under blankets, slept.

❦

Lunch at the top of the falls was an event. Louisa and Alice decided that boys away from their parents became barbarians and Lilly wasn't much better. They had no manners. Emil insti-gated a spitting contest. Much to Louisa's chagrin Lilly giggled and joined the boys. Emil walked on his hands all the way around the blanket. Hank told of drumbeats heard from these woods and the howl of werewolves when the moon was full. Angry about the spitting, Louisa withheld the chocolate bars but passed around the tin of cookies. The sun came out for a few minutes; the wind shifted and smelled of snow. Charlie and Lilly curled up with Owen and took a short nap. Hank stayed with Louisa and Alice; the twins, Emil, and Johnnie explored the west side of the falls on foot with Mayo.

Mayo, huge but still a puppy, acquired his name from Daniel after the chunky russet-colored Mastiff puppy licked clean an entire quart of Summer's mayonnaise. He stole the bowl right off the worktable, took it underneath, holding it between his giant-sized paws and licked the bowl clean. Calm, easy-going Summer chased him with a broom. "You big stupid dog, do you have any idea how difficult it is to make mayonnaise?"

Midway down the incline, an ancient ash tree had fallen creating a bridge ten feet above a shallow stretch of Whipping Creek. Fearless Emil marched out on the makeshift bridge and sat down astride the giant log. "Hey guys, the view is terrific. I can see the island, all the houses, the barns, and the dock at the Indian School. You should come out." He could see, too, most of the length of the falls.

The twins secretly agreed Emil was crazy, but Mac started and only lasted five steps before turning back, then Gus tried and also turned back. They wouldn't let Johnnie try. From upstream, the girls suddenly screamed. At the same time a little rumpled ball of dark blue and red rags with a mop of dark curls rolled, actually bounced, down the hillside opposite the boys. Lilly landed in a sitting position on a small, flat patch of dirt. Less than ten feet away, but with the deep chasm separating them, they could see her expression. For a long moment Lilly just sat there looking stunned, then she let out a wail loud enough to wake the bears.

As Emil inched his way across the log toward her, the patch of dirt and gravel surrounding Lilly folded in and the ground collapsed with a swoosh of dirt and dust. From his vantage point halfway across the falls Emil could make out the small round hole where Lilly vanished.

All four boys saw her disappear. The three on the far side of the chasm stood speechless. "I'm going across," yelled Emil.

"You go around. Tell Hank to fire the shots. Bring rope and the picnic basket. And a canteen."

Breathless, the three boys scrambled up the steep incline to the aspen grove in no time.

Hank kept his head. Most of the children did. Charlie came over and hung on his brother's pant leg while Hank and Louisa managed to get off the shots. Mac found the watch in his saddle-bag and started timing.

All talked at once. 'Where's the rope?"

"Emil said to bring a canteen," said Gus.

Johnnie said, "Your brother wants the picnic basket and a blanket."

Alice handed Johnnie the picnic hamper, then found the remaining rope. Gussie grabbed a blanket. Alice, Johnnie, and Gus raced down the eastside of the stream with the agility of goats. In unspoken agreement, Louisa, Mac, Hank, and Charlie remained at the grove. Hank and Mac diligently watched the time. Louisa sat cross-legged, her legs weak, limp as rope, on the ground, holding Charlie in her lap. He finally quit crying and sucked his thumb.

Louisa's heart beat faster than a cornered rabbit's. She felt sick for Lilly. *How did everything go wrong, so fast?*

Emil reached the sinkhole first, shortly followed by the dogs.

⚏

Lunchtime on the train passed unnoticed. Abbey slept. Tom and Violet didn't even think of food. With the freezing temperatures and the lingering odor of death, they had no appetite.

By late afternoon, the car was sufficiently aired to close the doors, the remaining horses calmed, and the train continued toward Pittsburgh. Joseph started a coal fire in the stove and warmth quickly filled the car. Tom finally cleaned the blood from his boots, washed his face and hands, and changed his shirt. Violet took it and put it to soak in the bathroom sink. Abbey groggily awakened. Still buttoning his shirt Tom walked over to the sofa and sat by her feet.

※※

Emil, lying flat on his belly wiggled to the edge of the hole. He had learned from his father at a very young age never to stand near the edge of a cliff. The same principle applied here. He looked down. The hole was still filled with dust. "Lilly. It's Emil. Answer me. Please?" Fear gripped his belly.

No sound came up from the depths of the earth. Up on the mountainside came the retort of a single shot. Hank had started the five-minute signals. Emil called again. "Lilly!" He called several times. Emil had never felt so frightened.

The dogs returned and sniffed around the area. Mayo's left front paw hit the edge of the opening to where Lilly disappeared. A chunk of earth broke loose. Emil heard a splash. A second later a scream, a Lilly scream, came out of the abyss, as Alice, Johnnie, and Gus slid down the steep path. Owen barked.

Emil's heart raced. Her scream was the best sound he'd ever heard. "Lilly, it's Emil. I'm coming for you."

Chapter 11

ALL THROUGH THE NIGHT

At the dinner hour, Violet arranged for Joseph to bring them mugs of steaming beef barley soup and a tray of toasted cheese sandwiches. No one felt energetic enough to walk to the dining car or to socialize with the other passengers. Half blamed them for the delay, the other half wondered just who they were?

Joseph kept looking at Abbey. "There's a doctor on the train. He's offered to come and examine her." He spoke to Tom, but looked to Abbey.

Tom and Violet shook their heads. They'd decided not to advertise Abbey's fainting spells. Her looks drew enough attention, she didn't need more. "Thanks, Joseph. Please thank the doctor. Just keep watch for that one-armed guy. If he shows his face again, I want to know it."

Throughout the light dinner, Tom spoke with various officials regarding the slain horse and the one armed man. Joseph kept the coffee hot, lit the lamps, and straightened the railcar.

As the train departed Pittsburgh, hours behind schedule, the car cleared of people. Joseph brought them a plate of warm gingerbread. When he left, the women changed into their night-clothes, robes, wool socks, and slippers. Tom stayed dressed just exchanging his jacket for an old wool sweater. No one wanted to sleep alone in the berths. Vi suggested, only half-jokingly, for Tom to sleep between them.

He chuckled and smiled charmingly. "Ladies, where did you get the idea that I'm a monk? You two sleep on the couch, I'll wedge open the door, and sleep with the horses. They need assurance, too. Trust me we'll all be safer this way."

Of course, Abbey who had slept all day stayed wide-awake now. She tossed and turned, tried to read, went over all the recent nightmare moments. About two o'clock in the morning, she donned her plain navy blue robe. At the last minute she arranged the covers over her pillow—a ploy to trick Violet into thinking she was still asleep on the couch-- then tiptoed in her socks to the horse stalls.

Tom awakened at once and wordlessly held open the blankets then pressed them around her, hugging her against his chest. The horses nickered.

She murmured in a raspy voice, "I can't quit thinking of Scout. Tell me animals go to heaven. If not, I don't want to go there either. Scout didn't deserve to die like that. Why would Ed do such a thing?"

"More than likely it was Ed, but we're not positive. Revenge? Meanness? I don't know." His hand caressed her cheek. "I'll join you in hell. No one I know would be in heaven anyway." He leaned up on his elbow; she turned onto her back then reached up and plucked straw from his hair.

Touching him, being alone with him, even the smell of him mixed with the sweet hay changed her good intentions. She didn't know where her resolve to stay away from him went or where the words now came from, they just bubbled out of her.

Her fingers brushed the side of his face. "Did you know I'm a bigamist? Married to two men at the same time and doomed for hell." She felt his smile; his hand caressed her hair. With no hint of humor she continued. "After I married Will, because he is a half-breed, I was told, privately, I was not welcome to return to Ft. Laramie or any army post. What would those officers' wives say now?

"Now, I'm married to two men at the same time, and there's a good possibility I've fallen in love with another man. Polite society will probably stone me." She laid her head against his arm. Her voice came out breathless. "Good Lord, Tom, I have tried to forget you. I don't want to be an unfaithful wife. I love Will, but I love you, too. What will become of us?"

Light from the cracked doorway provided a little illumination. He saw her tears; his arm tightened around her; he produced a handkerchief and wiped her face then kissed her sweetly, not demanding anything. When he finished he lay with his cheek against hers until her heart slowed to a soft patter. His right hand slid to her waist, his voice thick with emotion. "I have thought of you every waking moment since we parted. I have dreamt of you every night. I want you more than I've ever wanted anyone or anything. Ever. I love you, Abbey. I love you more than I've ever loved anyone. I'd marry you in a moment." His hand moved to her belly. "I've been worried sick that you might be pregnant. Are you?"

She didn't answer.

"Tell me, Abbey. I know Will must sleep with you. You're married. If not, he's either very ill or a fool."

After a long moment, she answered. "I was scared I might be pregnant, but when I discovered I wasn't I cried. I know we cannot be together. I cannot leave Will, but I thought if I had your baby I'd at least have something of you. Isn't that the stupidest thing you ever heard? With our coloring any child of ours would be fair. I think I'm going crazy."

His voice softened. "No, it is not stupid. I am honored that you would want my child. Part of me is saddened, too. We'd make beautiful children, but I am relieved. Any children of ours wouldn't pass for Indians, would they? I love you Abbey. I don't want you hurt." He leaned up on one elbow. "I want you, but there is no way for that to happen without hurting a lot of people."

He pressed a finger to her lips. "Hush. Hear me out." He took a deep breath and ran one hand through her hair. "I will not be the cause of destroying your marriage. Will is a good man. He loves you as much as I do. I saw it in his face. He's fighting for his life. This is bigger than just you and me. I like your children, your beautiful, brave children—I could love them. However, Will's their father. I don't want them to hate me. Your brother trusts me. Do you have any idea how good that makes me feel?"

He kissed her, just a breath of a kiss. "…Know this, Abbey Dupree, I'd run away with you to Canada this second if you'd give them up… but I love you too much to ask that."

She nodded, her face a crumpled knot of emotion. She leaned into his chest until her shudders slowed.

He stood and pulled her to her feet and brushed the straw off her navy blue robe. "Get yourself on the couch before Vi wakes up."

He chuckled and flashed his bad boy smile. "Good, clear-headed Tom Custer is about to fade into wicked wild Tom Custer who wants to ravish you." He swept her into his arms and kissed her hard then swung her around, pointed her toward the doorway, and gently swatted her bottom.

※

Daniel, Summer, and Lobo on winded horses arrived at the top of Switch Back Falls about four o'clock. An hour of daylight remained. Hank and Mac told what they knew. Mac said, "You can't take horses down there. It's too steep." He looked to his mother. His face contorted and his voice broke. "Lilly bounced down the hill like a ball. At first, we thought it was a ball then when she stopped rolling, she screamed. You know how she can scream when she's scared?" Tears erupted. "I am so sorry, Mama. The ground beneath her just disappeared."

Summer sank down onto the damp grass beside Louisa and pulled both children into her lap. "You've done everything right. We'll get her, but we need to stay calm."

She looked up to her husband as he bent and hugged all the children. "I want us to all stay together."

He stood, all business now, and turned to Lobo. "Secure the horses then follow us." To the children, he said, "Bring your lanterns. And your canteens. Someone grab a blanket." He asked Mac. "How far down the hillside is the sinkhole?"

"About half-way. Did you see the ash tree that fell across the creek? You can see it from the road."

Daniel nodded and held out his hand to Louisa. "Do you still have any of those chocolate bars?"

"Yes, they're in my pack.".

"Run and get them." To everyone, he said, "Let's move, we only have a little daylight left."

Chapter 12

A RED BANDANA

Daniel slid down the trail first then lifted each child and Summer over the last steep drop. He looked to the north. The light was fading fast and a damp coldness crept about them. The children, all wide-eyed and uncharacteristically quiet stood away from the sinkhole. They looked as frightened as he felt. "Gus, Johnie, you are in charge. That's good, stay away from the hole. Everyone gather some sticks for a fire. Stay in sight."

Emil sat cross-legged a good foot from the gaping hole singing *Brahms' Lullaby*. Still looking amazingly disheveled and dusty, he held up a finger to his lips and motioned for everyone to stay back. Cleverly he sang, *"Stay away, stay back, more dirt may cave in. She screamed for a while but now she's asleep."* He stood and pointed to the rope. One end looped around an overhead limb, the other was intricately attached to the basket.

With careful steps, he edged away from the sinkhole. He looked up to Daniel and Summer, his voice a whisper. "I had a little time to think about this. Except for Charlie and Lilly, I'm the lightest. I weigh about thirty-eight, maybe forty pounds. My Dad tells me I'm hollow. Uncle Danny, lower me down the hole. Once there, I will put Lilly in the basket, tug the rope, then you can haul her up. Then lower the basket for me."

"You're just five," whispered Summer. "We can't allow you to do that."

Daniel again looked to the sky. Darkness would be total within twenty minutes. Too much cloud cover would hide any moonlight. Summer's face appeared terrified; His heart pounded. He looked at Emil. Filthy in ripped white shirt with one tail hanging out, no jacket in sight, a red neckerchief wrapped around his forehead, he looked far older than five. He sounded far older too. Everything the boy said rang true, but he didn't want to risk another child.

"She's five, but acts three, and she's a tiny bit of a thing." His big blue eyes flashed to the sky. "You want to leave her there all night in the dark until you can get stronger rope and mules to pull up Lobo or you? It smells like snow. She's scared to death. I don't know if she's hurt. Who knows what could be down there?"

He pointed to Summer's lantern. "May I take that?" He looked around the little group. "I can do this. I am almost six, and I'm strong, I am smart, and I'm an Indian. I am Thunder Cloud's son."

The children with Daniel and Summer stood in a semi-circle, Louisa shifted Charlie to her other arm, reached in her pocket, and held out a chocolate bar. As Emil took it, she hung on to his hand "If anyone can do this, you can." She stuck her thumb up. The rest of the children did the same, even Charlie, who was clueless as to why, held up his thumb. Overhead, crows cawed as they came to their roosts, the air smelled of snow. The silence felt loud.

Summer handed him the lantern and raised her thumb.

Daniel gave him an unlit torch and matches and inspected the knots on the basket. "I have more matches. We'll start a fire here. Take a canteen. Are you sure, Son?"

As he put the canteen and unlit torch in the basket, the matches in his pocket, the lantern over his arm, he was quiet. When he picked up the basket and cautiously walked over to the sinkhole, he looked to Daniel, then as he stepped into the makeshift gondola. "Think of it this way. If something goes wrong, I'll be down there with her. She won't be so frightened. Draw that line tight, Uncle Danny."

The wicker creaked as the basket lowered into what proved to be a cavern. Summer's kerosene lantern didn't shed much light, but Emil immediately noticed the stalactites hanging from the ceiling. If there were stalactites coming from the ceiling, probably spears of limestone were rising from the floor. He hoped the basket could come to rest without being poked by one. He also noticed small patches of brown-gray fur dotting the ceiling. He sent up silent prayers to the great Christian God and to all his ancestors to keep all those bats sleeping. *Even brave Emil, son of Thunder Cloud, grandnephew of Red Cloud,* he thought, *is frightened of a huge swarm of bats!*

The basket came to rest. He took the canteen, the unlit torch, and the lantern, with him as he swung himself outside the little gondola. Fear made the muscles in his legs weak; his moccasins landed on damp but solid grit. With the light coming down from the opening he saw a little of the size of the cavern. It appeared endless. Emil with his father had explored the caves up on the Yellowstone and Rosebud Rivers near home. This cave smelled much the same, dank, full of decay, and ancient. Unlike the western caves he felt a draft against his cheek and heard a strange music, a distant chanting, which he thought was a trick of the wind or perhaps his imagination gone wild.

He took a sip from the canteen, more to quell his fear than his thirst. He then lit a match and the tar torch; he turned, moving an inch at a time, in a tight circle, allowing light to fan the area. He felt more than saw a slight movement in the distance, perhaps a bat, something else. Fear gripped his belly and he concentrated on the moment, a skill all Indian children learned from the cradle. There across the stream lay a motionless ball of red and blue with her thumb in her mouth. He sent up a prayer that she was alive.

Tears filled his eyes, he wanted to cry but he felt his father's hand on his shoulder and took a shallow breath. *First things first, Emil.* The stream was narrow, perhaps a foot and a half, maybe two feet wide. He heard his father's voice. *Never trust murky water. Test.* He knelt and poked at the water with the handle of the torch. It was only an inch or two deep. He edged across, testing every step, then ran to Lilly, planting the torch then kneeling beside the small body. He pulled her into a hug. Her eyes opened. Nothing in his entire short life ever felt better than the warmth in her cheek. Now his tears wouldn't obey.

She nodded and smiled, her short dark curls quivered. "Don't cry, Emil. I'm okay. One of the angels stayed with me. She was so beautiful." She motioned with her head. "Hear them singing?"

The only sound he heard was the thumping of his heart. He hugged her tighter and pulled the chocolate bar from his pocket, removing the wrapper with one hand. He broke off two pieces. As she greedily took a piece, he pointed to the circle of light in the ceiling. "Mommy and Daddy are up there."

He popped the other piece of chocolate into his mouth then lifted her. Holding her, the lantern, and the torch took some doing, but he made his way back across the stream. A small dark something scurried into the darkness. A few pebbles skittered. He concentrated on Lilly. At the basket, he placed her inside. He held out the canteen. "Take a sip. As soon as I tug on the rope your daddy will pull you up." He pointed to the opening in the ceiling. "Stay seated. Hang on tight, right here." He fitted her chubby hands on each side of the basket. "Hold on. When you're safe, Daniel will lift you out and send it back to me." Fearful that she might burn herself or worse spill the kerosene, he didn't give her the lantern or the torch, but just before he tugged the rope, he removed his red bandana and tied it around her forehead and dark curls. She looked nothing like an Indian. She reached up and touched it with both hands, then smiled, one of those enormous glowing smiles only young child can make. He pointed to where her hands should be holding the basket then tugged on the rope and watched the line grow taut. She waved and blew him a kiss.

He blew it back to her. "Hold on to the basket!"

⊨⊨

Abbey, still in her robe, lay curled on the sofa, sound asleep. Her blanket had slipped to the floor. Violet noticed the straw sticking from the back of her hair and on the bottom of her socks. She put two and two together and gave Tom, who was just entering the car, one of those looks.

He noticed the straw at the same instant and knew better than to attempt to buffalo this savvy lady. "Honest to God, Vi. Nothing happened." Under his breath, he muttered to himself, *"Not that I'm happy about that."*

He checked the lock on the door to the stalls then, ignoring her admonishing eyes, and said to Violet, "Everyone should be dressed in an hour. I will ask Joseph to send us some coffee and breakfast. "Do you know where we are?"

She paused for a moment as if she wanted to say something else then said, "We just passed Cleveland, Ohio."

"Good."

Abbey stretched and appeared half awake. His tone softened. "Honest Vi. Nothing happened. I love her too much for that." He picked up his valise. "I'll use the bathroom in the next car. You ladies have the car to yourselves."

When he returned, Joseph was setting up the breakfast table. Freshly shaved, with his moustache trimmed, Tom looked relaxed. He didn't wear a uniform again, but looked clean and pressed in khaki trousers, a white shirt, and a dark blue sweater. Over his arm, he carried his light-colored doeskin jacket.

"Where is your red bandana, the one you wore on the trip out here?" asked Abbey. She was half-afraid, the other girl, the flirty friend of Libbie's, had it.

Tom smiled as he pulled out a chair for Violet. "Your son talked me into giving it to him. Are you sure he's just five? He's quite the salesman. I'll have to get another. All the officers of the

7th wear them." He pulled out Abbey's chair, then sat, and passed the platter of eggs to Violet.

"You both look lovely." The women, too, had dressed in fresh outfits. Violet wore a pale gray suit of fine wool with a lavender silk blouse and three long strands of pearls, and Abbey glowed in a rich dark brown velvet riding habit with a cream- colored silk blouse with lace ruffles at the wrist and neckline. Brown leather gloves and a brown lady's felt riding hat with ostrich feathers and veil sat on the bar.

"When you exercise the horses, I'd like to go with you." She looked over to the older woman. "I've cleared it with Violet. I need some fresh air and exercise." Abbey lowered her eyes. "Don't either of you look at me like that. I'll go insane if I don't get off this godforsaken train. I feel as if I'm in a sausage casing."

Tom's eyes smiled. He let out a snort and arched his eyebrows.

"Sausage casing? I'd better take you for a ride." He looked to Violet. "Would you like to join us, Violet? We can hire another horse."

"Thank you, but no. I haven't ridden in years. Dress warm. The weather can change in the blink of an eye."

Violet picked up the newspaper. "I want to read about the accusations against your Secretary of War. I've been watching Grant's administration deteriorate. Did you know Mr. Belknap has been married three times? The other cabinet member wives call this last one, Queenie. She's his second wife's sister. She sounds like a real pip."

Tom chuckled. "Pip is a great word for her. I've met Mrs. Amanda Belknap. So the ladies call her Queenie? Do you want to know what the men call her?"

Both women looked up expectantly. They suspected it wasn't polite. A little gossip broke the monotony of the flat countryside and perked up their spirits. "If my charge here can swear, I suppose you can tell us," whispered Vi.

"Puss. Her reputation is far from pristine. My sister-in-law detests her."

"Libbie? Why?"

He expelled a long breath as he buttered his toast. "It's politics at its dirtiest. Ladies. Are you sure you want to know?"

Both women nonchalantly nodded. They were dying to know.

Tom acted equally blasé. "Secretary of War is a fancy title, but the salary isn't much, definitely not enough to pay for Paris dresses and New York shopping trips. I'm a bit of a clotheshorse myself, and I know what things cost. Amanda's sister, Carita—Carrie— Belknap's second wife, started the scheme. You know the trading posts at the army forts? There are several on the reservations, too. Only the War Department—Belknap's department—can assign traderships; they're very much in demand because they're money-making machines."

He cut the toast into small squares and ate one with a bite of bacon. "Carrie arranged a kickback on the tradership at Ft. Sill. She received six thousand that first year, but poor Carrie died of tuberculosis. Amanda, conveniently widowed, stepped in and married Belknap. The illegal dividends continued. And it's not just one fort. Imagine her receiving kickbacks from a number of army forts and Indian agencies." He ate another piece of bacon and toast. "That is a sizeable augmentation to Belknap's scant salary. They can live like royalty."

He finished his breakfast, pushed back his plate, and stood. "And to top that off the sulters sell cheap shoddy goods to the soldiers and the Indians for exorbitant prices. It's a monopoly. There's nowhere else to buy supplies so the soldiers and Indians buy wormy flour and spoiled canned goods." He pulled on his gloves as the train slowed.

"Queenie or Puss hinted to Autie that if he'd look the other way regarding cheating everyone, she'd ...show him a good time." His eyebrows danced. "Have either of you ever seen her?"

They shook their heads.

"She's a beguiling piece of goods. Not many men would turn her down."

Violet and Abbey's eyes grew huge.

Tom laughed at their expressions. "Don't look so shocked. Neither of you are naïve. Such things go on. Some women count coup on men like the Indians do with their opponents. You'll be pleased to know Libbie got wind of what was happening and nearly scratched Puss' eyes out. Had her escorted off the post."

Violet arched both eyebrows, tucked several newspapers under her arm, and refilled her coffee cup. "I think I'd like your sister-in-law. Now you've piqued my interest. Enjoy yourselves. Don't get lost."

"I grew up in this section of Ohio. Joseph told me the train will be in Toledo for at least two hours for repairs. We'll ride over to the home farm where my brother, Nevin lives." Tom had planned to detrain a few stops before Toledo, then race cross-country and pick up the train in Toledo.

Now, as he helped Abbey stand, he said, "I'm not sure Tontogany is ready for you. You look like the wife of an oil tycoon not a Sioux Warrior."

Abbey and Vi grinned like conspirators. "I found it in a secondhand shop in Philadelphia. Violet helped me alter it. Isn't it lovely? I haven't worn such an elegant thing since my debutante days. Is it too...? I can change."

"No need for that. I want to show you off. I'll wire Nevin. He and Ann can meet us in Toledo."

⊰⊱

When the weary party returned to Camelann, Daniel, Hank, the twins, and Lobo took the tired ponies to the barn for a rubdown and feed. Daniel directed the younger boys to the upstairs bathroom, "Johnnie, you're in charge." Summer oversaw the girls' baths in the downstairs bathroom. An hour later the infamous nine, smelling of soap and dressed in nightclothes, met in the dining room for Mrs. Love's fried egg sandwiches and hot chocolate. All proceeded without a hitch until Summer attempted to remove Lilly's red bandana.

Her little jaw squared, the chubby hands locked fists, and Pennsylvania's champion screamed yelled, "N-O-O-O-O! IT'S MINE!"

Summer looked aghast. All her children were strong-willed, but Lilly took the cake.

Emil said, "Keep it Lilly. You earned it. I'm just happy you're safe."

Daniel raised his cup of chocolate, the children and Summer followed suit. "To Lilly," he said, "We are happy you all are safe. I'm going into Philly tomorrow. I'll look for red bandanas for everyone. I think we all should wear one to commemorate the Camelann Nine's first grand adventure. May there never be one so exciting. Right Lilly?"

Lilly held up her thumb. "Hooray for Emil."

They all raised their thumbs. "Hip, Hip, Hooray for Emil."

PART II

Chapter 13

BEST THINGS

New Year's Day 1876

President and Mrs. Grant sank into two blue damask-covered wing chairs facing the Blue Room fireplace. On their feet, shaking hands, smiling, chatting since noon, they ached. The little clock on the mantle chimed five as the last guest left. The staff immediately started to clean up the debris, and the President groaned and massaged his right hand. It was swollen double. Mrs. Grant sent a maid scurrying for an icepack.

The President smiled. Julia was particularly good that way, anticipating his needs, never asking, just doing. With his blue eyes twinkling, his left hand plucked a red rose from the enormous bouquet which sat on a little table between them. He kissed the rose then bent forward and handed it to her. She was the best thing that ever happened to him. From Missouri, a member of the slaveholding Dent family, Julia had stuck with him through all the lean year, traveling from one dreary army post to another and through all the public criticism during the war. He was happy now to see her thrive as First Lady, a role she was born to do, and one in which she loved.

"Thank you, dear.

"Hamilton"—Hamilton Fish, the Secretary of State—"thought your party first class. He whispered to me that your reception outshone Mrs. Belknap's by a mile."

She sniffed the rose and beamed. The flattery pleased Julia. Outdoing Queenie at anything quickened Julia Grant's heartbeat. Young Mrs. Belknap's good looks alone irritated all the cabinet member wives. Elias Tanner, a handsome young waiter, approached carrying a silver tray with a linen-wrapped icepack, drinks, and a plate of finger foods. The competition among the wives of Ulysses' Cabinet members rivaled that of the Executive Mansion's staff.

She smiled at Elias as he finished tying the icepack to the President's hand. He passed the plate of tidbits, placed their drinks and the platter within reach, and bowed. As he backed away he winked at Mrs. Grant. Elias was a bit of a flirt but she didn't mind.

The crackling fire sent out waves of warmth as the first couple relaxed with heavy sighs. The President and Mrs. Grant's New Year's Day Reception had been a resounding success.

Mrs. Grant took a sip of champagne. This was not her first glass. She frowned. "I should care what that hussy does?" she said with uncharacteristic venom. "Queenie was all but falling out of her dress. I suppose you noticed. Every man here couldn't keep their eyes off her." She passed the little tray of appetizers to her husband and let out another big sigh. "She's his third wife, you know?" Julia nibbled on a cucumber sandwich and lowered her voice. "Makes one wonder what Mr. Belknap does with them?"

"Now, now, Julia. Be careful, we have no idea who might be on *Harper's* payroll."

She took another sip of wine. It certainly loosened her tongue. "The Cabinet wives wondered about that and they *all* want to know how Queenie affords her clothes, the trips abroad, that mansion—I doubt if you noticed, but that was a Worth dress she was falling out of, and Julia Fish told me Queenie served Black Sea caviar and strawberries dipped in Swiss chocolate at her little *soiree*, last night. And they had a thousand guests and a full orchestra."

She stretched and took another swallow of wine. "What must she have paid for strawberries in December? Mr. Belknap cannot possibly afford all that, and I know neither of them comes from money. His father was an army officer wasn't he?"

He took a miniature creampuff filled with chicken salad. Belknap was an old friend of the President. He commiserated with Bill. The Presidency had alleviated some of Ulysses' financial woes, but he knew all too well the burden of debt. "Be careful, dear, don't spread rumors. Mrs. Fish said the third Mrs. Belknap inherited a lot of money from her first husband."

Julia, usually the most pleasant and kindest of women, harrumphed. She whispered. "I heard she ran through Mr. Bower's money then laced his grits with rat poison so she could be first in line to marry her sister's husband when Carrie died."

Julia patted her chest and breathed deeply. "Her maid told my maid's sister that Carrie gave Bill and the child to Amanda just before she died…Quite a touching scene. I want to cry just thinking of it."

The President lifted one eyebrow and took a second cream puff. "Your maid's sister? Can one give away a husband? Please don't give me to anyone." His eyes flashed. "By the way, dear, that is hearsay. I wouldn't repeat that if I were you.

"Speaking of hearsay, Hamilton tells me young Lt. Colonel Custer wrote those anonymous articles for *The New York Herald*. They're all based on hearsay. That boy better be careful."

Julia's face paled. She had read the articles, too. They were ugly and all lies. According to the articles, her husband's administration was beyond corrupt. The army, the Indians, even the horses were being swindled. *You might,* she thought, *be forgiven for shortchanging the soldiers or even the natives, but heaven help anyone who cheats the horses.* She finished her champagne and Elias immediately replaced it with a fresh glass.

"Be especially reticent right now, my dear. Clymer's committee wants Belknap's head on a platter. And mine right beside his. This Democratic congress is a weight around my neck. Politics is not for the weak kneed." He finished his whiskey with a satisfying smack of his tongue. Elias had a fresh drink waiting.

"We all know Goldilocks is a Democrat. If Custer testifies against my administration, he may find himself deep-sixed."

"Hush, Ulyss! Someone might hear you. Don't even think such a thing." She looked around slyly, making sure no one was hiding behind a palm tree. "You'd never do anything like that, would you?"

The great savior of the Union and the eighteenth President of the United States stood and held out his left hand to his wife.

His right was still wrapped in ice. "Don't concern your pretty little head about such things." He chuckled. "That is a metaphor. Of course, I'd never do something like that. However, my staff is protective of me." He added, "Not that Sherman would ever permit such a thing."

He bent forward and kissed her softly on the forehead. She was and always had been the best thing in his life. "Now do you think the First Lady, the best hostess in Washington, could rustle up more of those chicken salad cream puffs?" He patted his expanding stomach. "A couple dozen would do nicely."

⚏

At Fremont, Nebraska, Tom stepped off the train and sent a telegram, which Abbey had dictated, to Mercy, Abbey's assistant teacher at the reservation school, giving her the particulars of their arrival.

So Mercy and her Cheyenne husband, Hawk, met them at dusk on New Year's Day at the deserted Pine Ridge railroad station with a borrowed wagon for their trunks. Snow and wind raged. Hawk and Tom rode the horses while Abbey and Violet followed, huddled in the wagon with Mercy.

After making introductions, Abbey said, "I forgot how bitter winter on the plains can be."

Violet in all seriousness said, "I just love it. As a girl, I lived north of Toronto. We used dog sleds in winter. Bundled to our noses in furs, we'd race across the frozen snow." She inched up her skirt to the top of her fur-lined boots, showing a quilted wool petticoat, long wool socks, and the edge of silk underwear.

"Canadians know how to deal with snow and cold." She patted Abbey's knee. "You have a sewing machine, don't you? I'll fix you both up with wool petticoats."

When they arrived at Abbey and Will's house, fires in the fireplace and both the pot bellied and iron cook stoves welcomed them. Mercy had cleaned the house to a sparkle, too. "I made a pot of chicken stew with dumplings and corn bread for you. There's fresh milk and butter in the larder."

"Thank you, Mercy," said Abbey as she looked around her sweet little home, which flooded her thoughts with memories of Will. He had built the house, one of the few houses on the reservation, laid the hardwood floors, painted the walls. Together, she and Will had picked out the colors, the materials. She'd made the white ruffled curtains, the cushions and needlepoint pillows for the sofa and rocker, and braided the rugs.

Tom stood in the middle of the living room and turned around. Unbeknown to Abbey, he had taken great interest in furnishing and decorating his officer's quarters at Ft. Lincoln. "This is perfect. You and Will built this? It is truly a home. It's hard to believe we're on the reservation."

Hawk interrupted. "Daniel wrote a long letter to Red Cloud telling him about you and suggested a truce while you're here. Tomorrow I'll take you for an official visit." Hawk knew all about the headstrong Custers. "It's best if you don't move around by yourself."

Tom nodded. Aside from living among hundreds of Indians, he knew the U.S. protocol. A United States Army Officer did not enter or leave a government post without paying respects to the commander-in-chief. However, Daniel had hired him to protect Abbey to and from the school. He assumed he needed to protect her here, as well.

He also was not prepared to leave her yet. And while they had resolved what had to be, he had no intention of parting with her yet. He smiled at the young couple. Hawk was full-blooded Cheyenne, dark skinned, well spoken, and likable. Mercy was white and quite beautiful. He could tell her blonde hair had been darkened with a dye made from walnuts. They looked immeasurably happy. An enormous pang of jealousy jolted him. He straightened his spine. "We appreciate all you've done. Thank you."

Violet, holding a lantern, walked toward the stairs. She looked exhausted. Hawk pointed to the trunks, and she told him which belonged to whom. He shouldered Violet's luggage and started upstairs. To Tom Custer he said, "You speak Lakota very well, but it's always wise to take an interpreter with you. I'll come by about eight in the morning."

Abbey stuck her head out of the kitchen doorway. "Violet, please take the yellow room, and Hawk, put Major Custer's trunk in Emil's room." The room she shared with Will was on the first floor.

When Hawk returned, Abbey walked the young couple to the door. She had asked them to stay for dinner, but they were anxious to return the wagon and settle the horses in the sulter's livery. She kissed them both. "Even though there's no classes tomorrow, let's go over to the school. Thank you again for your help."

※※

Tom walked into the kitchen carrying his boots. "Vi asked for a tray. She's wiped out. Would you fix it? I'll take it upstairs." He set his boots in a corner. "Do you mind those there? I'll polish them later."

She liked that about Tom. He was thoughtful. She noticed that the day they'd stopped in Toledo for lunch. She had worn her lovely secondhand riding habit, the matching brown hat all done up with dyed ostrich feathers and a veil. He decided a madcap race across northwestern Ohio would not do. Although she rode astride rather than sidesaddle, he didn't want to risk her or her outfit. Instead of going to the farm he invited via telegraph Nevin, his wife, Ann, and his parents to lunch in Toledo.

They arrived early to the small German brewery and delicatessen near the harbor, well known for its beer. Outside terns and gulls squawked and sailed on the breeze; inside the dim barroom, the aromas of rich dark bread, garlic pickles, pungent mustards, and brisket surrounded them. Tom walked into the one washroom, cleared all the men out of it, cleaned it up for her then stood guard at the door while she refreshed. No facilities were provided for women. He did the same for his sister-in-law and mother.

At first, his parents were a little standoffish, but once Tom made a point of mentioning Violet's presence as a chaperone on the train, they warmed up.

She liked his parents, Maria and Emanuel. In addition to helping Nevin on the farm, Emmanuel still ran a blacksmith forge and Maria assisted Ann with the children and the farm work. God-fearing Democrats and very proud of their boys, they were polite to her, but had a little difficulty understanding how she could be married to a savage, even if he was a half-breed.

Tom gave a good and succinct explanation. "Will is no ordinary Indian. His mother is Red Cloud's sister. She's also a shaman and headmistress of an Indian School in Pennsylvania. His father is a very successful French-Canadian fur trader. Will was educated in Toronto and Montreal. He speaks English, French, and Spanish, and he's fluent in most Indian dialects and acts as an interpreter. He saved Abbey's life when the whites abandoned her to winter and the wolves. They have two very bright children. You'd love them, Ma. Will, her husband, is currently staying with his sister, a medical doctor, in Philadelphia. The children are with Abbey's brother, who is General Charteris. You read of him during the war? He hired me to protect Mrs. Dupree who is returning to the West River Reservation to help the school carry on without her. She and Will are moving to Pennsylvania to be near her brother. He lives on a twelve thousand acre horse farm. She's going to teach at the school there."

Abbey smiled at Tom's mother. "It's mostly about being around family. I think you understand that."

Maria Custer patted Abbey's hand. "We certainly do. Armstrong and Nevin bought a farm together outside Monroe, Michigan. George and Libbie hope to retire there."

The visit was short. As they said goodbyes, Tom's mother reached up and fingered Abbey's hair. "Are your children blonds?"

Abbey smiled thinking of Alice and Emil. "No, they both have their father's dark hair. They don't have my curls either. Their hair is straight as an arrow."

"That's a shame. Your hair is beautiful, and I do so love tow-headed babies."

⚏

Tom and Abbey ate supper before the fireplace in her snug little house. They sat at the table Will had made. She put together a peach cobbler from her canned peaches. It baked while they ate their supper.

Dressed comfortably in robe and slippers, Violet brought her tray downstairs, and they all made short work of the dirty dishes. "The food was delicious. I feel much better. I think I was starved for a home-cooked meal and sick of the constant motion of the train."

Over coffee and cobbler Vi asked Tom, "Would you explain this Belknap Scandal to me? It's the top headline in every paper I read, and I've collected papers from San Francisco, Chicago, Washington, and New York."

While Abbey cleared the cobbler dishes and refreshed their coffee, Tom fetched a map from his trunk and spread it out on the table. It was a large-scale map of the upper plains from the Black Hills to the Big Horn Country, compiled from Autie's expeditions.

His hand brushed over the Dakota Territory, Nebraska, Wyoming, and Montana. "The history is important. The Great Sioux Reservation was established by the Fort Laramie Treaty of 1868 and includes the southwestern part of the Dakota Territory, commonly known as West River Reservation. One segment in particular, the far western quadrant of West River, came into contention. The Indians called it *Paha Sapa,* the whites called it *The Black Hills.*

"The Sioux Nation has claimed *Paha Sapa* since 1765, when they took the land from the Cheyenne, and have no intention of parting with it now. Autie led a large expedition into the Black Hills the summer before last. It's beautiful. There's nothing like it on the plains. I doubt if there's any place like it in the universe.

"The press always follows my brother. News of him and the 7ᵗʰ Cavalry sells papers. Only Indian atrocities, especially if women are involved, sell better." He shrugged. "The public likes nothing better than some damsel captured by the heathen; they eat up gory, scandalous, news.

"My brother possesses a zest, a flamboyance, which the public also loves, and he's clever. He's built amazing camaraderie within the 7ᵗʰ. He heard someone playing **Garry Owen** on a piano in a saloon. It's an ancient Irish drinking song, and he adopted it as an anthem for the 7th. Everyone except our enemies loves it. He gave all his officers red scarves and each company within the 7th ride like-colored horses. That's an ancient Cavalry practice, and the U.S. Cavalry used it during the war; Armstrong continues it. During battle the officers can spot their men easier, and the men can reassemble better. The band—he always traveled with a band—rides only white horses. Such a simple thing as like-colored horses not only creates camaraderie, we can see who is where easier.

"Eastern readers lap up such stories about him and the 7th Cavalry. Libbie helps, too. She's pretty and glamorous. Autie's the prince and she's his lady. Their story rivals Camelot and sells papers.

"So when the pressmen wrote of the 7th's expedition and fabricated stories of Black Hills gold clinging to the roots of the grass, of chunks laying in creek bottoms ready to be plucked up, the public devoured it. Because it was Autie's expedition, fortune-seekers by the hundreds flooded *The Black Hills*.

"Of course, the Sioux objected; the *Paha Sapa* is sacred. For once Red Cloud and Sitting Bull agreed. The Army made a show of stopping the miners, but they continued. The government also tried to amend the treaty. However, they discovered that to change the treaty required a three-quarters majority vote by the Sioux." Tom grinned. "Can you imagine three-quarters of the Lakota Sioux agreeing about anything?"

Tom stood and stretched and walked around the table. Abbey refilled all their cups. "To be candid, Ladies, the U.S. Government was not interested in stopping the miners. That's a little-known truth no one talks about. Our economy is depressed. In the East, factories have shut down, men are out of work. A good influx of gold would give it a boost. President Grant quietly suggested that what was needed is for the Sioux to break the treaty, thus the U.S. Government could take back *The Black Hills.*" He stretched and sighed. "Politics is dirty business."

"The Sioux starting a war over *Paha Sapa* would definitely nullify the treaty. Now, how do we get the Indians to start a war?" he asked.

The ladies shrugged. Violet jokingly asked, "Give them guns and whiskey?"

Tom pointed a finger at Violet. "Bingo. That's part of it. And that will be tomorrow night's lesson."

The wind whistled and shook the little house. Tom added logs to the fire and stoked the kitchen stoves. Vi stood. "I believe I will sleep tonight." She kissed Abbey then Tom goodnight. "I enjoy our talks. You're much more interesting than the lady doctors. They can go on about gall bladders and pancreases. Mrs. Belknap and what happens behind closed doors in Washington is much more interesting."

After Vi went upstairs Abbey fussed in the kitchen, making noise rather than accomplishing anything. Tom came and stood behind her, hugging her, kissing her lightly on the side of her neck. Swaying a little he sang in a soft baritone,

Brahms Lullaby, the words a little different than the one he sang to the children.

> *"Lullaby and good night to my sweet delight;*
> *May my love hold you tight all through the night?*
> *Lay thee down now and rest; may thy slumber be blessed*
> *Lullaby and good night may my darling abide,*
> *Snug and safe in my heart, all through the night.*

She turned around, her face wet with tears. "Oh Tom, what is going to happen to us?"

He kissed her forehead and smiled his quirky smile and wiped her face with his handkerchief. "Well, one thing is for sure. I'm going to run out of clean handkerchiefs soon."

She hiccupped and grinned a little. "What would I do without your handkerchiefs? Give them to me. I'll wash and iron them."

"Get some sleep. Life always looks better in the morning. I'll sleep on the sofa so I can watch over both of you, and keep that fire burning."

She touched his face. "No, no. It's cold. Sleep with me. We won't do anything. I just want you to hold me."

He chuckled and flashed his bad boy grin. "Sweetheart, it won't take five minutes, probably not two, for sensible, clear-headed Tom Custer to fade into wicked wild Tom Custer who cannot think about much else than those soft sweet whimpers you make. If I sleep with you we'd do more than hold each other, and that cannot happen. I've spent all my life searching for the perfect girl. I thought I found her in Lulie, but that wasn't meant to be. I refuse to compromise your marriage. You might love me now but you'd end up hating me. Will is the father of Emil and Alice. If I take you away from Will when he needs you, if I wish for the death of their father, I would hate myself. I cannot do that to Emil and Alice. The only choice I have is to step aside and allow God to make the choice. Just loving you is not enough. "

Tom cupped her face and lightly kissed her then said, his voice thick with emotion."I thought about this all day. You know John Donne's writings? I found it in a book Summer lent me: *No man is an island...entire of itself; every man is a piece of the continent, a part of the main...any man's death diminishes me, because I am involved in mankind. And therefore never send to know for whom the bell tolls; it tolls for thee.* Libbie first read those lines to me when she was making me presentable to the officer corps. I never really understood the meaning until today. We are all connected."

He kissed her temple. "Now scoot and stop looking like that, or I'll take my handkerchief back."

Chapter 14

THE LETTER

In their private Quarters Julia Grant, exhausted but happy, snuggled beneath the down comforter, closed her eyes, and let the champagne do its magic. She fell asleep within minutes. The President's whiskey did not work so well. After a half hour of tossing and turning, the President kissed his wife's forehead, again thanked his lucky stars for her, slipped on his robe and slippers, then lumbered through the dim corridors of the Executive Mansion to his office. His hand still ached but the swelling had gone down. He often didn't sleep well. Julia blamed his guilty conscience, and she no doubt was correct. Some nights his mind just didn't shut down.

The President slid open the bottom right drawer of his desk and retrieved a bottle of Kentucky Bourbon, a glass, an ashtray, and a Cuban cigar. Julia's first directive as First Lady had been to clean every nook, cranny, and corner of the great house as it never before had been cleaned. She banned smoking in the entire Mansion except for him.

He poured three fingers of whiskey into a short fat glass and lit his cigar. Usually he smoked a pipe, but he did love Cuban cigars. He again thought of how perfect a wife Julia was. Right now, he appreciated that she slept like a bear all night long.

From his center drawer he withdrew a dog-eared file, sat back, and put his feet on his desk. He began to review the activities of the past few months.

Grant read for twenty minutes then threw the file onto his desk. *How,* he asked himself, *has Belknap allow this to become such a mess?* He topped off his drink and walked to the window and looked out on the city. *I know firsthand what debt can do to a man. Desperate men do desperate things. Thank heavens, Julia is Julia, undemanding, a helpmate rather than…. Good Lord, Bill, three times! You picked the wrong woman each time?* He made a mental note to see Belknap tomorrow. *Perhaps something can be salvaged.*

Thank God, the Department of the Interior has straightened itself out. Delano went without a whimper and Chandler, the new secretary, is honest to a fault, but that's what's needed right now. Now if my brother stays sober…and that cheeky Custer keeps his mouth shut… I'll have Sheridan talk to him.

When he spoke with General Sherman, Sherman answered skeptically. "Sheridan is in Chicago. He's all worried that we have too many horses and not enough generals. He might put Custer in for promotion. I don't want that."

The President shook his head and groaned. He remembered Lincoln complained often of just the opposite: too many generals, not enough horses. *Sherman tells me our army is in bad shape: the veterinaries made more than doctors. The Indians buy breech loaders that use brass cartridges while our own soldiers carry single shot Springfields with cheap cardboard cartridges that jam consistently. Well, Chandler did direct his Indian agents to cease selling guns and ammunition to the roaming Indians. And since they would no longer be permitted to hunt on non-reservation land, they won't need guns or ammunition. If the Indians don't comply, their meager rations will be stopped. No meat or substance made hungry and angry Indians.*

The *LETTER's* unspoken intent was to mollify the public. No mention was made of how these harsh imperatives would reach the renegades. Already two to three feet of snow covered the northern plains; temperatures at Fargo and Ft. Buford have already reached 20⁰ below zero. And if by some miracle the *LETTER* does reach the roamers, how would the illiterate Sioux read it? And no consideration was given to how—if the Sioux wished to comply—would they move their families, children and old people, hundreds of miles in the dead of winter.

Clearly, the roaming Sioux tribes, with no place to live and no means to feed their families, had no choice except to go to war.

The President walked back to his desk, added a finger of bourbon to his glass, and looked at the last piece of paper in the file. He took special note of the dates. Today is January 1, 1876. Before a shot is fired or a tomahawk thrown the following directive was already written, carefully worded in legalese and slated to go out on the first of February: "Said Indians are hereby turned over to the War Department for such action on the part of the Army as you deem proper under the circumstances."

⧉

Red Cloud, great and longtime headman of the Oglala Sioux, had known of the *LETTER* since early December. A brave from the tribe of Tatanka Iyotake, the Hunkpapa leader known mistakenly as Sitting Bull to the whites, told him about the *LETTER*, and Jim Purvis, a new Indian agent, read it to him. News traveled, even in the great western expansions, by drums, smoke signals, mirrors, perhaps by wind whispers; however it moved, it moved fast. An important event happening in the morning in Pine Ridge would be known in western Montana or eastern Minnesota by noon. The Indians were neither stupid nor child-like innocents as most white people believed. They knew immediately of the *LETTER's* intent. The white man either wanted them annihilated or changed into docile farmers plowing dirt or herding sheep. Regardless all wanted their land.

The wind howled and rippled the elk hides of Red Cloud's tipi as the headman's son, Jack Red Cloud entered the lodge. He sat by his father. Both Indian men looked across the fire to Tom Custer and Hawk; Red Cloud politely offered a pipe. Daniel's letter had respectively informed him of news of his family and friends so this visit was no surprise. Red Cloud's fire reflected on their faces as the bowl of the pipe glowed red. Hawk translated until he realized they knew enough of each other's language to understand each other.

"Thank you for your assistance to Thunder Cloud's wife and their children when she took them east. I heard how you rode on the roof of the train with them." He smiled. "I like to ride up there, too."

Tom shrugged. "They're good kids. Very bright. I enjoyed talking with them."

"Daniel wrote that Thunder Cloud's health has improved?" Jack Red Cloud sat a little straighter. Thunder Cloud was his cousin; they'd grown up together.

Tom nodded. "Very much. In his last letter to Mrs. Dupree, Thunder Cloud spoke of taking short rides on a gentle horse. He and Daniel took his doctor, Dr. Cutter, to Buffalo Bill Cody's *Wild West Show*."

Red Cloud nodded. He'd seen *the Wild West Show* at Ford's Theater in Washington. Now, he asked of many of their mutual acquaintances: Armstrong, Phil Sheridan, Sherman, Grant.

"Did you meet my sister, Wakanda?" He asked after Daniel and Summer and their children. He inquired of Alice and Emil—except he referred to them as Fire Cloud and Running Cloud. He laughed with Tom, Jack Red Cloud, and Hawk, shaking his head. "Naming a Lakota boy, Emil! A coyote must have run off with Thunder Cloud's head!"

Red Cloud paused and passed the pipe again. On a day such as this when a thousand howling ghosts roared out of the north, when the tan elk hide of the tipi rippled like sand on a river beach, he wisely stayed warm inside his tipi. He mentioned the *LETTER* briefly, more to see what Tom knew than to complain. The men acknowledged the stupidity of the politicians.

Red Cloud studied his guest. *Young Custer seems preoccupied.* Red Cloud was a wise headman. He suspected as to why.

When the pipe came back to him, he asked, "How is my nephew's wife, the lovely Zizi, Yellow Bird?" He laid his hands against his bosom and smiled. "*Tanka!*" Red Cloud, like the majority of men, admired Abbey's exquisite figure. Jack Red Cloud nodded and smiled, too.

Tom knew to smile just a little and to nod. "Her heart is *tanka*, too," he said. "She misses Thunder Cloud and their children. She hopes to return to Philadelphia by the *Moon of Popping Branches*."

Red Cloud drew long on the pipe. "That is a good thing. Many braves want her moccasins beside their sleeping mats. They wait like vultures for my nephew's death."

Tom took a deep draw of the pipe and released the smoke in a long stream. He looked from father to son. "Tell them Thunder Cloud's health is improving. Their wait will be long. He will be strong again soon."

Red Cloud nodded. "Daniel wrote of their plan to stay in Pennsylvania. Daniel says that may be a good thing."

Tom told Red Cloud and his son of the incident on the train with her first husband. "Thunder Cloud's wife needs protection. Many men want her. I heard rumors that Kincaid's holed up in a cave on the Yellowstone."

Jack Red Cloud grinned. "I will tell Crazy Horse, Thunder Cloud's old friend. Crazy Horse hates Ed Kincaid, calls him a coward of the worst sort for abandoning her. He, too, would be happy to take Yellow Bird as his wife."

Tom's face stayed smooth and he let loose a breath of laughter. "How many wives does Crazy Horse have now?"

"Too many," said Red Cloud with a deep chuckle. "They keep Crazy Horse warm but they make him crazy." Red Cloud laughed at his play on words, then more seriously, he said to Tom. "'Keep close to Yellow Bird and none of you should wander about." He looked to Hawk. "Stay with them both." He nodded to Tom again. "You should have a wife or two by now. Eh?"

Tom shook his head and chuckled. "Not me. No. No."

The pipe mellowed Red Cloud; he leaned back against a roll of hides. On such days he often ruminated in his memories, and at least once a day Red Cloud thanked his ancestors for the wisdom given him to choose Pretty Owl as a wife. Anyone alive now who attended Red Cloud's wedding to Pretty Owl understood.

He pointed the stem of the pipe toward his son then, Tom. "I was a young man such as you. I had given little thought to marriage. Most of my older cousins had at least two wives, maybe three. I supposed I would someday get around to choosing a wife.

"However, my mother announced one day that it was time." He took another pull on the pipe, the bowl burned bright. He smiled his smug little smile. "Women take care of such things. Isn't that so, Jack?"

Jack Red Cloud nodded.

Red Cloud's chest plate of buffalo hump bones rattled. "Who to pick? How to choose? I must tell you many women wanted me. I showed great promise as a young buck, and I loved them all." He handed the pipe to Tom.

"Finally, I decided on two, Pretty Owl and Pine Leaf, both lovely girls, both from good families. Even after choosing two I still needed to pick who to marry first." He shook his head. "Unlike horses, a man cannot bring a string of brides to the ceremony." He held up one hand. "One wedding, one wife."

Hawk quietly added wood to the fire and poked the hot embers with a stick. The fire flared bright.

Red Cloud shrugged. "I don't remember choosing. I think my people picked Pretty Owl. The women took care of such things. My mother, *Walks as She Thinks*, told me to leave four ponies at the tipi of Pretty Owl's father, then four more, and finally four truly magnificent horses.

"The elders talked." He made a sweeping motion with his arms. "Much fuss was made, dancing and drums, a night of revelry. Our family and friends erected a lodge of cured elk skins, made a bed of willow branches, buffalo robes, and trade blankets. My many war trophies were displayed. Finally, a ritual where Pretty Owl, wrapped in a blanket, was carried through the village by four armed warriors, with drums and dancing. They deposited her at my feet and Pretty Owl made dinner for our friends."

He paused and took a long pull of the pipe. "The following morning when I rose to greet the day as a married man I stepped out of our tipi. There hanging from a low branch of the cottonwood tree swung the bloated gray body of Pine Leaf. Her bulging eyes stared at me."

He shook his head and touched his son's knee. "Even today I feel the horror, the shock. I had no hint Pine Leaf would do such a thing. I screamed and ran to my mother's tipi. Your mother, Pretty Owl, ran to her father's lodge." He shrugged again. "For days, weeks, I do not know how long, I was inconsolable. Our families took care of the details. "Pretty Owl waited for my sadness to leave. Eventually, I returned to Pretty Owl and my tipi. I vowed then to have but one wife. I never married again."

Young girls, who wore metal trinkets on their knee-high fur boots, chiming as they moved, brought in plates of roasted meat and bread, and an urn of coffee. When they finished eating, Red Cloud said, "Tell your brother that this *LETTER* the white men sent has angered the reservation braves. They vow to join their brothers who roam if the army comes after them. That *LETTER* was not wise."

Chapter 15

SHADOWS

Daniel brought home two dozen red neckerchiefs from Philadelphia. "I bought out the store," he told them. The children loved the scarves. Summer, Lobo, Daniel, even Mrs. Love wore one. The Camelann Nine became simply *The Nine*. The scarves gave them camaraderie. It pleased Daniel that they were red.

Lilly became Emil's shadow. He took to hoisting her up behind him on his pony. She became comfortable around horses. Sitting on the fence she curried them and combed their manes, and with Emil's help she spread fresh straw in the stalls and filled their feedbags.

Emil took her to his grandmother's school. She shadowed Wakanda, too. She helped with weaving, pulverizing corn, and setting out strips of salted meat to cure; she took to the Lakota language as if she'd been born to it. She perfected her own language, too; she knew the ABC song by heart and sang along with the other children, and she could count to a hundred. Reading then writing would not be far behind. Like Emil talked nonstop to Summer Rose, Lilly threatened to wear out Wakanda's ears.

When Emil asked his grandmother what they talked about, Wakanda smiled her mysterious grin, her dark eyes twinkled. "Little girl secrets, Running Cloud." She lovingly touched his cheek. "They wouldn't be a secret if I told you, now would they?"

However, Wakanda did tell Daniel. "She speaks of an angel, a beautiful angel who stayed with her while in the cave. Do you have any idea what she's talking about?"

"I may."

⁂

Half a continent away, winter roared into the Pine Ridge Reservation with subzero temperatures, strong winds, and, heavy snow. Tom and Hawk strung ropes from tree to tree between Abbey's house and the school. Such a thing was a wise practice on the northern plains. In a whiteout an occasional body was found feet from their front door because they walked in circles for hours lost in the world of white.

That first day of braving the impossible whiteout, she wore the knee-high and fur-lined moccasins Pretty Owl had sent over and the quilted wool petticoat Violet made out of a trader's red blanket. "This petticoat weighs a ton! At least I won't blow away," she said as she stepped into the wind and wall of white. The snow blew sideways. Fine as sand it whistled up their sleeves and funneled down the backs of their necks.

At the first tree, Tom stopped, twirled her around so his body blocked the wind, and they kissed a long hungry kiss that erased any thought of cold. Neither the snow nor the icy wind bothered them at all. When he pulled away, she said, "I want to stay here all day and kiss you."

"If only we could," he said, a note of sadness lingered in his voice.

The school stood next door to the trading post. After firing up the school's woodstove, sweeping a path to the privy, and filling the wood box, Mercy, the mothers, and children filed into the school. Tom wandered over to the trading post where Toledo and Shortcake were sheltered. He spent a good two hours grooming them, cleaning their stalls, feeding them hay and oats, breaking the ice in their water trough and filling it with fresh water, for it made no sense to exercise them in this fierce cold. The horses nickered and rubbed against him, loving the attention.

When finished, he slipped through the passageway to the sulter's store. Violet had given him a list. Yesterday he'd shot an antelope and a brace of rabbits but they needed flour, coffee, sugar, salt, and some canned goods. Tom read the list to the Indian woman behind the counter and handed her a gunnysack. He pointed to a mesh bag of California oranges and held up three fingers. The Indian woman understood.

Hawk and two other Cheyenne men nodded a greeting. Jim Purvis hollered down from the loft, "Help yourself to some coffee. I'll be down in a few minutes."

The *LETTER* was the news. "The natives are getting the message. The big fear," Jim Purvis told him, "is that the peaceful Sioux living on the reservation will sympathize with their free-roamer kin and join them when the soldiers come after them."

"How many free-roamers are we talking about?" asked Tom.

Jim thought for a long moment. Tall, square built, and blond with a weathered complexion, he used his big, rough hands to emphasize his words. "We're talking of half a million square miles: Colorado, Montana, Wyoming, and the Dakota Territories. The white trappers and squaw men tell me there are thousands, maybe as many as ten thousand including the families. Sitting Bull has sent out messages to all the Hunkpapa, Cheyenne, and Arapaho. He promises a Sun Dance. Let's say a thousand are free-roaming warriors. If their kin on the reservations join them—and that is a very real fear— you're talking about two to three thousand young, angry warriors."

It was food for thought, and Tom muddled it over through all the month of January and on the train ride escorting Abbey and Violet home to Camelann. It was a long, sad train journey for Tom and Abbey knew it was the end of the love affair they never really began.

Will, Alice, and Emil with Dr. Cutter and Daniel met them at the station. Tom's heart sank. He hadn't expected Will to be at Camelann. He had hoped for at least one more day with her. Will, too, looked so much better, and strong. One might even call him robust. A knot twisted Tom's stomach.

What a dichotomy. The opposing emotions threatened to rip out his heart. A part of him wanted Will healthy for Abbey and the children, and another part wished him dead so he could marry his widow. He managed to hide his anguish until it came time to retire. Just the thought of her walking into the bedroom with Will, and it would be the room right beside his, threatened his sanity. He made an excuse to go to the barn and check on

Toledo. Daniel followed him; they talked and drank whiskey from Daniel's reserve stock for a good two hours, relating all the world's woes.

Before he returned to Fort Lincoln, Abbey found him in the barn preparing Toledo for the journey. For a long five minutes she combed Toledo's mane and rubbed his forehead. At last, she took Tom's hand and led him into a small, dim room where Daniel stored jars and tins of seeds, next year's crops. "You know I'm torn apart," she said as she leaned her face against his chest and placed her arms around him.

His voice came out harsh, angry. "You? I'm close to insane." Wild, wicked Tom Custer kissed her savagely before sensible, clear-headed Tom Custer kissed her tenderly. They both cried. "I know we agreed not to write, not to torture ourselves, but if you need me for anything, write anytime. I'll come for you, for Alice and Emil."

She nodded and touched his face, wiping his tears with her lace-edged hanky. Her voice choked. "Know Tom Custer, I will love you forever."

They both heard Daniel whistling as he walked down the path. Tom took her sodden handkerchief and stuffed it in his sleeve. From his breast pocket he pulled a big, crisp, linen one with TWC stitched above crossed swords and a flag, all embroidered in navy and gold thread, and wiped her face. He pressed his handkerchief into her hand. His voice, thick and low, hitched and he whispered. "Take mine. Go, my darling girl," his fingers feathered her cheek, "go before I do something stupid. I love you. I will always love you."

❧❧

Despite blizzard conditions Tom arrived in Fort Lincoln in early February. Armstrong and Libbie were not quite so lucky. Their train became stuck in huge drifts just a few miles from Bismarck. Armstrong sent a trooper up a telegraph pole to wire news of their dilemma to Fort Lincoln. Tom and a few friends rescued them with his sleigh, mules, and supplies. The Missouri was frozen thick, and the men walked beside the animals. Libbie rode in the sleigh. She recognized immediately that something seemed amiss with her beloved "little brother." It was Libbie who had taken the rough sixteen-year-old brother of her husband when he first joined the army and molded him into officer material. She leaned over the side of the sleigh and held onto his arm. "What happened, Tommy? You are sadder than even when Lulie died."

Libbie was the model of the woman he was looking for: beautiful, intelligent, and intuitive. "I'm okay. Ask me again when I'm drunk. I might tell you."

"Oh, Tommy, are you drinking again? I don't approve. You know it's not good for you. Agnes and Nettie are coming up next week. They'll cheer you up." Libbie patted his arm again. "All will work out."

He dipped his head. "I doubt it." He spoke louder so Autie could hear him. "We have a lot of work to do. Right?"

Autie nodded.

⚔

That evening Autie briefed his officers on General Sheridan's plans for the coming campaign. Sheridan's vision was no surprise. He emphasized that to round up these rogue Sioux, the campaign must begin as soon as possible. "Early spring, Sheridan insists. Otherwise, once the weather breaks, they will be difficult to find."

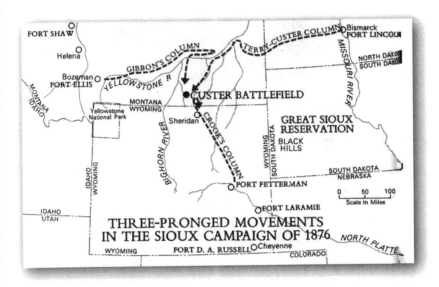

THREE-PRONGED MOVEMENTS IN THE SIOUX CAMPAIGN OF 1876

Armstrong pointed to the map tacked to the wall. "Sheridan's plan is classical Cavalry, a three-prong attack with Colonel Gibbon's column of eight hundred men, out of western Montana, staying north of the Yellowstone and preventing the hostiles from escaping north. Then General Crook with a column of eleven hundred men will come from Wyoming preventing escape to the south, and if all works well the hostiles will land in our laps."

Chapter 16

THE BEST LAID PLANS

The campaign to round up the roaming Indians, now dubbed *hostiles,* was set into motion. Of Sheridan's impressive three-prong attack, the Montana and Wyoming contingents were ready. Major General Sheridan formally ordered Brigadier General Alfred Terry, military commander of all the Dakota Territory, the okay to give Autie command of the Dakota column and a start date of April 6th.

The 7th Cavalry prepared to march. A great deal of work needed to be done. None of the twelve companies of the 7th were up to full strength in officers or enlisted men. Adjustments and shuffling positions needed to be made. Supplies were gathered, tallied, and ordered, and equipment evaluated. A hundred supply wagons buried under the snow with the wheels embedded in frozen mud needed to be collected and repaired. An army doesn't move on good wishes. The old adage from Shakespeare's *Richard III: For want of a nail, a shoe was lost, for want of a shoe, the horse was lost…*was as true now as it had been in Elizabethan

England. And as impetuous as the Custers were, they were not stupid. They knew the necessity of well-stocked and well-packed supplies and ammunition, oiled guns and axles, healthy animals and men. It was an enormous task, which George Custer and his able staff set about completing.

However, other interests were afoot. In mid-March Armstrong received a subpoena by telegraph demanding he come to Washington to testify before Hiester Clymer's congressional committee investigating corruption in the awarding of the lucrative army post traderships. Enormous amounts of money changed hands while feeding, dressing, and arming this military force. An army moves on its belly. Hannibal, Genghis Khan, and Napoleon knew that. The investigation centered on several members of the President's cabinet, mainly Secretary William Belknap.

George had raged to the press and fellow officers regarding the fraud in the trading post licensing and administration. Because of Armstrong's showmanship and popularity with the public, Representative Clymer demanded his presence. Although such a trip slowed the campaign, Armstrong eagerly wanted to testify. He had been complaining to the Department of the Interior for years. His soldiers and *his Indians* paid top dollar for moth-eaten blankets, rotten beef, and rock hard or wormy flour. The Army wives specialized in Sunshine Cakes, made by spreading trading post flour on a sunny rock. As the sun heated up the rock they watched the bugs run off. Then they used the debugged flour to bake the Sunshine Cake.

General Terry, Autie's commanding officer and overall commander of the western theater, and a Yale-educated lawyer, attempted to have the summons lifted. Furious, the Democratic Congress had no intention of releasing such a prime witness. The Republicans could wait to round up the natives. Haven't they been free roaming for centuries?

Belknap knew his goose was cooked so he resigned. President Grant's acceptance of his resignation infuriated the committee, and they filed Articles of Impeachment against Belknap anyway and intended to prosecute him. General Terry could do nothing to lift George Armstrong Custer's subpoena.

The evening before Armstrong departed for Washington, his staff, the majority of his thirty-two officers, threw an impromptu party to wish him well and perhaps pound a little sense into their fearless leader's thick skull. Autie's greatest characteristic, his willingness to smash headfirst into a fight, was equally his most limiting asset, barreling into an argument or fight without analyzing the pros and cons.

While the post sulters couldn't supply reliable flour or meat, bottled champagne and barrels of whiskey were in pristine and abundant supply. The party roared. Captain Myles Keogh, an Irish soldier of fortune, and one of the most senior captains of the 7th, confronted Tom, both of whom had already consumed more than enough alcohol. "Make sure, Tommy, your brother knows that under no circumstances should he badmouth the President, his friends, or his family. This Belknap Scandal—and Belknap is an old friend of Ulysses—-could bring the President down, and Tommy-boy, I know Ulysses Simpson Grant well enough to know he'll throw your brother to the wolves before he allows his administration to fail." Keogh opened a fresh bottle of champagne and filled Tom's glass. "You and I both know Grant has never been a fan of Armstrong. Is there any way you could go with him?"

⇥⇤

Autie waved off Tom and Myles Keogh's suggestion and left for Washington on the 21st of March 1876, with only an aide. He expected to return to Ft. Lincoln in a week. When he arrived in Washington, important Democratic congressmen wined and dined him, kept him out to the small hours, filling his head with great aspirations of how the Democratic Party adored him. He lapped it up, refilling his fragile confidence.

And with the political acumen of a day-old buffalo calf, he spent more time than he should have at Mary Ann Hall's place on Maryland Avenue. During the war her house had been by far the most elegant brothel in Washington, rivaling the New York houses. In addition to sporting a stable of lovely ladies with whom to spend the evening, it was the place to rub elbows with the rich and powerful. In 1876 Mary Ann's was still the place to be, but the paint was peeling and the roof leaked. However, Republicans prowled there too, and reported every activity to the President. So while Armstrong waited to be summoned, he enjoyed the city, partying with Democratic members of Congress. He angered the Republican President before he even testified.

The truth of the matter was the famous George Armstrong Custer's well of confidence bottomed out. He was frightened to the marrow of his bones. The entire quandary of would he or would he not command the 7th brought back those self-doubts and paranoia he usually hid so well. Ever since he graduated as the goat of his West Point class, he'd been the brunt of countless jokes and innuendoes. Just last week at the farewell party, he spotted Major Reno and Captain Benteen, his old enemies, whispering to a new lieutenant. He knew that miserable twosome told lies about him to the new officer. Usually such talk rolled off him like rain off a steep roof. After all, he'd married the prettiest woman, had one of the best commands, and his name made the newspapers more often than any other of his West Point classmates. The country considered him a hero. Rumor hinted he might be a surprise nominee on the Democratic ticket in the upcoming presidential election. He only had himself to convince.

Did Reno or Benteen mention to the new officer that I was a major general at 23, the first man to do so, that I alone held the line at Hanover defeating Jeb Stuart, and halting a Confederate victory at Gettysburg? Only my family and friends knew I'd been surprised with the early graduation and all the southern boys deserting the Academy. No wonder my class standing was so poor.

Usually he could shrug off gossip or bad press, but if he lost command of the 7th Cavalry, if he had to sit home twiddling his thumbs while his beloved 7th marched into harm's way, he'd die of humiliation and sadness. How could he watch his regiment, his friends, his brothers and nephew ride out to risk their lives and not be part of it? Armstrong, usually brimming with confidence and optimism, didn't know if he could prove himself again. Without a definite victory over the Sioux, he feared his career would be over.

Violet winced as Abbey walked into the sunny kitchen of Tilley's apartment. Will and Dr. Cutter had just left for their morning walk. Vi's gaze dropped to Abbey's wrist. *There she is again with Tom's handkerchief tucked in her sleeve. If Will notices it and discovers to whom it belongs, what might happen? My heart aches for her...for all three of them.*

On their trip west Abbey had become the daughter Violet never had. If she could have adopted Abbey and Tom as her children, she would have. She loved them that much. On the return trip from the west, they both separately, confided their feelings for each other and their resolve to end the affair honorably.

She's going to lose her looks if she's not careful, thought Violet. *She's lost at least ten pounds, her complexion is sallow, her eyes bloodshot, and her nose is red from crying. She loves both men and they both love her. You'd think everyone would be happy, but no one's happy except Dr. Cutter.*

Violet smiled. Dr. Cutter was becoming a close friend. *Elliott is so proud of his Indian. He should be. Will looks marvelous. When she first saw Will in Tilley's apartment she'd been shocked. Where was the stunning young half-breed who spent the winters of his youth in Toronto? The one the Toronto girls all flirted with? Then the handsome young Will Thunder Cloud sitting in Tilley's living room looked like a scrawny, gray-colored, hairless heathen.*

Now I can see it. With his chest and shoulders filled out he is a magnificent specimen of a man. Dr. Cutter has him working with clubs and weights and doing vigorous exercises. His chest and arms are huge. With a slight blush of rose slashed across those cheek-bones, his coloring is gorgeous, those blue eyes disarming. When Will Thunder Cloud smiles, he lights up a room. And his wife, with all her lush blonde beauty, looks ill. Oh, Abbey girl where's your grit? I cannot blame you for loving them both. Tom has more sexual magnetism in his smile than most men ever acquire. And your Will, well the maids are making eyes at him. Need I say more?

Violet sighed, a little color flushed her cheeks. In my day, I had my share of suitors and lovers. I broke a few hearts, too, and my heart shattered far too many times. Still to this day, I wonder whether or not Tennyson's poem is true.

"'TIS BETTER TO HAVE LOVED AND LOST, THAN NEVER TO HAVE LOVED AT ALL."

Love always seems to hurt. Those last few days on the train, watching them, had just about broken my heart again.

She fixed Abbey a cheese, bacon, and spinach omelet, rich with hollandaise sauce and coffee with cream and sugar. She set it down in front of her charge. "Eat all of it, miss. We are going to put a little weight on you. I have some exciting news you'll like."

Abbey looked up expectantly.

"After you clean your plate."

A touch of irritation entered Abbey's voice. "Stop treating me like I'm ten."

Vi didn't miss a beat. "You are going to have the figure of a ten-year-old unless you eat. Trust me. This news is happy news. Clean your plate."

Abbey pitched into the food, eating most of it. She looked up to Violet. "This better be good."

Vi refilled their coffee cups. "Actually, there are two things you'll like. First, Tom's brother is testifying in Washington at the Belknap scandal hearing." She handed Abbey the paper folded open to the article. "It sounds like he borrowed Tom's clothes."

Abbey grabbed the paper. Her finger slid down the column. "Colonel Custer appeared before the committee; he looked quite dashing in a black double breasted cashmere jacket with brass buttons and cream-colored trousers tucked into long black boots..."

Abbey beamed. "It does sounds like what Tom wore the last night on the train..."

"You'll like this even better. Dr. Cutter just this morning suggested we start packing. He and Will plan to leave for the Dakotas to visit Pine Ridge, then on to San Francisco. Will wants us and the children to go with them. School is almost finished."

Abbey jumped up and hugged Violet.

"Don't get your hopes up, dear child. You may not even see him."

Tears filled her eyes. "I know, Vi. I just want to breathe the same air he breathes."

❈

At Fort Lincoln, Tom and Libbie pored over the papers, too. They noticed the comment on the clothes Autie had borrowed from Tom, but ignored it for more pithy verbiage. Libbie pointed to an article in the *New York Herald*. "This one is done well."

Her finger skimmed down the column. "There are long paragraphs explaining that sulters are private contractors and how much money they make. And that their stores on the army posts aren't just some little hole in the wall where soldiers can buy candy and tobacco, but rather how they're similar to having a quartermaster on post." Her finger slid further down the column. "It explains how some sulters can cheat the soldiers and the Indians, how the traderships can only be appointed by the Secretary of War." She looked up. "This article doesn't mince words."

She read aloud to Tom, Boston, and her sister-in-law Maggie and her husband, Jimmy Calhoun: "The soldiers pay higher than market prices for goods. They have no other options. Stationed in the middle of nowhere, your sons can't run to the store in the next town. The traders also do an illicit business with the tribes, selling the natives weapons and other goods that could potentially be used against the troops."

Switching again to another paper, her fingers flew down the column. "Listen to this:" She read, "In 1870, at the urging of his second wife, Secretary of War William Belknap gave the trading post contract for Fort Sill to a man named Caleb Marsh. However, that fort already had a sulter named John Evans. They came up with an ingenious solution. They formed a partnership; Evans kept the trading post, with the provision that he give Marsh twelve thousand dollars a year in profits, through quarterly payments. Marsh then split that money with Carrie Belknap."

Libbie stopped for a sip of water and said, "It's hard to imagine that much money. A decent house costs what-seven hundred dollars? No wonder she can afford that mansion and those clothes." Libbie shuddered and looked up at her sister-in-law. "Do you think he's good looking? What's the attraction?" She made a face. "That beard! I keep expecting a bug to fly out of it."

She continued reading: "Carrie Belknap died of tuberculosis later that year, but her husband kept receiving payments for the care of their child. However, then the child died, and still, the money kept rolling into Belknap's pockets. After he married (for the third time) Carrie's sister, Amanda—you all know how I feel about Queenie—the cash flow continued. With the details of this plot exposed, Belknap had no choice but to resign as Secretary of War. Regardless, Clymer's Committee drew up Articles of impeachment." Libbie lowered the paper. "Here's the part about Autie "A series of articles in a New York newspaper exposed the schemes, using anonymous sources. One of those sources is rumored to be George Armstrong Custer, with an accusation that he may have even authored one of the articles. Colonel Custer testified on March 29 and then on April 4. He described the scheme at his own post, Fort Lincoln. His testimony rocked the Senate chamber.

"'During the prior year," Colonel Custer testified, 'I noticed my men paid higher than normal prices for their goods and supplies. Upon looking further into the matter, I discovered the sulter only received twelve thousand for every fifteen thousand of profits. The other thirteen thousand must go to either some illegal partnership or to the Secretary himself. The real surprise, however, came when I discovered a percentage of the funds went to Orvil Grant.'"

Libbie choked and turned pale.

After a sip of water she looked to Tom. "Didn't you warn him about that Tommy? I should have gone with him." Rage flashed in her eyes. "What has he done?" She looked around the room and handed the paper to Tom. "I cannot read any-more. God help us, Tommy. Orvil Grant is the President's brother."

Tom picked up the paper. Here the reporter inserted,"A silence hung for a long moment over the Senate Chamber then a collective gasp arose, as the reporters stumbled over each other to make it out the door to file their copy.

"Orvil Grant had been an investor in what appeared to be legal partnerships with three trading posts, one of them supposedly Fort Lincoln. Colonel Custer further told the committee that a fellow officer, who had tried to expose these arrangements, had been transferred against his wishes to Fort Buford on the Canadian border."

Chapter 17

WESTWARD HO

Tom stood and wadded Autie's letter to Libbie into a tight ball and hurled it against the dining room wall.

"What are you doing?" cried Libbie as she rescued the precious piece of paper. She kept all Autie's letters, tied up with blue ribbons and stored in a hatbox.

"Better you ask your husband what the hell he's doing. Doesn't he understand what a hornets' nest he's stirred up?"

Libbie sat back in her chair, her mouth in a tight line. Her hands worked methodically to smooth out the precious letter. "How many times do I need to tell you, Tommy, not to use profanity in my house? I'm serious, Tommy; I won't have it."

Tom sat back down. "I apologize, Libbie, but where is my brother's head?"

In the past, Armstrong didn't always see the repercussions of his actions. He'd gone eagerly to Washington to vent years of anger. He fully expected to be back in North Dakota in less than two weeks. He testified then relaxed with friends waiting for the committee to either summon or dismiss him. 1876 was the centennial year of America's birth. The big events would commence on July 4th, but soldiers especially didn't need much of an excuse for a party.

In mid-April when Clymer's committee finally released Armstrong, nearly a month after he left Ft. Lincoln, General Sherman stopped him in a hallway outside the hearing room. "You'd better pay your respects to the Commander-in-Chief and skedaddle back to Ft. Lincoln and get your column underway."

However, President Grant refused to see him, and furthermore the President asked his new Secretary of War, Alphonso Taft, who replaced Belknap, to appoint a new commander for the 7th.

If the President had his way, George Custer would be twiddling his thumbs when the 7th took to the field. In Grant's mind, accusations against his brother went beyond contempt. Grant had given his blessing to his brother's deals. In his mind, nothing appeared askew.

Stunned, Armstrong appealed to Sherman again who told him to see the President. Sherman then wired General Terry in St. Paul and suggested he prepare himself. "You may have to make do with a new commander of the 7th."

Again Grant refused to see him. In shock, Custer felt thwarted of any chance for redemption. Confused, frightened, and left with no place to go, he departed for Chicago to see General Sheridan.

To further humiliate him, President Grant, Commander-in-Chief of the Army, ordered Custer's arrest for not following Army protocol, for not seeing his Commander in Chief before departure. Upon Armstrong's arrival in Chicago, General Phil Sheridan, Autie's mentor, had him arrested.

Stone-faced, Sheridan said, "I regret this more than you do."

"Who will lead the 7th?"

"Major Marcus Reno."

Color drained from George's face. "Good Lord Almighty, you cannot allow that to happen."

All parties agreed. Reno did not have the *savoir faire* to replace Custer, let alone fight Indians. Frustrated himself, Sheridan sent Custer to Fort Snelling, Minnesota, to meet with General Terry, who was on leave. George Custer spent four days in a St. Paul hotel room under house arrest waiting for Terry's arrival.

When General Terry returned, he took one look at George Armstrong Custer. His heart filled with pity. To see a man of such boundless energy, courage, and confidence reduced to begging for his career hurt. And Terry wanted Custer back. The entire operation of herding the roamers onto the reservations fell on General Terry's shoulders, and he knew defeating the growing numbers of Sioux required boldness and a true Indian fighter like Custer.

Using his civilian skill as a lawyer, General Terry helped Custer compose a *soldier-to-soldier* letter to the President. Terry also wrote pleading for Custer's return. He convinced Sheridan and Sherman to do the same. No one, including any officer in the 7th, wanted Major Marcus Reno in charge of the 7th.

Custer's luck turned. In addition to his superior officers wanting him reinstated, public pressure regarding such poor treatment of an American hero caused Grant to reverse his stance. With the Centennial upon the nation, America needed to secure a victory against the Sioux, and it needed to be done soon. Putting aside the insult to his family, President Grant acquiesced.

George Armstrong Custer again commanded his beloved 7th Cavalry.

⚔

At first, when Will found the big linen handkerchief embroidered in navy and gold under his wife's pillow, he didn't realize the significance of TWC. Later in the day when Elliott wrote a prescription, he saw the doctor's initials, ETC, and suddenly he knew who TWC was, and the probable reason such a thing was under his wife's pillow. Abbey's tears, her depression, the dark circles under her eyes, her sadness, all made sense.

Will's heart skipped a beat and tears stuck in the back of his throat. *Oh, my brave, beautiful girl, he stole your heart, did he? And you came back to me? My precious girl, I am so sorry. You know I adore you. You should have told me. If you truly want him, I'll let you go.*

He walked from Tilley's living room back to their bedroom. A tear slid down the side of his long nose. He shook his head and sat down on a bench. *I love you, Abbey. I talk brave, and I don't know if I can really bear to let my Yellow Bird go. Talk to me, darling. Do you really love him? Perhaps it is just an infatuation?*

⚔

In bed, under the covers, at Camelann, Daniel leaned over Summer; his big hands softly massaged the bulge of the baby. Daniel loved making babies, the babies themselves, but with each of Summer's pregnancies he worried more. She suffered two miscarriages after Lilly's birth. He knew childbirth killed more young women than disease. He felt very responsible for putting her at risk.

While in Philly, he'd purchased some expensive cream which promised to help her skin retain elasticity. It not only smelled great, it gave him an opportunity to erase stretch marks and ease the aches of her pregnancy.

Summer moaned happily and asked, "Do you think a seven year old can really fall in love?"

"You mean Alice?" Tall, willowy Alice looked and acted far older than seven. He dipped into the jar and took another glob of cream and worked it into her left hip and leg. "What makes you think she's in love?"

"That feels marvelous. Ever since you told them they're leaving this week for the West, Alice has been floating around as if on a cloud. At first, I thought she might be happy to spend time with her parents, or see her old friends, but when I asked, she said, "Oh No! I'm excited to see Tom."

Summer rolled onto her other side. "My right hip and leg feel neglected."

"They do, do they?" He took another glob. As he started to work on her right hip, he said, "In my experience women or girls like men or boys who give them attention. Tom spent time with all the children to hide his feelings for Abbey. I will tell you, our sweet, little Lilly will be inconsolable when Emil leaves. She spends every minute she can with him. I plan to give her riding lessons when he departs."

He positioned Summer as flat on her stomach as possible, moved her long hair from her neck, and massaged along her spine. "Is there any place I've missed?"

Summer snuggled closer into his arms. "Daniel, you, who are brilliant about Alice, Lilly, Emil, Tom, and Abbey, know the answer to that question. Don't you?!"

⚞⚟

In mid-May Lt. Colonel George Armstrong Custer returned to Fort Lincoln with General Alfred Terry. All twelve companies of the 7th Cavalry were present and camped on the rolling plains just south of the post. Row after row of white tents stretched into the twilight. As Armstrong and General Terry arrived, the band played *Garry Owen*. Armstrong and Libbie and General Terry gathered for a short reunion in Tom and Boston's tent then left for their own quarters. Reveille, scheduled for four in the morning, would come too soon.

Fog delayed departure, but once the tents were loaded on the wagons, General Terry ordered the command to march through Fort Lincoln. For the first time all twelve companies of the 7th Cavalry mounted on horseback stood together, totaling thirty-two officers and seven hundred and eighteen enlisted men. Several companies of infantrymen with three Gatling guns and Lt. Charlie Varnum's thirty-nine Indian scouts plus the dozen or so Ree scouts of the Arikara tribe accompanied the regiment. One hundred and fifty wagons, a mule train, a cattle herd with teamsters, herdsmen, and packers waited at the rear. Generals Terry and Armstrong with Libbie and Maggie watched the review. Tom rode at the head of Company C.

The morning was still damp with a chill, the guidons barely moved, the horses snorted, as Lt. Colonel George Armstrong Custer turned and barked, "Forward!" Each company commander in turn shouted, "Forward!" As they moved toward the fort they first passed the women and children of the Indian scouts, who stood by their tipis, singing and chanting. The deep voices of the Indian men answered with singing and beating of their drums. The dirge continued as the troops passed by Ladies Row where the enlisted men's families stood. As they moved into the fort proper, the band struck *The Girl I Left Behind Me*", a song which had sent men to war for centuries. Armstrong halted the troops on the parade ground and ordered the married men to dismount and say goodbye to their families. Only a few eyes remained dry. *"Boots and Saddles"* sounded. Just as the column left Fort Lincoln and converged with the wagon and mule trains, the sun burst through the mist.

That night they camped along Heart Creek. By starlight, Tom wrote to Abbey.

My Dearest, My Golden Girl,
I know we promised to not write, to not prolong the agony. I find myself needing to tell you one last time how much I love you and to thank you for touching my life. I find since we met there's a peace inside me I never before knew. The skies are a little bluer, the air a little crisper. The stars here on the

high plains are thick and bright enough to read by. My one regret is you are not beside me. I can just imagine the color of your hair in this light, the scent of you. Please know dear golden girl, you're in my heart and will be forever.

With all my love,
Always, Tom   *May 1876*

He slid the single sheet into an envelope addressed simply 'Abbey', and then slipped that envelope into one addressed to Mrs. Violet Montour in Philadelphia.

When he walked over to where Libbie and Maggie were staying, he gave the letter to the sulter who would escort the ladies back to the fort in the morning. The sulter had accompanied the regiment this far to collect what the soldiers owed him. Autie had wisely waited until twelve miles from the fort to have the paymaster pay the men. Otherwise, a lot of the soldiers would have blown their pay on whiskey and showed up drunk this morning.

Tom warned him to keep his letter from Libbie or Maggie. "They'd probably steam it open. I don't want that. It's just a thank-you note to a dear lady."

※

Violet and Abbey had already left Philadelphia when Tom's letter arrived. Tilley tossed it onto the growing stack of Violet's mail.

However, Abbey's spirits rose considerably just getting underway. They stayed one night at Camelann in order to pick up the children and say goodbye. Mrs. Love, in addition to serving them a delightful roast beef diner with Irish potatoes and Yorkshire pudding, gave them a huge hamper full of ham and beef sandwiches, hard boiled eggs, pasties, donuts, pies, and cookies, all the foodstuffs to which Dr. Cutter objected.

As they stood on the platform about to board, Summer, Daniel, Wakanda, and all the children gathered around them, all talking at the same time.

"Wire us when the baby arrives. I think it's another boy."

"Bite your tongue Abbey Dupree. It's a girl. Let us know you are all safe."

"Alice, watch him. Keep him off the roof."

While everyone hugged and kissed, Daniel held Lilly in one arm and handed his sister and Will a small notebook. "I copied down some cipher and router codes for telegrams."

Will nodded. He had just finished reading Anson Stager's book about secret ciphers and codes used during the war.

Daniel lowered his voice because Lew and Martha were within earshot. "From now on send all telegrams in code, and send them and any mail to the Emmitsburg, Maryland, post office. A few acres of Camelann dip into Maryland, so I'm able to arrange mail delivery there. I am sick of you-know-who knowing our business. I know she steams open our letters."

With Lilly sobbing against his shoulder he hugged the ladies and shook hands with Will and Elliott, then hugged Alice and Emil. Emil looked as upset as Lilly. At the last minute he reached up and forced Lilly into a hug. It was painful to watch.

To all but looking directly at Abbey, he said, "Stay safe. You will always have a home at Camelann."

⊰⊱

Daniel had been right. Lilly sobbed when Emil boarded, and Daniel held her tight against his shoulder while she cried all the way home. Once there, as prearranged, her brothers and Louisa brought out a smart looking black pony, just Lilly's size.

She wiped her eyes with her fists and looked up to her father. "For me?"

"For you. It's an early birthday present. Emil helped me pick her out."

She squirmed down, stretching out a hand, allowing the pony to smell her.

She instantly loved the pony and insisted on naming her Sooty because the mare, except for a white star on her forehead, was black as soot. Although her brothers and Louisa tried, no one could talk her out of the name.

With her face snuggled against the pony's neck, she said with her jaw set, "Soot is not dirt. It is coal dust. It's black and shiny, just like Sooty."

Daniel insisted, as he had done with all his children, she learn to care for Sooty. He didn't make her muck Sooty's stall, that would come later, but he taught her to rub down the little mare, curry her, comb her mane and tail, and clean her hooves. She learned to measure the grain and spread the clean straw and to do so on a schedule. "Animals learn to love those they trust to care for them," he told her. "How would Sooty manage to get her oats if you forget? If you cannot care for her, make sure someone else does."

No one needed to teach her to ride. Daniel planned to smooth out the rough edges, but she knew the basics probably from all the time she spent with Emil.

⚍

The travelers didn't have a fancy railroad car for this trip, just facing seats, where Abbey and Will sat across from Dr. Cutter and Violet. Emil and Alice when they weren't roaming the train sat with them. Elliott Cutter proved to be an excellent traveling companion. In addition to being a fascinating conversationalist, he told wonderful stories and jokes. He played cards with them all. After asking permission of Abbey and Will he lent a huge book about Human Anatomy by Henry Gray to Alice and Emil. Every morning he assigned them a small section to study and every evening he tested them. They excelled and loved it.

"It's the best thing," said Abbey. "Otherwise, they'd be running about on the roof of the train."

Violet giggled, "Oh dear Abbey, they go to the roof. Will takes them. Elliott and I went up yesterday while you napped. You should come with us sometime. The weather is beautiful. So is the scenery."

At night, Alice and Emil shared a berth, as Abbey and Will did. Vi and Elliott had separate berths across the aisle. Will whispered to his wife, "I heard Elliott's voice coming from Violet's berth. Do you think...?"

Abbey grinned, "I wouldn't be surprised, but perhaps they're playing cards."

Now Will laughed outright, snorting loudly, as he pulled his wife into a big hug. "They may be playing but it is not cards."

⊹⊱⊰⊹

To Abbey, Will could not have been sweeter or more attentive. After much deliberation, Will decided not to mention the handkerchief. He did put an Indian agent in Custer's camp to spy on Tom. Perhaps Tom Custer would just fade away. After all, the west was a very big place.

And although Tom's handkerchief stayed tucked in her sleeve, at times Abbey almost forgot him for a minute or two. Riding on the roof improved her color; she began to eat better.

Will thrived. He spent time with his children testing them on human anatomy and explaining codes and ciphers. He and the children concocted simple codes and sent them to Camelann. All the adults stood in awe of their brainpower. Once more they felt like a family. The ride from east to west became a healing time. She didn't faint once.

Chapter 18

ANGELS

As Daniel led his small troop around the mountain to Emmitsburg, Maryland, Lilly on black Sooty rode beside Louisa on cream-colored Feather, both directly behind Daniel on Chester. The twins and Johnnie on three frisky pintos followed with Lobo on a powerful paint at the rear. All wore their red headbands. Misty spring sunshine filtered through the pale green canopy, and splashes of wild plum and mountain laurel peeked around the thick tree trunks. Songbirds twittered, gathering twigs and feathers, hawks circled overhead. In the distance, a woodpecker rat-a-tat-tatted. Spring bloomed around them.

"We used to come *this* way to visit my mother when she was ill," said Louisa to Lilly. *The Sisters of Charity* took care of her at their sanitarium."

"She died, didn't she?"asked Lilly.

Louisa nodded. Her bright blue eyes grew bigger and wet.

Last week, the children had scared off three coyotes from the remains of a dead doe they found in the woods. The crows had already taken the eyes.

Now Lilly thought of Emil's leaving. In a soft voice she asked Louisa, "Dying is worse than someone going away on the train, isn't it?"

Louisa nodded. Lilly cried herself to sleep most nights. "You'll see Emil again. I have to die in order to see my mama. I miss her every night."

Just the thought of losing her mother brought tears to Lilly's eyes. Her young mind whirled with heavy thoughts about life, dying, and death. "Emil said he'd write a letter to me. I can't write very well yet. Will you teach me?"

"You'll learn to write in school, but you can tell me what to say and I'll write it down. We can do that tonight. I'll write to Alice, too."

The path suddenly opened into a bright grassy field, so green it made them blink. Below a road shot straight as an arrow to a village of white buildings. Beyond the little town smoky, blue, mountains seemed to stretch forever. A church bell rang, and the aroma of baking bread reached them."

Daniel turned Chester and faced his troops. Unfortunately, he had not packed a lunch. "I smell it too, and I can hear your stomachs growling. Hold your horses. I want to stop at the post office here then we'll see about lunch."

They followed Daniel across the Mason Dixon Line into Emmitsburg, Maryland. A few dogs barked, a woman ceased beating a rug, which hung from a clothesline, and a blue-shirted man hammering atop a house, stopped and stared. Two little girls pushing a miniature baby carriage waved. Lilly and Louisa waved back.

At the post office, gravel crunched as they dismounted and hitched their horses. Then leather boots clunked against the wooden steps and onto the porch as they followed their father inside; Lobo stayed outside, as the self-appointed guardian.

Inside the small post office, Daniel introduced the children by name and each child walked up and shook hands with the postmaster, Mr. George Grundy, a thickset man with huge hairy black whiskers, which covered all but a small patch of his face and neck.

"What good handshakes," said Mr. Grundy. "Did your father teach you?"

Lilly shook her head. "No Sir, our mother taught us." She looked at the others. "No dead codfish, right?" With her hands on her hips, she looked up to the big man. "That's what she whispers to remind us to shake hands like she taught us, not like a dead codfish."

Mr. Grundy's black eyes twinkled; his belly jiggled. He turned to Daniel. "You have your hands full. She reminds me of Summer. You know, we played together as children then her father sided with the Yankees." He shook his head. "Please give my regards to your wife. How can I help you General Charteris?"

"Please call me Daniel, George. The war is over. I want to open a post office box and introduce you to my children and the Indian boy who is standing outside. These children and Lobo will pick up the mail and any telegrams."

"I can help you with that."

Daniel smiled at his children. "Go outside and keep Lobo company. I'll be out in a few minutes."

⚉

As Mr. Grundy flipped the little sign from OPEN to CLOSED and locked the post office door, Daniel said, "We can leave the horses here. Mr. Grundy suggested *Aunt Sally's* down the street."

Lilley and Johnnie, their eyes wide, both saw a bug fly out of Mr. Grundy's beard. She went to tell her father, but he shushed her.

At *Aunt Sally's* a blast of chatter, clanging crockery, and the aroma of frying bacon greeted them as Daniel held the door for Mr. Grundy, the children, and Lobo. Of the children, only Louisa had eaten in a restaurant, so their excitement ran high, especially the boys and Lobo who eyed the platters of meatloaf, mashed potatoes, and gravy. Lilly from her perch on her father's arm took in the blue oilcloth-topped tables, the white crockery, the display of pies in a glass case, and the rebel flag pinned to the back wall. The rich aromas made her mouth water.

A pretty girl with her red hair pinned up and wearing a white apron over a brown-checkered dress approached; she smiled at Daniel and pinched Lilly's cheek. "Aren't you a sweetie? Come this way, Sir."

A white-haired old woman with enormous popped eyes and a black shawl flapping at her elbows, hustled toward them. Her crablike claws grabbed Lobo's arm. "You'll have to step outside. We don't serve your kind."

Daniel's free hand clamped on her wrist and removed the claw from Lobo's arm. With his voice deep and smooth as cream, and to people who knew him, dangerous as acid, he answered, "That's unfortunate. You won't be serving us either. Come children." He nodded toward the postmaster. "Is there anywhere else?"

"None that serve heathens or niggers. Relax Daniel, we'll send out a sandwich. He can eat it out back."

Daniel shook his head and motioned for the children to go outside. "We eat where Lobo eats. I won't promote such prejudice." He followed the children out the door, easing it shut. "I know just the place, a place where they don't use ugly words."

As the door slid shut, Louisa whispered, "You did very well, Daniel. You didn't lose your temper."

He expelled a deep breath and whispered back. "I've been working on that."

⚓

As the train rolled into Pine Ridge, Emil and Alice stood first in line, ready to launch themselves off the train. Dressed in buckskins, red headbands, and feathers, he and Alice anxiously awaited the reunion with their friends and their Great Uncle Red Cloud.

They were not disappointed. Red Cloud, Crazy Horse, and half a dozen Indian men waited with Emil and Alice's friends. Once their party detrained and clustered about their luggage, the greeters raced their ponies around them, whooping, yelling, blowing their eagle bone whistles, making a racket and sending up clouds of Dakota dirt.

The Indians wore their eagle bone whistles on a string hung around their necks. They were made from the long wing bone of an eagle and emitted a high-pitched haunting scream, which in war intimidated their enemies.

Red Cloud dismounted and embraced them all. He motioned to the riders. "They wanted to see for themselves if Thunder Cloud is as healthy as the drums foretold."

Will laughed as he greeted his friends. "They just want to see if Yellow Bird still puts up with me." He tucked an arm around Abbey. "She does."

A string of several spare ponies trailed behind the chief; Mercy and Hawk again borrowed the sulter's wagon for the luggage. After greetings and introductions, Abbey, looking fresh in a sunny yellow dress with a white straw hat, chose to ride on the wagon with Violet. Memories of Tom threatened to overwhelm her as she suddenly realized it was here at the Pine Ridge train station where she'd first met Tom Custer. How kind he had been.

Violet took her hand. "Easy child, they're all watching you. Who is that big, foreboding man wearing a red trader's blanket? He's staring at us. He's very handsome in a frightening way."

With her face turned, Abbey said, "That's Phizi, in Lakota, Gall in American. He and Crazy Horse are the warrior headmen of the Hunkpapa Lakota. Sitting Bull is the spiritual leader of their tribe. Gall, Crazy Horse, Jack Red Cloud, and Thunder Cloud were all born the same year, they grew up together. Don't look directly at Gall or Crazy Horse or any of the ones talking with Will."

She exhaled a long breath. Her Will looked robust, excited. He wore buckskin trousers and vest. The muscles in his bronze arms rippled. Jack Red Cloud handed him a bone breastplate, a rifle, and a tomahawk.

He looked over to Abbey and smiled. The other men glanced too, and Crazy Horse said something; they all laughed. Abbey understood all too well that in some ways Indian men differed very little from white men. And not for the first time did she regret her full breasts and hourglass figure. If Will died, Gall, Crazy Horse, and others would want her as a wife.

She shuddered. Most natives had a stable of wives. They would marry one woman and if she proved a good wife, they'd marry all her sisters, creating one big family. Marriage to Will had been different; they'd lived off by themselves, in a house, with books, a wooden floor with braided rugs, and an iron stove, not a tipi with a buffalo robe floor. She and Will lived away from the general population. Will was educated, his father was white. In her presence he acted white although he could be as Indian as the rest of them. Their marriage was altogether different than marriage to a full-blooded Sioux.

She nudged Violet. "See that young man off to the left in the long coat and bone plate and all the feathers? That is Wolf Tracker also known as Beau Farro. He's a promising medicine man; some say he's Sitting Bull's protégé. He sees visions and knows the weather before it happens." Abbey arched her eyebrows. "I haven't seen this but he's rumored to catch bullets in his bare hands."

Will walked over to the wagon; he possessively planted his hands around her waist and lifted her, holding her in midair, making a show of kissing her, smiling at his old friends, silently announcing to whom she belonged. After situating her on the wagon seat, he chose a gentle black and white spotted pony to ride; Dr. Cutter, a polo player in Philadelphia, entrusted his doctor's kit to Violet, then mounted a spirited bay with white stockings. He looked to be having the time of his life.

⹅⹅

In Morgan's Corner, Ed Kincaid watched Lew Graves walk toward the town to the saloon. He did so most afternoons. Then the former military officer entered the general store. He stood by the stove reading a newspaper until Martha entered and nodded to him. He returned her gesture. They knew each other from the war. A general hatred of the Charteris family gave them a common bond.

"She left for the West last week. She took her half-breed and their Injun brats with her. Want a ticket?"

He held up his good hand and flashed his West Point ring. "How far will this take me?"

Martha smiled. "Down to that, are you?"

She didn't wait for an answer. "Keep your ring." She slid a cross country ticket to him and a twenty dollar bill. "Teach the bitch a lesson."

⹅⹅

Daffodils ruffled the fine gravel path to the convent. Daniel yanked the bell pull at the high gate. The children ignored their growling stomachs and stood back with the horses. The scent of fresh bread had their mouths watering again. As they had ridden out of Emmitsburg, Daniel had explained that he had planned to visit *The Sisters of Charity* after lunch. "I want to introduce you all to them. If you are ever in trouble—a lame horse, a sudden storm, anything—stop here and they'll keep you safe. In the winter Lobo and I shoot several deer for them. We'd do anything to help them. Right Lobo?"

Incredibly shy, the young Indian nodded and looked down at the ground. Daniel continued. "They were tireless nurses during the war, and they took wonderful care of Louisa's mother." He reached over and squeezed his half-sister's shoulder. "And they are our neighbors. They wear black or white dresses and great white hats." And," Daniel paused with his eyes twinkling, "they gave us a starts for our rhubarb bed at home."

All the children made faces. Rhubarb, a ritual of spring, was not a favorite. Mrs. Love mixed it with strawberries and ruined the pie.

A woman, dressed in black as Daniel had described, opened the high gate. Lilly grew wide-eyed and uncharacteristically still. Another woman came who Daniel introduced as Sister Mary Agnes. She knew Louisa and kissed the girl. "What are you feeding her? Oh, my, haven't you grown."

She shook hands with all the children and made a special fuss over the boys. She studied Gus and Mac. "You are twins? You look nothing alike. You must be Johnnie and you're as big as your brothers." She came to Lobo, taking his hands in hers. I know you're good at hunting. Can you climb trees?"

All the boys nodded. So did Lilly.

She gestured to a shaggy barked sycamore. "Well, after lunch will you rescue a kitten from that large sycamore tree? He climbed very high."

Daniel piped in. "We'll be glad to help." He explained what happened in town.

Sister Mary Agnes crossed herself. "I apologize for their ignorance and rudeness. Will that horrid war ever end? You all must be starved." She took Lobo's arm and led the troop into a lovely arbor where pale grape vines and lavender pods of wisteria threw sharp shadows on the flagstone floor. She directed them to sit on benches along a white linen-draped table. Within five minutes and making no sound, other sisters placed plates, silverware, and napkins in front of them and served cups of steaming potato soup, silky smooth with flakes of carrot and chives. Other sisters passed large platters of sandwiches, egg salad on dark bread and ham on rye. Others sisters served sweet tea and a platter of pickles and condiments.

Silent and on their next-to-best best behavior, the children struggled to sit straight and still on the benches while the sisters served them. Mac and Gus squirmed and giggled until Louisa pinched Gus and shot a sharp look at all the boys. Although starved, they settled to wait until everyone was seated. Sister Mary Agnes bowed her head and said grace.

No sooner had Sister Mary Agnes said, "Amen," when Lilly shot off the bench like a pea out of a shooter, nearly taking the table cloth with her, and jumped into the arms of a sister so tiny she appeared as if her winged wimple might carry her aloft. Louisa saved the tablecloth and dishes while both Lilly and the sister cried and carried on, hugging and kissing and laughing.

Lilly danced her to Daniel. "Look Daddy, this is the angel from the cave."

Daniel stood and Sister Mary Agnes walked over. "General Charteris, I'm pleased to introduce Sister Mary Clare, our newest novice. She stayed with your little one when she dropped from the ceiling of the cave practically into our laps." She frowned. "I guess our secret is out now. We hope you will keep it."

She slowly allowed her eyes to drift over all the children and Lobo. "That cave runs between our grotto and your lake. Before the war we used it as part of the Underground Railroad. Summer's parents helped us. We keep it secret. I don't know how many poor souls hid in our caves. Only God knows the future." She looked to Lobo. "Evil people still do evil. We may need it again."

Chapter 19

GATHERING STORMS

Bivouacked along the Little Missouri, Captain Myles Keogh nodded toward General Alfred Terry, who sat sound asleep in a camp chair with chin to chest, and whispered to Tom Custer, "War is a young man's game."

Tom and Myles sat on a hillside enjoying the hot spring sunshine and sharing a cigarette. Their horses watered nearby. Before them the spring grass undulated beneath a pale yellow sky that stretched all the way to the mountains. It was difficult to believe that just three days ago snow had kept them immobile for two days.

"He does look beat," said Tom and handed the smoke to Keogh. "How old is he?"

"He's forty-nine, and he's been sitting behind a desk in St. Paul far too long. Grant had no business sending him out here. Twenty-five to thirty miles a day over wild country, sleeping rough is hard on me, and I'm only thirty-one." He took a long pull on the cigarette. "How far have we come from Ft. Lincoln?"

Myles knew the engineers for map-making purposes attached an odometer to the wheels of one of their wagons, and he knew Tom checked the mileage each day.

"One hundred and sixty-five miles and we haven't seen one hostile." He took the cigarette from Keogh. "Grant just sent Terry along to remind Autie he doesn't trust him. Why can't Grant just leave him alone?"

Myles Keogh stood. Tall, handsome, fit, often called the heartthrob of the 7th. After leaving a long trail of broken hearts, he recently had settled down with one girl he hoped to wed. Around his neck on a rawhide cord hung the medal, given to him by Pope Pius IX for gallantry during the papal wars. He seldom took it off. Now, he fingered it. "If I've learned one thing, Tommy, nothing is as it seems. Grant is America's hero; he saved the Union. Remember, too, he ordered us to burn the Shenandoah, ordered Sherman to destroy Atlanta and South Carolina then he hounded Lee until he surrendered. He only redeemed himself by being fair to the conquered, but I'm sure you noticed he wasn't at all kind before they surrendered. Your brother crossed Grant. Paybacks may be forever."

He motioned toward Major Reno and Captain Benteen, who sat on a rock near where their horses watered. "Take those sneaky bastards. They should slide under that rock rather than sit on it. They've been passed over more times than they can remember; they're in their forties, they're useless. No one trusts them. Reno made an ugly pass at my girl." He spit disgustedly.

Tom raised his eyebrows.

"For Christ sake, the little lily-livered rat reached under her skirt, way under it. Granted, he was drunk, but that is no excuse.

I nearly killed him, but your brother stopped me. Thank God. I'd have hated to swing on the end of a rope for him. Reno's an incompetent leech, but Benteen's dangerous. Someday, someone is going to wipe that sneer off his moon face. He detests Armstrong and makes no effort to hide it."

He ground out the cigarette butt. "How far is it to the Yellowstone?"

⚞⚟

Tatanka Iyotake felt his 45 winters. His subordinate chiefs, Crazy Horse and Gall, managed the camp, sent out scouts and spies, developed war strategies, and protected the people. Daily new families joined the Gathering. Leading this enormous village through the great rolling plains was a huge undertaking, so when Tatanka Iyotake's ancient mother, Her-Holy-Door, stopped him just outside his tipi and gave him advice, he listened. "Allow the younger headmen to fight the *wasicu*. You, my son, have wisdom and experience to offer. Seek guidance."

Abbey and Violet felt honored to sit among the headman's wives. Abbey knew some Lakota, the Indian women knew a little French and English, and if Emil or Alice were about, they translated. However, they communicated by showing and doing. While the Indian women knew basics sewing, Violet gave them slender steel needles and taught them to wax these fine needles and embroider wildflowers on their babies' blankets. She shared from her trove of embroidery thread and taught them to make various embroidery stitches: chain, feather, blanket, herringbone, French knots, and more. Soon strings of lavender violets and white daisies with delicate yellow centers and green leaves, golden sunflowers, and brown cattails with spears of green, decorated the edges of their blankets.

Just as Abbey and Vi knew to look away at some of the grosser practices of food preparation, they knew to talk of just women's work. They realized they knew much more than even the chiefs because of Tom's lectures. Way back in Philly and Camelann before they embarked, Dr. Cutter and Daniel advised them not to advertise their knowledge.

"And above all," added Will, "do not mention you know any of the Custers."

From the corner of her eye, Vi watched Abbey's fingers quiver and said, "Tom Custer did go with us to Pine Ridge. Jack Red Cloud is aware we know him."

Will's eyes, Vi noted, searched his wife's face. He said, "Just don't mention him. Pretend he is dead."

Vi's gaze dropped to the throbbing vein in Abbey's neck; she watched the girl's shaking hands searched for the edge of that handkerchief. *Just once*, Vi thought, *I wish she'd forget that damned rag.* However, even here in the camp with thousands of Sioux studying their every move, that handkerchief ended up tucked in her sleeve. Violet suspected Will saw it also.

Dr. Cutter had become informed through Jack Red Cloud, who spoke excellent English. One evening sitting around their fire, Dr. Cutter and Jack Red Cloud explained, "The Sioux chiefs blame their current woes on the *wasicu,* the Americans. They feel their troubles began when the yellow-haired, Colonel George Armstrong Custer took twelve hundred soldiers, a geologist, and miners into the Black Hills, the

Paha Sapa, the sacred land of the Sioux, and discovered *Maza Zee,* gold ore.

"Little Phil," Elliott further told them, "promised to abide by the Treaty of 1868, but somehow 15,000 miners seeped into the sacred *Paha Sapa.* Little Phil's soldiers chased them out but for every miner that left two more showed up."

Jack Red Cloud leaned forward and stirred the fire. "My father met with the *wasicu.* The United States Government made an offer to purchase the Black Hills. I heard Red Cloud ask for seven generations of basic subsistence for his people and six hundred million. The government man counter-offered six million and negotiations failed completely which didn't surprise us. These are the same people who announced to the world that the only good Indian was a dead Indian.

"Then the LETTER was sent out this past December demanding all hostiles report to a reservation. If they refuse, no ammunition will be sold to them and no basic supplies will be given. Unable to hunt and with no subsistence supplies, the hostiles will think the *wasicu* government plans to starve them into submission." He paused and studied each face. "It's been done before."

Another night, Dr. Cutter situated himself cross-legged on a blanket with Emil and Alice. He took an offered piece of antelope, ate it enthusiastically, and drank cool spring water from his tin cup. He wiped his mouth then said to his small audience. "Then *Three Star Crook,* commander of the Yellowstone column made a stupid error." Elliott again wiped his fingers on a cloth. "George Crook is no three star general. He's a brigadier." Elliott chuckled. "The Indians dubbed him such because he wears three stars, one on each shoulder and one on his hat. *Three Star Crook* carries a rabid hatred of Crazy Horse. He took a thousand horse soldiers out in search of him. Instead *Three Star Crook* found the camp of Chief Two Moon, a peaceful Cheyenne. *Three Star Crook* attacked and his men brutally murdered men, women, and children." He motioned with his big head to a bedraggled group of Cheyenne further along the stream.

They looked and saw them huddled around small fires even though the day was warm. Near them Hunkpapa women erected tipis. "The survivors have found refuge here in Sitting Bull's camp. They are angry and their kin are angry. I am angry, too. How can they kill children?"

As Dr. Cutter spoke, the great Tatanka Iyotake returned from a three day fast and meditation. He stood on a slight rise and, in his deep resonate voice, announced to his people. "I promise you not only a Sun Dance, but also a red blanket."

⚑⚑

Dear Nines,
Greetings from somewhere near the Montana Territory!
Alice and I wonder whether or not you are still the Nines.
Although there are only Seven of you now that we are trav-
eling the West, we decided Nines should stand because we
plan to come back to Camelann. The West is beautiful, but
we miss Pennsylvania's trees.

The train ride went very fast. Dr. Etcetera made the trip
fun. He knows all kinds of card games and tricks, and he
taught us human anatomy and all about ciphers and codes.

Most days we rode on the roof of the train. The weather was so fair even our mother, Yellow Bird climbed up on the roof with us. With a little color on her cheeks now she looks a great deal healthier.

We stopped for two days at Pine Ridge in the Dakota Territory. We stayed in our old house, which seemed so small. Mama said it just seemed that way because I've grown. We visited a few of our old friends and Red Cloud. Most of Red Cloud's camp went west with Sitting Bull and the Hunkpapa tribes. A great Sun Dance and Gathering are promised so the Cheyenne and Arapaho tribes have joined Sitting Bull. Red Cloud did not go with the tribes. Rumor says he's too old. I think he's pouting because he's not the leader. However, his son Jack Red Cloud and his family, against his father's wishes, plan to join Sitting Bull.

Sitting Bull is not a true translation of Tatanka Iyotake. A better translation of his Indian name would be 'Buffalo Bull Sits Down.' The whites won't change their thinking, but to be clear and correct I will call the man the white's call, Sitting Bull, Tatanka Iyotake.

Our father, Thunder Cloud, insists we all follow the tribes to the Grand Gathering and Sun Dance. He said both are part of his heritage and we should know of it. Dr. Etcetera especially wants to see this Sun Dance.

At first, Mama and Violet were to stay behind in Pine Ridge, but our father's friend, Crazy Horse, supplied us with horses and found a large-wheeled buggy for Violet and Mama. Sometimes they need to get out and walk because the land is too rough, but most days they stay in the buggy.

It looks like a sawed off Conestoga wagon. Alice and I ride miserable ponies, they are both stubborn and long in the tooth. Gall promises better horses for us as soon as we get into the Montana Territory. Thunder Cloud's health improves every day.

When we camp, our tipi is set near those of Tatanka Iyotake, Crazy Horse, and Gall; Thunder Cloud and Dr. Etcetera sit around the fire and talk long into the night with these and other Indian leaders.

Mama and Violet now wear beaded buckskin dresses and moccasins. The Indian wives fixed them up. From a distance, Violet could pass for a gray-haired Indian grandmother with her hair fixed in long braids, but poor Mama. They darkened her hair with a dye made from a mixture of boiled tree bark and smashed walnut shells. After dying it, they smoothed it down with goose grease, which smelled like dead fish and rotten eggs. She cried and Thunder Cloud took her upstream and helped her wash her hair. They stayed away for a long time. Alice and I worried about them until Gall came over and told us they were okay and for us to go to sleep. In the morning, there was Mama, all smiling and smelling much better. Her hair is still dark, but curly. Our father found a ragged slouch hat for her. He sat behind her locking her tight between his knees as he tucked her dark curls under it. The both laughed. We all are happy she smells better.

Alice and I translate for the women. When not helping them, we spend our days playing with the other children, but it's not nearly as much fun as the Camelann Nine. We see Tatanka Iyotake but he walks off by himself to consult with the spirits.

Today is a day of celebration. Fire-roasted antelope smells delicious, and we all are promised honey cakes. Today we stay in camp with soft drums, games, and dancing. Dr. Etcetera saved the lives of one of Gall's wives and her child. The baby had a terrible time being born. Dr. Etcetera somehow turned the baby, and he came out right. The whole camp rejoiced. Even Beau Farro, Wolf Tracker, a Medicine Man, congratulated Dr. Etcetera.

Chief Gall looks fierce, and can be, but to his family and us he is very kind. I'm teaching him to play chess, and his youngest wife, the one with the hard to pronounce name who we call Sunny, likes Alice.

Lilly, how is your pony? I thought her beautiful and just the right size. Pick a good name for her. Alice and I wish you were with us. Please write. Send your letters to Fire Cloud or Running Cloud in care of Red Cloud at the Pine Ridge Agency, Dakota Territory. I'm not sure exactly where we are going, but the agent at the Red Cloud Agency will know. I'm sending this letter back there with a scout. He will mail it from there.

Tell Mrs. Love I miss her donuts. Tell Aunt Summer I pray her baby comes easily. I'm learning a lot about Indian and white medicine from Wolf Tracker and Dr. Etcetera. Alice sends hugs and kisses. She misses everyone. So do I. Emil

Chapter 20

BIG BIG SKY

After dinner General Alfred Terry stepped onto the river steamer, the *Far West,* now docked beside her sister ship, *Josephine,* at the confluence of the Yellowstone and Powder Rivers and greeted Captain Grant Marsh. Like Sitting Bull, General Alfred Terry felt his forty-some years. Unlike Sitting Bull he had no wise mother traveling with him and giving sound advice.

Instead he vented to Captain Marsh. "I have half-a-dozen generals vying for attention, arguing, interpreting orders as they like." He took the offered whiskey and grimaced as he took a seat. General Terry suffered with boils.

Captain Marsh, a legendary riverboat captain had been piloting these rough northwestern rivers on specifically built river steamers with shallow drafts for nigh on thirty years hauling troops, supplies, even horses. Tall and powerfully built,[' he got along well with the natives and knew this country almost as well as they did.

"Too many cooks in the kitchen," said Grant Marsh. He'd brought up supplies from Ft. Lincoln for the entire command. As they spoke the steamer was being off-- loaded. He poured himself a coffee and sat opposite General Terry.

"Well said," answered Terry, "Too many cooks and they all insist they know best." The general chuckled. "Gibbon argues that his interpretation of Sheridan's orders is to just keep the hostiles south of the Yellowstone, to not attack unless they moved north. Considering that the Yellowstone is raging from spring rains and that eight horses drowned yesterday, no one could move across the Yellowstone if he wanted to. And," continued General Terry, "yesterday, Custer's scouts managed to get lost. We backtracked twenty miles, and Major Reno failed to follow orders again."

General Terry groaned. "Reno actually reported, in writing, that he could tell me where the Indians weren't, but he had no idea where they were."

Grant Marsh chuckled and shook his head. "That's important to know."

The tired general laughed sardonically. "The highlight of the day was watching Benteen's crew attempt to saddle the pack mules. Saddling a buffalo might have been easier."

Just then one of the 7th Cavalry's contract surgeons, Henry Porter, stepped aboard the river steamer and greeted both men. "Where's a good place for me to lance those boils, General?" He nodded toward the general's drink. "Might want to sip on a couple more of those, Sir."

From her spot under the fly of their tipi, not fifty miles away from the *Far West*, Abbey Dupree glanced inside and smiled at her sleeping children. One lay on each side of Violet, all snug like a vixen with her kits. Outside the lodge, brilliant starlight bathed the prairie in ambient light, a wind chime made of polished buffalo bones rang from the branches of a nearby ponderosa pine, soft drums beat in the distance. Sunny, one of Chief Gall's wives, had told her there were now 800 tipis laid out in circles around them. The people had come for the Sun Dance.

Abbey looked out now at dozens of amber-colored tipis, which dotted the landscape like flickering lamps; closer she heard both Will and Elliott's voices as they laughed by another fire, sharing a pipe with Will's boyhood friends. Crazy Horse, Gall, and Jack Red Cloud, all born the same year as Thunder Cloud, all possessed small blue lightning strikes tattooed on the inside of their wrists, a symbol of their brotherhood. She tried to imagine the four Indian men, now in their prime, as ten-year-old boys. She shook her head and rubbed the scar on her own wrist, the one where Will had cut her flesh and mixed her blood with his so many years ago in a rite of their marriage.

Tears came unbidden, and she shook her head in astonishment. Her Will was truly an extraordinary man. She couldn't in a thousand years have found a better man, Indian or white or mixed. Would any other man in the world have forgiven her?

As she aimlessly studied the stars through the blur of her tears, her mind tripped to the other evening when Will had led her upstream to a private cove to wash her hair, to rid it of the rotten smell. They'd slipped out of their clothes and into the chilly stream where he'd soaped her hair a half dozen times until all the grease was gone and it squeaked with cleanliness. Gone were the gagging odors, too.

They'd cavorted like otters and afterwards made gentle, sweet love wrapped in a buffalo robe. Still later Will lit a small fire, and as they lay there skin to skin, with owls hooting from the nearby pines, without any warning, Will asked, "Tell me about Tom Custer? I found his handkerchief. I suspect he's important to you. What happened?"

Her heart stopped. For a moment she thought she might die. Another part of her wanted to die. Will took her hand. "Tell me. I'm not upset, darling. You are here with me now, not with him. It's important, though, that I know what happened."

The tears wouldn't stop. When she could breath, she answered. "It just happened. Remember that evening on the train when you sent the children to dinner with Bear?" She stopped and blew her nose. She sniffed. "And we ordered from menus and dined in our car, and the waiter kept refilling our wineglasses and we all drank too much. You fell asleep. Tom helped me get you to bed." She sat up tightening the blanket around her. "Then I fell asleep in the chair, and he helped the children to bed, sang them a lullaby, and saw to cleaning up the dishes. When I awoke, he stood to leave and when we shook hands, t-t-he train jerked…"

Her shoulders gave a little shrug, and her voice dropped to a hoarse whisper. "I fell into his arms. It just happened." Shuddering sobs shook her now. "He feels as badly as I do. Neither of us intended to…"

She tried to gloss over the details, but Will patiently dug out every snippet of her shame, all of it. His voice always stayed calm, his tone kind. "You love him, don't you?"

The tears came in a gush now. Her voice, thick with emotion, said, "No, no, I never loved him." Her head however kept bobbing up and down.

"Here..." He handed her Tom's handkerchief. At the time she'd been too upset to wonder how it was in his possession.

When she'd calmed a little he handed her the buckskin dress and pulled on his clothes then helped her with her moccasins. "We'd better get back before they send a search party." He bundled the robe about her then took her hand and led her through the circles of glowing golden tipis toward their campfire. When they neared their fire, he stopped at a spring and soaked Tom's handkerchief. Handing it to her, he said, "Here, clean your face."

His kindness threatened to overwhelm her. She continued to cry.

When they came to their tipi, he ducked inside and returned with a ragged slouch hat. He kissed her tenderly. "You smell much better," he said as he handed her the hat and helped her tuck her dyed curls out of sight.

He grinned. "You still don't look like an Indian, but if we put some feathers on the hat and from a distance..."

He spread the robe and pulled her to it and held her. "I'm not angry, my darling Yellow Bird, my brave Zizi. I understand. Those were dark days for both of us. I feel honored you came back to me." He fixed the robe around them both and looked up to the stars. "Let's sleep outside. The night is perfect."

She hiccupped and another shudder coursed through her.

He chuckled then pulled her against him. "This will cheer you up. Sitting Bull asked me if he could marry you. What do you think of that?"

Gulping, she sat up with a jerk. "Oh, no, no, I could never... he knows we're married... never..."

"Sitting Bull doesn't care if we're married or not. One thing about Sitting Bull, he likes women. He claims to have had fifteen wives. And he especially likes white women. He has seduced many of those missionary ladies who come to save him. Notice how his voice softens and purrs when he talks to you. Let me assure you he doesn't purr to his braves. I told him he absolutely could not marry you. However, if something happens to me you now have your choice: Gall, Crazy Horse, and Sitting Bull. Or would you prefer Tom Custer?"

She didn't answer but he felt her heart skip a beat and her body quiver at the mention of the last name. He kissed her temple. "Now, my darling Zizi, go to sleep. I promised years ago to keep you safe, even from Sitting Bull. I always will. Thank you for telling me. I feared he might have forced you." He took Tom's handkerchief and held it up to the light. He pointed to the embroidered shield and flag with his initials, TWC, on it. "That's the tattoo on his arm, isn't it?"

She nodded as she watched her husband pocket the damp cloth.

She reached up and kissed his cheek, allowing her fingers to rest there. "No, he didn't force me. I was equally at fault."

He didn't tell her Tom Custer slept under the same night sky not forty miles away. Rock Hard Head and Little Wind, young scouts, had spotted Little Hair, the Indian's name for Long Hair's brother, on patrol with the 7th west of the Powder River. Will knew all hell would explode around here soon. Neither he nor any of the Sioux warriors planned to

go gently onto the reservations. At least 1,500 Sioux warriors, and the numbers grew daily, would eventually find
the Cavalry, and every one of them salivated for Long Hair's
scalp. If they couldn't capture his, the scalp of one of his
brothers would do.

Will rubbed the lightning strike tattoo on his wrist. He had
already talked with his blood brothers and Elliott. Crazy Horse
had dispatched two braves to the Yellowstone caves. A plan took
form. After the Sun Dance, Elliott and four scouts would take
Violet, Abbey, and the children north and east, back toward the
Missouri River and the Dakota Territory.

⚏⚏

Dear Alice and Emil,

Greetings from Camelann.
Yesterday, Daniel, Hal, and Lobo built an enormous
bonfire—even bigger than the one at Thanksgiving—on
that same spot above Forty Foot Falls. All of Camelann and
a few neighbors turned out, and we had a great summer
feast of roast beef, ham, and early vegetables from our gar-
den, all topped off with Mrs. Love's Strawberry Shortcake
with whipped cream. Do they have strawberries in the
Montana Territory?
I read your letter aloud to all, adults and children. We
all wish we were with you, but only if you have strawberries.
The Montana Territory sounds beautiful. The Gathering
must be a wonder to see. Wakanda told us the warriors

paint themselves and their horses and parade around the circles. She also wondered if you've seen a grizzly yet? She told us how big and fierce they are. None of us would want to meet one. Our small black bears which are more frightened of us than we are them are scary enough.

Thank you for mailing your letter to Emmitsburg, Maryland. Have you ever been there? It looks like a storybook town, a happy village of white buildings, houses, and two churches, but it isn't. Lobo, Lilly, and I take the shortcut through the mountains twice a week for the mail. Mr. Grundy, the postmaster acts nice, but he has this gigantic beard. Tiny bugs, fleas or gnats, fly in and out of it. Like the bugs, we dash in and out of the post office as quickly as possible then race to the convent to say hello to the sisters there. The town is unfriendly. No one has thrown rocks at us yet, but we feel they might. I suppose they don't like us because we had different sympathies during the war. They are not, however, as mean as Mrs. Graves. I miss you. Louisa.

I'm still writing but Lilly is telling me what to say:

Hi, I miss you both terribly, but I've stopped crying. The pony helps a lot. I love her. She's perfect. I named her Sooty because of her shiny coal black coat. The first thing I do in the morning before breakfast is run to the stable and feed her and give her clean water. When she finishes her oats, I saddle her, and Sooty stays with me all day. I don't know what I'll do when school starts.

The babies—yes, the babies—Wakanda and Dr. Ray told us they are twins and are expected any day now. I am so excited. Mama's tummy is huge. I think they will be girls.

They will have to have flower names like Mama and me. I like Pansy and Petunia or Primrose and Peony, but no one else likes those names. Louisa likes Iris and Daisy. What do you think? My brothers all want boy babies. Mama thinks they are elephants; Daddy just smiles and says that if they are he gets to name them.

I love visiting the nuns at Lourdes. When you get home I'll introduce you to all of the sisters. I've told Sister Mary Clare all about you.

Hugs and kisses,

Lilly

Chapter 21

THE LONG DAYS OF SUMMER

The next evening General Terry and his senior staff met aboard the *Far West* to devise a strategy. They decided the strongest fighters, Custer's regiment, should ride south along the Rosebud Creek to a position east of the Indians. Generals Terry and Colonel Gibbon together will follow the Yellowstone to the Big Horn River then follow it to the Little Big Horn. General Terry stuck a line of pins across the map outlining the proposed routes. The hostiles will be caught like a wolf in the steel jaws of a trap.

As Grasshopper Jim Brisbin, commander of the 2nd Cavalry, followed General Terry's pins and marked the route with blue ink, he said, "I worry that you're not strong enough, Armstrong. Why not take four battalions of mine?"

George didn't respond. Terry in an avuncular tone said, "Armstrong took quite a verbal beating from President Grant and feels the need to vindicate himself."

George nodded. "I believe the 7th can handle anything Sitting Bull throws at us."

"Well," added Major Brisbin, "at least take a couple of the Gatling guns."

A crack of lightning crashed overhead, followed by the loud din of hail smashing the *Far West,* the dock, and the water. It silenced the men; they sat for a few minutes. Then George nodded.

A short time later, though, as they crunched over the hail-stones back to Custer's tent, he changed his mind. "Those guns cause more trouble than they are worth. Pulling them over the divide will be difficult."

General Terry agreed. He'd dragged those cumbersome guns all the way from Ft. Lincoln. They caused numerous delays.

⊰⊱

The following morning the 7ᵗʰ passed in review before General Terry and Colonel Gibbon. As always Custer's regiment looked smart, a fine fighting force. As they parted Colonel Gibbon, who had been Armstrong's artillery instructor at West Point and who knew him well, said as an afterthought, "Now, don't be greedy Armstrong, wait for us."

⊰⊱

Tatanka Iyotake knew war with the *wasicu* was inevitable; he knew too the battle would be soon. Daily, Hunkpapa, Cheyenne, and Arapaho families joined the roamers. The pony herd, sleek and healthy from feasting on the spring grass, now swelled to ten thousand; they needed fresh pastures every other day. The village became a sea of moving people. Never in recent memory had the Gathering been so large. The people felt powerful, too. Well-fed, strong, with adequate ammunition, they had met and sent *Three Star Crook* and his soldiers fleeing north.

Scouts under Crazy Horse reported evidence of a large number of bluecoats on horseback. Sightings increased daily.

Today Tatanka Iyotake left instructions with Jumping Bull and White Bull to find the correct cottonwood tree and create a sixty-foot circular arena with a bed of the traditional sharp gravel. Soon Tatanka Iyotake would dance the *Wiwang Wacipi*, the Sun Dance, and give the Great Spirit a red blanket.

⁂

At first light, just as pale yellow sunshine crept over the eastern horizon, he took his sacred pipe, some tobacco plugs, and a buffalo skull over the divide toward the Valley of the Little Big Horn. Plum, pink, and white flowers splattered through the long grass; the blossoms damp with the dew delighted Sitting Bull's senses. Bees feasted on the nectar. Today, on this day of long sunshine, he walked until he reached the hillside where two whirlwinds met and became one.

Here he arranged the offerings: the polished skull, the pounded meat, and the tobacco. He rested his sacred pipe on the skull and began to pray to the *Wakan Tanka*. He spoke the words through his eagle bone whistle. The notes, shrill like the cry of a diving eagle, drifted upward to the Great Father for hours.

Emil and Alice, always wise to the whispers of the camp, squeezed through the swelling crowds and found front seats on the perimeter of the arena. Their parents had disagreed about their presence at the event. Abbey argued they were too young to see such violence. Will countered. "It's their heritage. I want them to know it." So Will joined them while Violet and Abbey sat further back on a hillside. Elliott stood near the women with Jack Red Cloud and watched with binoculars.

When Tatanka Iyotake emerged from his tipi, the crowd silenced. Emil squeezed his father's ankle and Alice wiggled under Will's arm. Sitting Bull wore his hair loose with eagle feathers standing up at the back of his head; on his body he wore only his eagle bone whistle, which hung on a cord around his neck, a breechcloth made from a buffalo hide, and bracelets and anklets made of sage. Few had seen the scarred flesh of their leader's chest and back. A huge hiss of a breath arose from the crowd as scars on his torso, some stood out thick like rope, became visible.

The great chief walked to the tree, placed the ivory buffalo skull facing east, laid his pipe nearby, and sat on the blanket with his back to the tree, looking east as well. He began to pray again through his eagle bone whistle. The piercing music floated toward the great Montana sky. His Hunkpapa brother, Jumping Bull, began to cut strips of flesh from Sitting Bull's arms, fifty pieces from his left then as many from his right. Blood flowed profusely. When the blanket was red, he rose. Jumping Bull held it up for the crowd to see, and the macabre dance began.

Tatanka Iyotake danced with strips of rawhide and long splinters of wood sewn into his flesh, deep behind the muscles of his chest, and tethered with no slack to the cottonwood tree. In certain positions Sitting Bull's toes barely touched the ground. Always staring at the sun or when dark to the east from where it came, he danced for the rest of the day and all night and into the early sunlight, at times suspended by the rawhide cords, and the shrill eagle bone whistle echoed through the valley. Emil and Alice slept in their father's lap. In daylight Sitting Bull stared at the sun, after dark he stared to the east.

Midway through the second day he grew faint and stumbled to the blanket, very close to where the children sat. His great friend, Black Moon, caught him and they whispered. As others came to tend Sitting Bull, Black Moon told the Gathering of their great leader's vision.

He told them. "A voice spoke: 'Stare just below the sun.' As Sitting Bull did, he saw, Long Knives by the hundreds fall through the air with their feet to the sky looking like grasshoppers and without ears." Black Moon continued. "The voice told him: *I give you the Long Knives. They will die, but do not take their belongings.*'"

Later that day, Beau Farro came and told the people of a great antelope herd in the valley of the Greasy Grass on the banks of the Little Big Horn. The people prepared to move.

Abbey, Violet, and Elliott gathered their belongings and packed the shortened wagon. Will helped them, and then Chief Gall came with his wives and his children, and presented Emil and Alice with healthy pinto ponies. When they first met Gall, the children had been terrified of him, for his countenance was fierce. Grown men would not meet his stare. While his enormous upper body, shaped like a beer barrel, showed powerful shoulder and chest muscles, he smiled and oozed kindness to children, but never to his enemies. Jack Red Cloud and Crazy Horse with their families came to say goodbye. Others brought packets of food and grain, a bouquet of flowers, beaded moccasins and headbands. Goodbyes were painful. Emil hated that he cried like a girl when goodbyes were said.

Gall knelt and hugged him. His large hand covered all of Emil's back. "You'll be a grown man for many years, cry now while you can. I never leave my family without telling them I love them. I cry often."

Will kissed his children and wife. "We'll meet near Black Rock on the Yellowstone. Bear knows the place." He shook hands with Elliott and kissed Violet's cheek.

"I love you," he whispered to Abbey and kissed her again.

"Stay with us. Don't go with them." She held him close and begged him again to come with them.

Will shook his head and tucked wayward curls under her hat. "There is something I must do. I'll come in three to five days. I'll find you."

⊨⊨

In Pennsylvania, Summer, beneath mosquito netting, lay soaked in sweat. The heat and humidity made breathing difficult. Hard labor had begun almost a day ago. Both water sacs had ruptured and sharp stabs of severe labor pain had not let up. Everyone knew something was difficult and dangerous. Daniel and Ray had stayed by her side continuously.

While Wakanda helped Summer change into a fresh nightgown, Ray sent Hal with the children across the lake to the Indian School so they would be out of earshot, and Daniel wrote a quick note to Sister Mary Agnes asking if Sister Mary Clare could come and stay with the children. "If you can spare the time, we'd appreciate your presence here, too."

Lobo saddled his pony making a mad dash to deliver the note to the Sisters of Charity. Lilly had been near hysterics in fear for her mother, and Daniel was almost as fearful as Lilly, but he had more experience at hiding such feelings.

❈

That first night away from the huge gathering of tribes, Abbey and the children felt unaccountably homesick, as if they didn't belong in either the white or the red man's world. The Montana sky, a blanket of stars, loomed above them, huge and ominous. They camped downstream from where the *Far West* was docked, and they smelled other fires so Emil and Alice gathered wood; Bear lit a small fire for making coffee and cooking bacon and pancakes. The Yellowstone River and its tributaries, the Tongue, The Redbud, The Powder, and the Big Horn, all oddly flowed north.

As they ate, the four Indians and the five whites heard violin music and men's voices from the wharf where the *Far West* docked on the Yellowstone. It seemed unnatural not to contact the white men there, but Elliott again reminded how their presence could jeopardize Sitting Bull's tribes. And Will. To Emil and Alice being of mixed bloods had never been so difficult. Their loyalties went both ways.

Fortunately nothing untoward happened overnight, and in the morning they continued northeastward following a path along the Yellowstone. Eagles and hawks careened in the huge sky. Bear pointed in the distance to enormous bears, which must be grizzlies, fishing in the river. Three small bundles of fur played on the shore. Alice sighed. "They are so cuddly. May I have one for a pet?"

Bear grunted. "Mama would rip you to pieces if you touched one."

Alice didn't argue. She knew the West was a dangerous place.

⁜

The Indians knew the 7th was near, and the 7th knew the Sioux were close. Neither knew exactly where. Armstrong's big concern wasn't finding them. What he feared the most was the Indians slipping away, scattering to the four winds, thus preventing his chance of vindication.

Now, he allowed campfires for coffee. As much as the seven hundred men on horseback and over a hundred pack mules attempted to be quiet, it was impossible. Hooves scraped rocks, fry pans knocked against tin cups, and the mules brayed incessantly. Likewise the Indians left a mile wide trail of debris. Thousands of ponies, hundreds of circle imprints left by their tipis, and ruts made by their travois created an unmistakable trail. However, like ghosts the natives could dissolve like mist.

Boston Custer, Tom and George's younger brother, and Autie Reed, their nephew, stuck close to Tom. They were civilian helpers who had come with the brothers for a summer adventure. They wanted to take home souvenirs, maybe a couple good Indian ponies, a buffalo robe, but today they seemed unnaturally skittish. "What's wrong with him, Tommy?" asked Boston. "Doesn't he know hordes of hostiles are all around us?"

Tom shook his head. *I can't figure him out either,* he thought. *Does he not sense them? Christ, I can smell them. Maybe he doesn't want to admit he's frightened? He never in his life lost at anything. He thinks he's invincible. But Grant's cold shoulder unnerved him.*

I know a secret too. Libbie swore me to secrecy. The Democrats in Washington told him, if he rounded up the Sioux, he just might find his name on the Democratic ticket for President. She thinks that is why Grant, a Republican to the bone, was so hard on him. The Democratic convention starts next week in St. Louis. He's under pressure from them and his wife. Tom shook his head. *I love and admire my sister-in-law, but… Libbie's parents, Judge and Mrs. Bacon, had groomed her to be First Lady from the day she was born. She's ready to put the bit between her teeth and go for it.*

And a lot of the men, officers, enlisted men, even the Ree scouts are grumbling behind his back. The men wonder where Autie's usual overabundance of confidence is? Where is all his nervous energy? And the Ree guides ask if he's lost his medicine? I wish to hell Libbie was here. If anyone can ground my brother, it's Libbie, but Libbie is in Ft. Lincoln.

And Tom knew he could be the problem. He was a different man, not so willing to risk limb and life. The magic moments he'd shared with Abbey had profoundly changed him, freed the softer side of him. Just speaking her name inside his head warmed him all over like a good coming-home hug warmed his soul. *Having a girl like Abbey love me, want me, and trust me gives me such confidence. I want to be the man she sees. I want to live. I'm not a dumb Ohio farm kid or a heartless Indian killer. I may not have gone to West Point but I feel as smart and knowledgeable as if I did. I know now Autie isn't always right. He's smart and capable. I'll give him that, but sometimes he makes stupid decisions. He's not perfect, but I love him.* He looked over to his brother's tent.

The shadow of Autie's slump-shouldered stance squeezed at his heart. *I sure as hell hope he knows what he's doing.* To Boston and Autie Reed he said, "Why don't you two go up to the *Far West* and stay there for a few days? I'm sure Captain Marsh wouldn't mind. He'll find some work for you."

Both boys shook their heads. "Nay," said Boston. "I want to be around family."

Chapter 22

GOING HOME BY A DIFFERENT ROAD

With the ban on silence lifted, George Custer's officers and a few of the scouts stopped by his tent after dinner. George was fond of saying, "My regiment is the best fighting unit in the entire United States Army," and his men often referred to him as *Old Iron Butt*. George Custer could ride all day, rest for a couple hours then ride for another ten hours. Every day more of his men, officers included, called him *Old Iron Butt*, which secretly pleased George.

Tonight, however, the mellower sides of these hardened soldiers surfaced. His men surprised him with a serenade. *Old Iron Butt* smiled as they sang a number of his favorites: *Aura Lee, Little Brown Jug, Oh Susanna, Auld Lang Syne,* and ending oddly with *The Doxology*. Rather than sound out of place, this ancient hymn seemed appropriate in the grand expanse of Montana, and brought peace.

> *Praise God, from Whom all blessings flow;*
> *Praise Him, all creatures here below;*

Praise Him above, ye heavenly host;
Praise Father, Son, and Holy Ghost.

Bloody Knife, Armstrong's favorite Indian scout and guide, knelt by his general's chair during the serenade. He wore his trademark clamshell and bear claw necklace along with the black neckerchief emblazoned with blue stars that General Custer had given him. As the general's officers finished the serenade with *For He's a Jolly Good Fellow*, Tom, who stood near his brother, overheard Bloody Knife say to the general, "I think tomorrow we'll both go home by a different road than we've gone before."

⚔

Lobo hitched the buggy belonging to the Sisters of Charity to the post at the Indian School; he helped each sister down from the wagon; four had insisted on coming to Camelann. His pony was hitched to the back. To Sister Mary Clare he pointed to the end of the dock where Lilly sat with her arms around Louisa, both girls staring across the lake at their home. Off to the left of the school the Reverend Tuttle and Hal supervised a baseball game with his two sons, Lilly's three brothers, and a few Indian children from the school.

When Lilly heard the hard leather shoe on the wooden boards of the dock, she turned around and saw Sister Mary Clare. She raced with her arms wide open, outstretched. They sat on a little bench where Louisa joined them. The three girls hugged and cried. Sister Mary Clare finally hushed them and offered a short prayer. "Dear Father above, please be with Miss Summer and the twin babies."

Hal, Reverend Tuttle, and the boys walked over to the other sisters, who still stood near the wagon. Hal took Sister Mary Agnes' extended hand. "Wakanda and Daniel would like your assistance at the house. We'd appreciate if the rest of you would help with these children."

Sister Mary Agnes motioned to all the boys and the girls, and when they all gathered around her, she prayed.

> *"Angel of God, our Guardian dear,*
> *To whom God's love commits us here,*
> *Ever this day be at our sides,*
> *To light and guard, to rule and guide.*
> *Be with our sister, Summer, and her children here*
> *And those about to enter our world. Amen."*

As the sister finished, a woodpecker perched above their heads on the white oak tree let loose a rat-a-tat-tat and flew toward the house across the lake. All eyes followed the red-headed bird. Sister Mary Agnes made the sign of the cross and said, "The Lord always answers. We must watch and listen." She turned to the Indian boy, "Lobo, will you please follow that bird and take me across the lake in the canoe?"

Lobo swallowed hard; his dark Indian skin turned yellow. Images of the billowing black habit and white winged wimple in the canoe or worse toppled into the lake frightened him. "I can take the wagon…"

Holding onto her winged wimple with one hand and hiking up her skirts with the other, she ran, very un-nun-like, toward the dock, yelling, "The canoe is much faster."

Lobo looked to Hal and the Reverend who both shrugged, then followed at a run. At the last second Lilly attempted to jump into the canoe with Sister Mary Agnes, but Lobo caught her and gave her to Sister Mary Clare. She and Louisa held the sobbing girl until the canoe reached the opposite shore.

⚔

Crazy Horse's young braves returned from the western caves on the Yellowstone with a bloody gunnysack, which they deposited at the opening of Crazy Horse's tipi. One of Crazy Horse's wives fetched Beau Farro, who took the sack containing Ed Kincaid's dismembered body and Tom Custer's handkerchief to Blue Veined Woman. The young medicine man told her what to do.

⚔

George Custer's nervous energy returned; he couldn't sleep so around ten o'clock he roused his orderly, John Burkman. "Cut my hair, John. Short, just below the ears. It's too hot for long hair. And I will wear my uniform. Do I have a fresh red scarf?"

John Burkman laid out his general's uniform with a clean pressed scarf and heated water, then shaved his general and cut his hair, cut it shorter than he had ever done before. "That will be much cooler, Sir. A lot less blond, too."

George looked in the mirror and ran a comb along his receding hairline. He was not happy about his thinning hair, but he quickly turned the loss of hair around. With a half laugh, half snort, he said, "That's less for those heathen's to grab. Right John?"

When he finished dressing, he ordered John to strike the tent. John objected but *Old Iron Butt* insisted. "Take it back to the supply depot. You stay there, too. I won't be coming back this way."

⚅⚅

Abbey, Alice, Emil, Violet, and Dr. Cutter with their Indian protectors and guides made good time. Pressed hard by the natives, they traveled long into the night, camping nearly forty miles north of the *Far West*. They watered the horses and fed both horse and human from their packed provisions and slept rough on the ground, the women and children beneath the wagon.

⚅⚅

Although night in Montana Territory in June was short, the moonless sky crawled at a slug's pace. The general first sent Lt. Charles Varnum and his Ree scouts and Crow guides to the Crow's Nest, a well-known Crow lookout.

Charlie arrived at the foot of the Crow's Nest about 3:10 a.m.. He noted faint light at the eastern horizon, but could barely see his hand held in front of his nose. Word filtered down from command suggesting they unsaddle the horses and try to get a little sleep. He first sent two Ree scouts to the top of the Crow's Nest then actually slept a little. At sunrise, just after 4:00 a.m, he awoke and climbed to the lookout. His scouts pointed excitedly. The clear early light showed an enormous village; hundreds of tipis could be seen about fifteen miles distant. Off to the right of the village was a herd of thousands of ponies. Lt. Charlie Varnum immediately sent a note to General Custer.

The general didn't come right away. He first rode clear around his regiment, speaking with each of his thirty-two officers and their sergeants. He relieved Tom as captain of C Company and made him his aide-de-camp. Lt. Harrington took over for Tom.

He spoke for some time with Tom, Adjunct Cooke, and a few other officers discussing and finalizing strategies. While Captain Cooke set about carefully writing out the orders, Armstrong climbed the lookout. The light had changed and the mass of tipis and the large pony herd were no longer visible.

"I don't doubt your word, Charlie. I'm just worried they may have scattered."

At noon, written orders were delivered by Adjunct Cooke and Armstrong divided his regiment into four battalions for reconnaissance and deployment purposes. Of course, Captain Benteen complained but he always complained, so no one paid attention to him. George simply said, "You have orders."

Captain Benteen's orders instructed him to take one hundred and twenty troopers four or five miles up the Little Big Horn in search of Indian villages, which could possibly be hiding in the ravines ready to attack the main body of the regiment from the rear. The moonfaced captain with the premature white hair and condescending attitude could be heard deriding the orders as ridiculous.

Charlie Varnum's scouts would go first toward the village to check for surprises and scatter any ponies they came across. Major Reno with 150 men would sweep into the valley on the south side of the Little Big Horn. Custer would take 218 men on the north side of the river. Captain McDougall was put in charge of the ever-important mule train hauling supplies and the spare ammunition. Custer sent Bloody Knife, who did not want to go, along with Major Reno.

"He's inexperienced. Stay next to him and keep him on the right track. Do not allow him to abandon the wounded." With a wink General Custer said to Bloody Knife, "Teach him how to fight Indians."

Bloody Knife shook his head. "Reno's medicine is bad. I do not trust him."

Custer insisted and Bloody Knife finally acquiesced. General Custer and a few officers watched Major Reno's battalion cross the river, reform, and set off at a gallop toward the village.

Chapter 23

CYCLE OF LIFE

When Mrs. Love opened the kitchen door to Sister Mary Agnes, the sister looked to Ray who stood over an obviously unconscious Summer. Wakanda held the chloroform mask over Summer's face. Daniel sat in a wooden chair turned toward Summer, holding her one hand. He looked terrified.

Ray raised his head. "Ah, Sister Mary Agnes." He had worked with her during the war and since then at the sanitarium. "Another set of hands and Lobo too." He nodded toward the sink. "Scrub up, Sister; Lobo, would you be so kind as to keep any wayward fly or insect out of here. Sister Mary Agnes will show you how to scrub. After scrubbing, put on clean aprons."

Lobo looked toward the table and suddenly realized that the large dome of white which Dr. Ray smoothed iodine over and surrounded by white sheets was Summer's naked belly. His cheeks flushed for half a second then paled as he saw the scalpel in Dr. Ray's other hand. Suddenly, the young Indian understood Miss Summer's babies were about to be born in an unnatural manner. His Adam's apple bobbed, but he nodded and swallowed hard.

Ray said to everyone, "Okay, once I make the incisions, things happen with amazing speed." As he drew the scalpel across Summer's belly, a thin line like red ink on paper appeared on her flesh. Then Ray quickly cut the wall of the exposed uterus. A mass of blue flesh popped out of the opening. Ray's capable hands grabbed the slippery infant, at the same time removing the thin film from the tiny blue face. A cry came from the baby then Sister Mary Agnes' flannel draped hands took the bundle as Ray tied off and cut the umbilical cord. Mrs. Love thumped to the floor.

Ray's eyes never left the open womb. "Leave her be. Sister, give Daniel that child."

"Danny, just bundle her up against your chest and sit there and hold your daughter. She's a beauty. Lobo, go stand beside him. Make sure he doesn't pitch over and hurt the baby."

Another blue mass came more gently into the world, but screamed just as robustly. Again, Dr. Stone slipped that child into Sister Mary Agnes' arms. "Danny, how are you?"

"Good. I can feel her little heart beating. Good Lord, she's precious."

Ray turned to the Indian boy. "Lobo, you've done great with the flies. It's important to keep those dirty pests away from Summer and the babies. Now please help Mrs. Love sit up." He looked to Wakanda. "You're perfect with the chloroform. We want her asleep while I finish all this. Another twenty minutes." To Daniel, he said, you now have another son, too."

⊣⊢

Abbey's party reached Black Rock in the late afternoon. Bear and his men caught a huge salmon which he cleaned and wrapped in leaves and roasted in the coals of a cedar wood fire along with wild dill and sage. The Indians dug tubers and wild onions found in the bank of the river and tucked them in the coals, too.

Emil and Alice felt as if they'd reached another world. They'd not seen, heard, or smelled another human for two days. Wildlife, moose, elk, antelope, deer, otters, and coyotes appeared well-fed and tame. The river rippled with big fish.

While supper cooked, the women and Alice walked upstream and bathed and put on fresh clothing. As they returned to the fire, they gathered baskets of blueberries and cherries. Vi and Alice picked immense bouquets of flowers. Back at the fire, Abbey braided Alice and Vi's hair. She allowed her own dark curls loose to dry near the fire. As it dried, a little of the natural blonde reappeared. She would be happy when the color was again just blonde.

After the feast, when the sun dipped below the horizon, the air grew chilly. They wrapped up in blankets and watched the sky erupt with a glorious blanket of stars.

Bear laid on his back, looking up to the celestial display and said, "Good food, good sky. Not a bad place to wait for Thunder Cloud. I'm very happy to be here, not with the tribes." No one asked why. They all knew why.

⊣⊢

Custer ordered Reno to charge the southern end of the village, stir up a panic, send the women and children running and screaming. The remainder of the 7th watched from a plateau. As planned, the women, children, and elders ran screaming from the tipis, very quickly followed by warriors. The horde swelled.

Reno ordered his men to dismount and form a skirmish line. Now, however, some Indians rode ponies back and forth creating huge clouds of dust, and from behind the billowing dirt, their Henry and Winchester repeating rifles proved dealy accurate. Reno quickly ordered his men to remount and move into the cover of the thick timber.

Bloody Knife and his Ree scouts, obviously up to no good, came racing from the village where the warriors were now wide awake; a hail of bullets followed the scout. He thundered toward Reno. Bad blood between Bloody Knife and Gall raised hackles on both sides. Now a bullet from Gall's men found Bloody Knife's head and killed him instantly. Red, pink, and gray matter exploded all over Custer's favorite Indian scout. Chunks of skull and gray matter caught in his elaborate necklace, the blue stars on his neckerchief, and splattered all over Major Reno's face, straw hat, and the front of his uniform.

Major Marcus Reno went berserk, screaming "Dismount... Remount... Dismount..." Attempting to clean himself, he spit Bloody Knife's brains and pieces of bone out of his mouth. His men watched in abject terror at their leader's breakdown.

⧼⧽

From his vantage on the plateau, aided by Lt. DeRudio's excellent Austrian-made field glasses, General Custer observed Reno's men engage. "What in the hell is he doing? He's supposed to be on the offensive." He lowered the glasses. "If he can hold out for an hour, we can... Tom, have we heard from Benteen? We should have by now. Send orders for him to return immediately. Tell him to bring the ammunition packs."

Tom turned to Sergeant Kanipe who saluted and took off at a gallop.

Custer's column moved forward down the coulee to the river; the soldiers seemed excited, anxious to attack the warriors from the rear.

Clouds of heavy red dust shrouded the timber line. In the meantime, General Custer took it upon himself to send another message to Benteen. He called up the bugler, Giovanni Martini, a recent Italian emigrant. Adjunct Cooke knew Giovanni spoke sporadic English, so he scribble in his notebook: *Benteen, come on. Big village. Be quick. Bring packs. W.W. Cooke. P.S. Bring packs.* He tore it out and gave it to the bugler, who spurred his horse to a gallop.

The general called all his officers to discuss their options. Even without binoculars they could now see the dust; they watched the women, children, and ponies scatter. Heavy gunfire echoed off the hills. No sound came from where Benteen should be.

Custer's officers didn't dismount. The horses snorted, stomped. Even they sensed the excitement and were ready to take the bit between their teeth.

George lowered DeRudio's field glasses then handed them to Lt. Jimmy Calhoun, his sister Maggie's husband.

Jimmy surveyed the landscape and grinned ear to ear. Returning the glasses, he said, "We got them, Sir. Once the chiefs realize their families are in serious jeopardy, they will surrender like lambs, and the 7th in one fell swoop will meet the objectives of the entire campaign."

Clouds of red dust gave Reno's battalion some cover as they left the relative safety of the woods and scrambled up the bluffs. But Gall and Crazy Horse's sharpshooters still killed and wounded a great many of Reno's men. The wounded followed the best they could, on horseback, crawling, clawing their way up the hundred foot cliffs, or pulled along by friends. To stay in the valley expecting mercy from Gall or Crazy Horse was folly. One of the last commands given by General Terry to all his officers was not to leave the wounded behind. No code of honor existed between the two cultures. A fate far worse than death would meet those left behind. Indians tortured those too weak to fight. Even the greenest soldier knew to carry a mercy bullet.

Dr. Porter and his orderlies gathered as many wounded as they found into a makeshift field hospital situated in a depression behind the center redoubt. He made assessments, cleaned, stitched, and bandaged wounds, splinted broken bones, made the hopeless comfortable. He gave each of the wounded a teaspoon of whisky. For severe pain he dispensed opium but sparingly for the big medicine chests still remained with the mule train.

⚏⚏

Custer's battalion, gathered along the north bank of the Little Big Horn, could hear the heavy gunfire from Reno's men. They also saw the red clouds of dust rising along the bluffs, and with Lt. DeRudio's glasses Custer made out men climbing the cliffs. "Where in the hell is Benteen?" he asked Tom.

They heard no gunfire from Benteen's battalion. Enough time had elapsed for him to have explored the upper reaches of the valley. Tom knew Benteen's orders clearly stated to pitch into anything they found and send written word to command, or to return to Custer if they discovered nothing.

⚌

Emil took his blanket and moved beside Bear. "Why," he asked in a whisper, "did my father stay at the village?"

The old Indian didn't answer for a long time. Finally, he said, "I'm not sure. Sometimes fathers need to do unexplainable things to care for their wives and children. I do know Thunder Cloud loves your mother, you, and your sister very much. Sometimes, we must trust the Great Spirit." He fixed the blanket around the boy and rubbed his back. "Pray for him, Running Cloud. He's a good man, one of the best I've known. Remember not all Indians are good and not all white men are bad. I think Thunder Cloud has the best of both races. Sometimes it's best to not think. Just pray."

⚌

When Captain Benteen first came across Reno's forces, he asked, "Where in the hell is our boy wonder?" He had never attempted to hide his hatred and disgust of Lt. Colonel Custer. He particularly found offensive that some men still referred to the upstart as General.

Reno's eyes had a strange cast and he smelled of alcohol; he shrugged, looking as if he were about to cry, and said, "I've lost half my men, Benteen. Help me."

As Captain McDougall, Company B and the pack train arrived, heavy gunfire could be heard from north of the river. A frantic Captain Weir appeared on Benteen's left, "I request permission, Sir, to take my company and go to the aid of the general, Sir. They sound as if they're in trouble."

Captain McDougall added, "I request permission to go with Captain Weir. They'll need ammunition."

Benteen snorted then refused permission. He'd already ignored Sergeant Kanipe's shouted command and the written orders from Custer's Adjunct Cooke carried by Bugler Giovanni Martini.

Custer was to come to his and Reno's aid, not the other way around, thought Benteen. No way was he about to run the gauntlet through the teeming mass of bloody savages and give aid to *Old Iron Butt.*

⊣⊢

Gall had awakened with a jolt. Women, children, and old people ran around like an entire flock of decapitated chickens. From the river came gunshots. Crazy Horse burst into the tipi where several warriors had slept after a night of revelry. He hollered, "Bloody Knife and his Ree scouts are at the southern end of the village." They both detested Bloody Knife. In addition to considering him a traitor to his people, bad blood had existed among the three of them since childhood.

Now the barrel-chested Hunkpapa ran toward his family's tipi. There among the debris of his home, Chief Gall found the bodies of two of his wives and three children, all brutally murdered. When he saw that Sunny's throat had been slashed and her breasts cut off, he howled. He knew whites used cured squaw breasts for their filthy coins. Such a practice sickened him. Thoughts of their foul fingers touching her boiled his blood. He dropped to his knees and buried his face against his dead family.

After a long moment, he lifted his dead wives and children to the Great Spirit and roared. Tears streamed down his face. His braves gathered round him. He lowered the bodies to the earth. "We will kill them all!"

Gall and Crazy Horse knew tactics; their braves would follow them to their death. And most were armed with Henry or Winchester repeating rifles which had been issued through the Indian agencies by the United States government for hunting, and which the natives knew how to use. They easily made out Reno's men scrambling up the hundred-foot bluff, taking cover where they could, and in the distance another cloud of dust rose above Medicine Trail Coulee.

Although enraged, Gall kept his head and signaled to Crazy Horse. They understood that to scale the cliffs and attack Reno's troops would be suicide. The soldiers would pick off their braves like straggling buffalo heifers. Instead, a horde of experienced and furious warriors held back their mounts. They were not only well-armed, but flush with confidence from their victory over

Three Star Crook's regiment, and they were the finest horsemen since Genghis Khan rode the steppes of Asia.

They left behind a contingent of experienced warriors to keep Reno's troops on the hilltop. Gall's men came up on Custer's right flank, Crazy Horse and Two Moon's braves galloped toward the left, swallowing Custer's five companies. Mayhem and chaos ruled. The fighting quickly closed into hand-to-hand combat; hatchets, bayonets, knives, war clubs, and tomahawks flew. Thick dust and blood blocked out light; the primal war cries of warriors, the soldiers' shouts, the shrill eagle bone whistles, the screams of men and beasts, mad with fear, the gunfire, obliterated the senses of both sides. Sweat, blood, body fluids of man and beast, the scent of terror and death did nothing to ease Gall's fury or the rage of his braves. Crazy Horse let loose years of hate, Two Moon's abhorrence was new and raw, just days since Three Star Crook had attacked and killed Two Moon's peaceful tribe. A thousand braves, maybe two thousand, overwhelmed the less than three hundred bluecoats, the bloody fighting ended too soon. An occasional gunshot, a scream, punctuated the dust and the mass of dead and dying men.

Crazy Horse did stop Rain-In-The-Face from finishing off Little Hair. Years ago, Tom Custer had captured and imprisoned Rain, embarrassed him, and Rain had vowed to cut out Tom Custer's heart and eat it. Crazy Horse expected Rain to take this opportunity for revenge and stopped him. He motioned to Will Thunder Cloud, the old women, and Beau Farro.

The Great Spirit had spoken through Sitting Bull after the Sun Dance and specifically told the people not to take the belongings of the Long Knives. Greed however ruled. The people did not listen. All around the long hillside, the women, children, and elders stripped the two hundred plus corpses of their clothing, guns, ammunitions, and valuables, checking to make sure each enemy was dead, mutilating bodies in symbolic ways but for no rationale except a long-festered hatred, contempt, and latent rage. For unfathomable reasons, a few bodies, except for killing wounds, were untouched; others were pulverized to an unrecognizable pulp. Nothing made sense. Young boys used the glistening naked bodies for targets. Many corpses, so riddled with arrows, looked like porcupines. The general and Captain Myles Keogh, except for fatal wounds, lay untouched. Most horses had been killed for defensive breastworks or had run off. The battlefield looked like an artist's rendition of hell.

※

Few Indians had any interest in paper; letters, notes, money, pages of diaries, books, the Bible, Last Will and Testaments blew like dry leaves among the dead; the Greasy Grass of the Little Big Horn Valley bled red.

Will and the old women, Blue Veined Woman and her sisters, quickly stripped Tom Custer's unconscious broken body. Beau Farro splinted his broken leg and arm then wrapped him carefully in a blanket to minimize his injuries and fitted him on a travois, made of discarded lodge poles and padded with buffalo robes. As Will mounted his horse, he watched the old women, all blowing their god-awful whistles, dump the chopped up body of Ed Kincaid from the gunny sack onto the battleground. The women had stone mallets, used for breaking the large joints of buffalo. They easily pulverized just about every part of the body from the gunny sack, smashing the skull flat to the depth of a man's palm; they did leave untouched their handiwork of the tattoo of a flag with the initials of TWC on the body's arm. Blue Veined Woman handed Will the heavy gold ring from the body, engraved: *West Point, Class of 1863,* marked with the initials, *EJK.* Will studied the ring then tossed it back to the Indian woman. He wanted no memento of the dark time of Yellow Bird's life.

Carefully, he guided his mount through the bodies, which already swelled in the hot sun. Flies by the thousands covered the corpses of man and beast. The stench choked both men. Beau Farro, who led the horse pulling the travois, rode beside Will. The sadness was unspeakable.

At twilight north of the *Far West,* they met up with Little Wind who took their horses. Beau Farro nodded toward Tom Custer, using the name the Indians called Long Hair's brother. "Little Hair will be more comfortable now," said Beau Farro to Thunder Cloud as they wrapped a robe around Tom Custer's body and lowered him to the bed of the canoe Little Wind had found. "I know no one who ever rode a travois who thought it comfortable." He nodded toward the front seat. "Take it easy, Thunder Cloud. I will guide the canoe and we will go with the current. Today had to be a strain on your heart."

Thunder Cloud didn't comment as they pushed off, catching the current of the north-flowing Yellowstone, but he didn't pick up the paddle. The canoe easily kept pace with Little Wind and their horses. This leg of their journey proved much more comfortable for all of them. Here on the river, the stench of death and the flies no longer bothered them. The sadness remained.

‡‡

At the farmhouse in Pennsylvania everyone except mother and babies worked. As Ray finished his stitching and bandaging, Lobo helped Mrs. Love place hot bricks in the bottom of the cradle and padded them with flannel blankets, while Sister Mary Agnes and Daniel carefully cleaned the beautiful babies and rewrapped them tightly in soft blankets then tucked them in the warm cradle. Because they'd not squeezed through the birth canal, their small faces were not bruised or misshapen. The boy had a full head of blond hair, the girl had Summer's distinctive nose. Both now pink, they slept snuggled together. Before moving Summer back to their bedroom, Ray, Daniel, and Mrs. Love carefully scrubbed the floors and furniture with a solution of strong soap and bleach; they wiped all the books, lamps, and any objects in the room with that solution, too and changed the sheets again.

Ray spoke to Daniel and Mrs. Love. "Hire some Amish girls to help with the wash and cleaning. I sent for a wet nurse. No one, especially the children, should sit on the bed or even hug Summer for at least a week. I'll give her Epsom salts to dry up her milk. She will want to hold the babies, but we need to keep them away from her too. Even you, Danny, stay on the outside of the mosquito netting. Infection is what kills the mothers." He held up his hands. "Some of the worst disease carriers are doctor's hands. The old timers don't believe us. They go from one patient to the next carrying dirt and disease with them. No one listens to me.

"I'll speak with the sisters and the children. Everyone wash his or her hands. We'll keep Summer alive." He paused. "Keeping everything clean... I wish we had a hospital here. I could control that."

"Do whatever you need, Ray. Keep Summer alive and I will, somehow, some way build a hospital here. I cannot lose Summer." An ugly bottle green fly landed on Daniel's wrist. He killed it with a quick slap. To Mrs. Love he said, "Ask Ezra to start making screens for all the windows as soon as possible. A patent for wire screening was just filed. I plan to screen the porch, as well. Thoughts of those filthy flies touching her sicken me."

Chapter 24

THE KILLING FIELDS

Like an angry Bantam rooster, Major Marcus Reno strutted about, his dark eyes flashing, his mahogany-colored hair almost white with dust, yelling, "Dig rifle pits! Protect yourselves. They'll murder all of us." And with few proper digging tools, his men wildly threw dirt using cups, spoons, forks, meat cleavers, empty food tins, anything to break the baked earth. The sun broiled down on the frenzied soldiers. When Reno melted down, ready to abandon his command and the wounded, Captain Frederick Benteen who had just arrived on the scene, took charge. He put a stop to the ranting and further ordered breastworks built. Here too, the soldiers used anything available: saddles, crates, sacks of beans, corn, oats, clumps of sagebrush, even dead horses, dragged by the men into position. Despite the scorching sun, every man worked frantically. Marooned on the hilltop, abandoned by their leaders, and surrounded by a swarming sea of bloodthirsty savages waiting for their scalps, the soldiers worked with manic speed.

Dr. Henry Porter, the youngest of the 7th' Cavalry's three surgeons, spoke to two of his orderlies. Dr. Lord had stayed with Custer's battalion, and Dr. De Wolf, Henry Porter's friend, was missing. Rumor reported him killed on the mad dash up the cliffs.

"Private Murphy, please remain with the wounded. Conserve what water we have." To the rest of his band of helpers, he said, "Let's make another reconnaissance of the area for wounded. Keep your heads down. Don't take any risks, boys."

They found several wounded and helped them back to the field hospital, now further protected by the picketed circle of horses and mules. In his search, Dr. Porter found the body of Dr. De Wolf, riddled with at least seven bullets. There was no way to retrieve his body now. A stab of grief for the loss of his friend quickly passed to the sickening realization that he was now the sole medical officer responsible for the combined forces of Reno and Benteen's battalions, a total of approximately three hundred and fifty officers and enlisted men, of whom fifty some were wounded with thirteen seriously so.

Dr. Porter shook off thoughts of the heat, the lack of water, and his abject terror of what might await them, and said a short prayer for his friend and vowed to gather Dr. De Wolf's personal effects to send to his wife, a task he did not relish.

On return to the field hospital, his orderlies, in addition to unpacking the crates of medical supplies, cared for their patients while he evaluated the wounds, gave opium to the hopeless, and doled out the little water available. A few patients needed surgery, which under the current conditions was daunting. In the back of Henry's mind, however, the thoughts of moving the non-ambulatory men off this hill and to civilization seemed impossible. All his training emphasized not abandoning the wounded. General Terry had over and over reminded them to care for the damaged men.

Late in the afternoon, a small band of brave soldiers, suffering themselves from horrid thirst, risked their lives by filling a few canteens and buckets for the wounded. Indian sharpshooters from a distant ridge of a higher elevation put a stop to that.

Where was Custer? Terry? Gibbon? Crooke? No one had heard from Three Star Crooke since the 17th, almost ten days ago. Late in the afternoon all shooting except for an occasional retort from those Indians guarding their hill, ceased. The stench of dead horses and men, the unrelenting heat, and the filthy flies compounded the desperation of the moment.

Captain Benteen, never one to mince his words or to hide his fury, said, "That son of a bitch probably took off on another of his wild goose chases. Someone should put a bullet between his eyes." Everyone within earshot knew who he meant.

⚔

The Yellowstone ran swift from spring runoffs. Estimating that Black Rock could be another half-day away, the medicine man at midnight insisted on beaching the canoe. Little Wind picketed the horses and built a small fire for coffee. Will and Beau Farro carefully lifted Tom to the grass. In the dim firelight, the medicine man cleaned and treated Tom's wounds. He dug a bullet from his right shoulder then bathed the incision with a weak solution of carbolic acid which the Indian Agent had given him.

After bandaging Little Hair's wound, he spooned water between Tom's parched lips.

"He's burning up. It's best if he sleeps," said Will as he sponged Tom's forehead and neck with cool river water.

"Best if he sleeps," repeated Beau Farro. "When he wakes he'll remember the death of his entire battalion."

"And his brothers and a nephew. His brother-in-law, too," said Will.

Little Wind had made coffee and warmed hard tack and fixed dried antelope, and tinned beans. They ate in silence. Listening to the rushing water and Tom's even breathing, Beau Farro said, "Rest Thunder Cloud. I'll take first watch and Little Wind will take the next." He shook his head. "You must be crazy about Yellow Bird to do this. I would roast Little Hair over a slow fire."

Will shrugged. A sly smile slid across his face. "Part of me thought of even worse things…" He finished his tin of beans and sat back. The light from the fire flashed on his profile. "I remember the first time I saw her." He sighed and stretched out his arms. "I was no naïve boy, but my knees went weak. Never had a woman affected me like Yellow Bird did. I wanted her more than I had ever wanted anything. The Great Spirits smiled on me. I married her and have been the happiest man alive.

"I've been able to protect her, but once I'm gone…" He shook his head then nodded toward Tom Custer. "He's an Indian fighter and, for a white man, a great horseman; he will protect her and my children when I cannot. My children and Zizi like him." He swallowed and a strange look moved across his face, and his fist tapped against his heart. "You see …" He paused as if searching for just the right word but couldn't find it, "as I said, I cannot explain it."

⁂

At Black Rock, Abbey and the other whites slept peacefully while a light rain pattered against the tented tarp which sheltered them. The cottonwood leaves sang their sweet music. Bear and the other Indians took turns sleeping under another tarp and guard duty. During the day Bear tried to teach the children how to make baskets, a desperate attempt by Bear to keep Emil's curiosity and boundless energy from killing the boy. Just yesterday, Running Cloud had swum across and back through the roaring Yellowstone to the admiration of all his Indian guardians. Dr. Cutter with the same purpose in mind tried teaching the boy ciphers which couldn't compete with daring escapades. Emil just couldn't sit still long enough to weave baskets or create codes. Alice, however, braided reeds beautifully and listened ardently.

⁂

Wakanda and Sister Mary Agnes slipped a clean cotton gown onto Summer and tucked her into the fresh linens. Daniel fixed the mosquito netting as Ray gathered his tools and scalded every instrument, including his hypodermic needle. "I gave her a heavy dose of opium, enough to knock her out for a few hours. The babies are fine. In fact, they're amazingly healthy. Sister Mary Agnes will watch them." He nodded toward the sister now.

"Hot water and a full size tub!" Ray chuckled. "That was clever of you, Sister, to suggest the Mrs. Byler take a bath. I bet she jumped at the chance." They could all hear the wet nurse humming and splashing in the bathroom.

Mrs. Love said, "I took her clothes and left her a clean robe while I wash her things. Can't have her nursing our babies in filthy clothes."

Ray smiled at Mrs. Love. "You're getting as devious as the rest of us."

As Ray finished packing his bag, he said to Daniel, "Come with me across the lake while I lecture the kiddoes on how to behave around their mother. Realize, Daniel, I do not support fairy tales. In my book babies aren't brought by the stork. Most children raised around animals know more than adults realize. I just want you to know I'm telling them straightforward what happened with their mother and how the babies were born, and I want all the children to stay at the school for a week."

Daniel stood and stretched. "Lilly is not going to like that."

⌘

On Reno's Hill, an agitated Captain Weir without permission led his men in the direction of where he'd heard the shooting earlier. "Who else could it be? The general must be in trouble."

Benteen shrugged. Thinking Major Reno had given Captain Weir orders, he and his men reluctantly followed. Reno, still shaken up by Bloody Knife's skull, brains, and blood exploding all over his face and uniform and who had not given his okay, ordered Dr. Porter to prepare non-ambulatory wounded to be moved. With Indian sharpshooters peppering the baked earth with bullets, a difficult ordeal became close to impossible. It took four to six men to carry one wounded man on a stretcher, and another to lead the rider-less horses. Just as they prepared to leave the hilltop, Captains Weir and Benteen's troops returned at gallop, halting any hope of escape.

Darkness brought a twenty-degrees dip in the temperature, and Dr. Porter became aware of scraping and digging noises coming from every direction. He realized the soldiers were improving their rifle pits and further building the breastworks around the perimeter. The stench of death permeated the entire hilltop, and especially the field hospital. He wondered if the men realized they may be digging their own graves. He overheard snorting horses and the soft voices of officers as they moved among their men whispering to them to try and get some rest. Hopefully, sleep would relieve them of a little of the terror and the horrid thirst, and the stench.

Lack of water also prevented Dr. Porter from properly cleaning the wounds of debris or providing cold water compresses to promote healing. And although he knew the importance of cleanliness, about all he could do was wring out the bloody bandages and reapply them. What water they had they doled out by the spoonful.

Benteen quietly told a bugler that he wanted revelry sounded at 2:00 a.m. He wanted those bloodthirsty savages to know they were ready for them. Reno was still useless but he'd quit talking about sneaking out the back way. Captain Benteen told the officers, "At least, the pack train found us, and we have ammunition.

Hopefully, tomorrow Terry and Gibbon will arrive. And Custer, well…"

Two of the hopeless abdominal wounded mercifully died which gave the rest of them relief from their moans and cries of pain. The night seemed at the same time both unbearably long and much too short.

※

No human heart beat on the long slope by Medicine Tail Coulee where two hundred and ten some men of the 7th lay bloating in the stifling June heat. One horse grazed nearby, Captain Keogh's beautiful bay, Comanche. Buzzards flapped from one naked body to the next, two coyote pups tugged at opposite ends of a thigh bone, beetles and ants did their grisly work beneath the corpses, and flies by the thousands hop scotched from one mound of flesh to another dropping eggs. Except for the wind and an occasional caw from a crow and the hum of the flies, silence ruled. A huge ball of hot orange-red sank behind the mountains.

※

Darkness had settled into Camelann when Ray and Daniel gathered the children and the three Sisters of Charity around a small fire Hal had built. Fireflies winked all around the edge of the lake as marshmallows, made earlier in the day by the sisters, were threaded on pointy sticks the boys had whittled. Golden orange light shone on the children faces as they roasted the treats. A very sticky Lilly dropped Sister Mary Clare's hand and climbed onto her father's lap. Louisa sat by his side.

He ran his hand through Lilly's dark curls and kissed the top of Louisa's hair. While Louisa biologically was his half-sister, in his heart she would always be a daughter. To all gathered about the fire, he said, "Your mother just gave us two new babies, a boy and a girl. They are beautiful and healthy and your mother's resting."

Ray removed a roasted marshmallow from a stick, ate it then licked his fingers. Sister Mary Clare handed him a damp cloth. She passed another to Daniel.

Ray took his time cleaning his hands, getting his words just right. "The babies didn't want to be born so I had to carefully cut them out of your mother's abdomen, her tummy." The look on the children's faces prompted him to hold up a hand and add, "Your mother would have died otherwise. I didn't hurt her. We used chloroform to keep her asleep. She felt no pain. Out popped the babies then I sewed up her tummy."

He sighed deeply. "We have worked very hard to keep everything clean. It's very important that no one sits on your mother's bed or hugs her, not for at least a week. I want all of you to stay here at the Indian School. This is for your mother's safety. Dirty hands carry sickness. I don't want any dirt near your mother."

Tears soaked Lilly's face. "Can't I at least see her? And the babies? Do we get to name them?"

Daniel hugged Lilly and put an arm around Louisa. "We thought tomorrow we'd take you all over to meet the new babies." Daniel noticed Ray's scowl, but ignored it. "The important thing is that you do not go running to your mother for a hug. She's going to be as sad as you. Summer would love to gather all of you in her bed."

"And," said Ray, looking fierce in the firelight, "that cannot happen." He looked from one to another of the children. "Can you stay away from you mother? You can kiss the babies. We," said Ray, "thought the boys could name the boy and Louisa and Lilly the girl. Now can you abide by those rules? Sleep here tonight?"

Ray studied Daniel for a moment. "You look beat Danny. Stay here with your children tonight. I'll stay with Summer." He patted the revolver he wore in a holster. "I'll fire three shots if we need you."

❈

At dawn on the 26th on what had become Reno's Hill, the day promised more blistering heat. Just after noon, another team of volunteers set about making a run for the river. This time they took four sharpshooters with them to provide cover from the Indians and quickly gathered several kettles and buckets of water. Just as they finished an Indian bullet blew a big hole in Sergeant Mike Madden's leg, just above the ankle.

Back at the field hospital, Dr. Porter evaluated the injury and as he gave big Mike some opium to dull the pain, enormous clouds of gritty white smoke billowed over the field hospital. Word soon spread that the Indians had set fire to their village and the prairie grass. Terror struck everyone for they had expected some kind of Indian devilment. Much to their surprise, when the smoke cleared, a spectacle no white man had ever seen confronted them. At least ten thousand Indian, men, women, and children, dragging travois filled with tipis and all their belongings, moved in an orderly manner, surrounding on all sides by magnificent painted warriors. Their dogs and the enormous pony herd accompanied them. Dr. Porter thought of Moses leading his people out of Egypt. They watched the mile wide sea of natives until they blended into the distant Big Horn Mountains. Henry found himself wanting to cry. Relief flooded him. While still filthy, sunburned, starved, and lost, in the middle of nowhere, their odds of survival had just increased by seven league proportions.

Major Reno ordered the compound moved closer to the river. The horses and mules moved eagerly for water. Cooks started fires and made coffee and began frying bacon for the soldiers. And at last Dr. Porter could take proper care of his patients.

PART III

Chapter 25

DAYS OF RECKONING

June 27th dawned as hot and dirty as the day before. Dr. Porter bent over Mike Madden, evaluating his wound. He started to say, "I can't put off amputation much longer... Mike," when cheers rang out along the perimeter of the bluffs. Private Murphy, Dr. Porter's orderly, ran over then returned. "It's General Terry's column, Sir." The joy on Murphy's face spoke with the relief they all felt.

Henry Porter squeezed big Mike Madden's shoulder. "I'll be right back." To Private Murphy, he asked, "Is Custer with him?"

Private Murphy shrugged. "I didn't see any grays." Custer's regiment was the only one that rode gray horses.

Just as Henry Porter approached Terry's column, Lt. James Bradley, Colonel Gibbon's, chief of scouts, rode up. He looked ill, and his horse exhausted and lathered. He saluted the commanders. "Sir, I'm profoundly saddened to tell you General Custer, all his officers and men have been slaughtered. It appears that they've been dead about two days, Sir."

Except for the snorting and stomping of all the horses and the creaking of their leather, silence hung like the pause between the tolls of a bell.

General Terry spoke first. He asked, "Where?"

Jim pointed northwest. "About four miles, Sir." He paused and wiped his forehead with a neckerchief. "It's about as bad as you can imagine, Sir."

General Terry in his cool, fatherly manner first ordered his men to relieve the suffering soldiers on Reno's Hilltop. While he consulted with Major Reno and Captain Benteen, his cooks started coffee and breakfast for everyone. With the help of Drs. John Williams and Holmes O. Pauling, Porter's field hospital was moved to the shaded timber on the far side of the river, as daunting and difficult a task as anyone imagined. Once accomplished, however, the wounded were laid on clean tarps, and adequate water made huge differences in their comfort. In spite of his tiredness, Henry Porter carried through with big Mike Madden's amputation and another delicate surgery on a soldier's face which had been riddled with fragments of bone and shrapnel. He was grateful for Dr. William's assistance.

❦

Emil ran down the ridge path with his arms stretched wide, his wild hair streamed behind him. "Canoe, canoe! It's Daddy!" Sure enough, a large canoe glided toward them. Bear held up a hand and the whites knew not to move, except Emil. He stood right beside Bear as the canoe pulled up to the small patch of pebbly beach. Will Thunder Cloud stepped out of the canoe.

He waved to Abbey, Alice, Vi, and Elliott then lifted Emil to the crook of his arm. He nodded to Bear, who moved in front of Will. He and Beau Farro lifted the bundle and carried it up the slight rise to the hillside camp.

Dr. Cutter knew who was in the makeshift litter, and he knelt opposite the medicine man. Elliott had clued in Violet, too. She stood between Abbey and Alice, an arm around both.

⚓

As Lilly wiggled into her underwear and stockings, she shot a scowl at Sister Mary Clare as she inspected her elbow. "Did you need to scrub me so hard?"

"I didn't mean to hurt you. I just wanted…"

Louisa came into the girls' bathroom in the Indian School. She glowed with cleanliness and excitement. Daniel had ordered baths for all the children, and Mrs. Love had sent clean clothes for all of them. Louisa wore a blue and white stripped dress with a starched white apron and white stockings. "Everyone else is ready. Listen to Sister Mary Clare. Here," she held out a dress and starched pinafore identical to hers but in a smaller size. As Lilly slipped into the clothes and stood still while the small nun buttoned the dress and tied the sash, she asked, "What about Larkspur?"

Louisa giggled. "Larkspur? I doubt if she'd ever forgive you." In a high pitched voice Louisa mocked: "Here Larkspur, come here Larkspur! That's downright silly. I like Iris best. It's much more dignified. Wait until we see her. We'll know then." She sounded very confident which irritated Lilly. She loved Louisa but she was only an aunt to the new baby. *I,* thought Lilly, *on the other hand, am a sister and I should be the one to name her.*

Lilly frowned again but allowed Sister Mary Clare to tie a red ribbon around her hair. She grinned into the mirror, inspecting her teeth. "I'm so excited. A brand new baby sister!"

"Two new babies," said Louisa. "Hurry, everyone else is in the wagon."

※

The first of the burial teams returned from the site of the killings. The first thing they did was drop into the stream fully dressed. They scrubbed themselves and their clothing to remove the stench of mortification and death. Lt. Bradley had been right. The site of the massacre, a long slope where the proud five companies of the 7th Cavalry met their death, was far worse than anyone could imagine.

"Be glad you weren't there. I doubt if the sight ever leaves my mind. Body after body, all naked and shining like hundreds of fallen white marble statues, sprawled across fields and ravines. Not everyone is accounted for," said Captain Moylan to a group sitting in the shade of a cottonwood near the river. He ran through the names of the officers they recognized. "We found Lt. Jack Surgis' blood-soaked undershirt, but not his body. The mutilations were... There's no rhyme or reason to it. Neither the general nor Captain Keogh was mutilated. I think just about everyone else was, some just a little, others brutally."

He grimaced and shook himself. "All of C Company was wiped out, but we found no trace of Lt. Harrington. Now," he let out an exasperated breath. "Tom Custer was just pulp. We had to scrape him up with a shovel. The only reason we knew him was that tattoo on his arm, the one with a flag and his initials. We buried what we found of him with his brother. Lt. Calhoun was scalped. Most of them were naked except for their socks. The savages took just about everything."

He suddenly choked, forcing back tears. "We do have one survivor: Comanche, Captain Keogh's bay. Private Lynch found him. When Denny called his name, the damn horse nickered and came trotting over. Denny took him to the hospital. He has a number of wounds."

Half the men stood and walked over to the hospital, and from that moment Comanche was a hero. Pvt. Wayne petted Comanche's nose. "Trust me boy, you're coming with us when we head back to Ft. Lincoln."

"Denny Lynch promised to take as good care of the horse as he would any of the other wounded in the hospital."

A short time later, General Terry announced solemnly, "Major Reno and Captain Benteen's wounded, approximately fifty-five men, will return to Ft. Abraham Lincoln via the *Far West*." General Terry cleared his throat. "As you all know there were no survivors from Custer's Battalion. We've buried and marked the graves of those we identified. We didn't find a trace of Lt. Harrington. We have slim hope he may have escaped." He left unsaid that Lt. Harrington may have been taken captive, truly an unimaginable fate. "I'm sending a long text to the telegraph at Bozeman. I've instructed that it be sent to both Ft. Lincoln and to General Sheridan. By our nation's centennial birthday, the world will know of this horrid blunder."A long moment of silence hung over the hillside as the finality of what happened set into the men's minds. A horse nickered, an eagle screeched, and General Terry continued with departure times and ended by suggesting the men write to their loved ones assuring them of their safety.

Relief and anxiety ricocheted off each other in Dr. Porter's mind. To see his wounded safely on board Captain Marsh's river steamer quelled his anxiety for their safety, but thoughts of the effort to get them the fifteen rough miles to the *Far West* sent his heart to racing.

⚿⚿

When Beau Farro removed the bandages covering Tom Custer's face, Abbey fainted. Will went to pick her up, but Elliott stopped him. He nodded to Bear. "Please take her up by the cottonwood trees." He handed Alice an ammonia capsule. "You know what to do with these, right?"

Alice nodded. A dozen questions rattled around in her mind, foremost of which was why had her father brought Tom Custer here? Wasn't he the enemy? Perhaps all her traitorous prayers for Tom's safety had been heard and answered. She understood why he was all bandaged. After Gall and Crazy Horse chased Three Star Crook back to his fort, the children in the village had talked of little else than how they'd kill all the bluecoats. But for now she kept quiet and ran to get blankets for her mother.

⚿⚿

Dr. Ray stepped onto the porch. "I'm pleased to report your mother slept all night, and this morning she sat in a chair for a short time and ate a small breakfast, a half piece of toast and a soft boiled egg. She's now back in bed ready to take a nap. She's very angry with me for not allowing her to see you or hold the new babies. Thank you for cooperating. It's important."

He motioned with his chin for Louisa and Lilly to sit on the big wicker chair and for the boys and Daniel to spread out on the long swing, then he reached beneath the netting and brought out one of the tiny bundles.

Louisa smoothed her blue striped skirt and graciously said, "Let Lilly hold her first. She's been so excited." Lilly squeezed Louisa's hand and wiggled deeper into the chair and held out her arms. Although bundled in a flannel blanket, the baby felt warm and Lilly marveled at the strong heartbeat. From the corner of her eye, she watched Dr. Ray hand the other baby to her father. She looked up to Dr. Ray. "Which one is the older?"

Ray nodded to the girl baby in Lilly's arms. "She popped out first so she's older by a minute."

Louisa and Lilly looked at each other and said in unison, "Poppy!"

Sister Mary Agnes said, "Why yes. Poppies are blooming all along the garden walk. I just love their big orange blooms."

Ray looked to Daniel who said. "Poppy is perfect, much better than Larkspur or Iris. Now fellows, what do we name your new brother?"

Dark-haired Gus, usually the quietest of the three brothers sat on Daniel's right. His big blue eyes took in the full head of golden hair on his tiny new brother. It was longer and thicker than Gus's hair. Someone tossed out Harry for a name.

Gussie tugged at his father's sleeve. He bent his head and kissed the baby's cheek. "Harry is okay, but I think we have to call him Leo. "He looks like a little lion with that mop of blond hair."

Daniel hugged Gus and slipped the baby into his arms. "Leo Charteris. That's a fine name. What do you think, fellows?"

The children took turns holding Poppy and Leo. Finally, Ray carefully eased the babies back into the cradle and Sister Mary Agnes ushered the children into the dining room where a breakfast of blueberry pancakes, sausage patties, eggs, and, of course, Mrs. Love's delicious apple cider donuts waited for them. Soon Hank and Charlie joined them. Later, they changed into play clothes and spent the afternoon on the baseball field then donning swimsuits and enjoying the lake. No one noticed Mrs. Millie Byler nursing the babies or their mother watching them from her bedroom window. Ray did allow Daniel into his bedroom where he sat outside the mosquito netting and talked to his wife.

"Nice work today, Danny. You deserve a medal," said Ray. "You've been great."

Daniel nodded to Ray, and inched his fingers under the mosquito netting and squeezed Summer's hand. Immense relief filled his chest. No words could describe the joy he felt. He knew she'd only managed one hurdle, and that many more lay ahead. To Summer, he simply said, "I hope you like the names, Poppy and Leo. We'll have to come up with middle names, but we'll do that later. They're beautiful babies. How are you?"

"I'm exhausted and sore. All I want to do is sleep. Tell the children I love the names. I miss them. I miss you."

"Ray threatened to tie bells to the netting if I as much as lift a corner. Ezra is working on window screens and I told him to go ahead and screen in the porch. We'll get you all better then you can sit on the swing with Leo and Poppy. Thank you for them. Do you think we have enough now?"

⚏

"Why, Vi? Why in God's name did he bring him here?" Abbey rolled to one side and looked down at the men doctoring Tom Custer. She had settled down enough to not be gasping for breath but she was by no means anywhere near calm.

Violet eased Abbey down on the blanket and sat beside her, holding her hand, patting it as if Abbey were a small girl. A soft breeze surrounded them making music in the cottonwoods leaves. Vi knew Will's intention but she also was not about to tell Abbey. Vi's voice came out quivery and hoarse. "Hush, child. He's busy with the medicine man and Elliott. I only know it will be a good thing. You know your Will only does good things."

She gestured to the group hovering over Tom. "But our Tom is in pretty bad shape: bones in his lower left leg and his right arm are broken—thank God they're not compound fractures. I saw three bullet wounds, plus he was knocked senseless. Personally, I'm happy he's unconscious. We don't know if he knows his brothers are all dead, his friends, even Toledo, are gone. He loved his family and that horse."

Violet squeezed the water from the cloth and sponged Abbey's forehead. "Little Wind said the battle was fierce, worse than anything we could imagine. He said all the bluecoats with General Custer, over two hundred, were killed, every one of them. Crazy Horse saved Tom. A lot of Indians died, too. Gall's wife, Sunny and her children were all killed."

Abbey abruptly sat up with her hands covering her ears and shaking her head. "No, no," she shrieked. "Stop. I don't want to hear anything more. I can't stand anymore."

Will heard her cry and came running up the hill, a good twenty-five yards from where Tom lay surrounded by Beau Farro, Elliott, Emil, and Bear. He slid to a stop beside Abbey. For a long minute he could not catch his breath which got Abbey's attention away from herself. "What, Will?"

Vi sensed she shouldn't be privy to what was about to be said, and she moved toward Tom. She signaled to Alice who ran to her side. They embraced and walked arm in arm toward the water.

This has to be difficult for Alice, thought Violet. Vi had watched the girl mature during their weeks with the tribes. Indian culture was so different. On one hand they could be so kind, almost childlike in their generosity, on the other hand so cruel. The natives expected more, much earlier, from their children than whites did. Boys became active predators from the moment they could clutch a spear, girls were not coddled or sheltered from the raw aspects of life.

She led Alice to the river, where they sat and dangled their feet in the water, and Alice started to cry. "I heard Little Wind say Sunny was killed." Her voice hitched. "Why do they do this?"

Violet pulled the girl into her lap, rubbing her back. "I don't know."

On the hillside, Will leaned against the cottonwood tree and gathered his wife close to him, snuggling her cheek against his shoulder, with his nose buried in her darkened hair. Here above the rushing Yellowstone, the late June day was glorious. Hawks circled above the rolling hills, a gentle breeze ruffled through the long golden grass. He plucked a spear and tickled her cheek with it. "How happy I'll be when your hair is once again all blonde." He smoothed the brown curls away from her face then kissed her eyelids.

"Remember, I told you Sitting Bull asked me if he could marry you? At first, he joked about it, but he continued asking me every day. He's now telling me all the amazing sexual antics he'll teach you once I'm gone. Gall and Crazy Horse noticed, too. Beau warned me to be careful. I am half afraid the old coot will slip an arrow my way just so he can have you. It's been done before."

He sighed deeply and held her tighter. "I know I'm fading. My heart grows weaker every day. Even Elliott cannot keep me alive forever, and barring death by Sitting Bull's order, I cannot expect to live for many more months." He kissed her cheek. "To be candid, I'm grateful for every day."

She started to cry. He pressed a finger to her lips.

"Hush, Yellow Bird." He pulled back and studied her hair. "Perhaps I should call you Brown Bird." He chuckled and hugged her again. "Allow me to finish. I talked with my blood brothers and we came up with a plan. I trust my brothers even though they each would take you as a wife. Elliott tells me it's the price a man pays for marrying a beautiful woman."

He shrugged then kissed her forehead again. "I intend, my darling girl, to enjoy these final times. I don't want to worry about you being abused after I'm gone. I want you and my children protected."

A touch of irony laced his voice. "I admit. I'm vain. I want to arrange the future. I want to keep safe what I hold precious even when I'm not here. Listen carefully. Our children are to be reared as whites and in Camelann. Wakanda will educate them enough to the ways of the Lakota. They should spend some time with my father in Toronto. I know Daniel and Summer will be good to you and my children. Tilley will probably be bossy and annoying, but you can manage her." He smiled, his blue eyes twinkled. "I told you years ago you would never pass for an Indian. I don't think you would do well married to a full-bloodied Indian either. The other wives would be too jealous of you." He made a face. "They'd give you all the dirty work: pounding buffalo brains and chewing gristle." He tightened his arm around her shoulder.

"Elliott thinks Tom must give up his Custer name. Otherwise, he'll be hounded by newsmen, the government, and every gunslinger west of the Mississippi will come after him. Elliott has other ideas, too, that will help Tom ease into the world under a new name. First, though, he needs to heal and grieve and I must convince him to cooperate."

He wiped her tears away then lifted her hand and kissed it, a smile danced in his eyes. "From what I've noticed when he looks at you I doubt I'll have a problem there. The children like him too. Thank the Lord, he is not the man his brother was. *Old Iron Butt could* never give up his killing ways; Tom already has.

We had spies watching him all summer. I want him to be able to protect you, but to never harm you or our children." His fingers again brushed her cheek. "Can you do this?"

He felt her nod and squeeze his hand. He asked, "Can you love him?"

Through her tears, she leaned close to him and pressed his hand between her breasts over her heart. Her voice came out hoarse, her throat full of tears. "I could never love anyone like I love you. Chemistry does exists between Tom and me---I guess that is a kind of love--but the deep trust I have with you isn't there yet Perhaps overtime, that will come.. From the beginning, from the one time we... we both understood that what we'd done was so wrong. Tom was adamant. I think he would want you to know. He, not I, was the strong one. He felt the children would hate him if they knew he betrayed you, and he did not want to dishonor you anymore than he had already done so. He holds honor close to his heart.

"I am amazed you do this. You are giving me to him. How do you keep from being jealous? I'd be all tangled with what others expect. What the Bible says... I never wanted to ...it just happened."

Will chuckled. "Thoughts of Sitting Bull with you motivate me. Never forget, Yellow Bird, I am very much a white man, too."

Chapter 26

HAZARDOUS DUTY

"You're sure this contraption will work, Doc?" asked big Mike Madden. The burly sergeant had just been loaded on a mule litter, an amazing innovation made of two parallel aspen poles with a lattice of woven horsehide strips strung between the poles, which created the litter. The litter with Mike in it was then fitted between two parallel but staggered mules. "If Betsy goes south while Nelly decides on north, I could be …"

Dr. Porter patted big Mike's shoulder. "Trust us, Mike. There's a man leading each mule. We've been training them for two days. Just close your eyes and enjoy the ride. Holler if you need more opium." He had given each of the five patients on mule litters a generous dose of opium. His other patients, fourteen on travois, and the rest on horseback were given lighter doses.

The distance to the *Far West* from Reno's Hill was nearly fifteen miles. No trail existed and the terrain was rough. Someone had sketched a map on the back of an envelope and the route took them along the Little Big Horn and up and down ravines and along a ridge trail to the Big Horn River where Captain Marsh's *Far West* waited.

General Terry made the final decisions. Because of the blistering heat and the inherent vulnerability of a long line of wounded men in hostile territory, they departed at twilight. At the time it seemed like a good decision, but soon heavy clouds covered the moon and a light rain made the trail slippery. Within five miles they were lost and one of Mike's mules stepped in a rabbit hole. Big Mike Madden with his fresh amputation tumbled into a cactus patch. To Mike's credit, he didn't cry out, but when they dropped him again he let out a string of swear words, many of which his comrades didn't know.

Colonel Gibbon and a staff officer dismounted and descended the ridge on foot and eventually found the *Far West*. With the help of the crew they lit a string of small fires along the way, and by dawn Dr. Porter's wounded came alongside the steamer. Captain Marsh's boatmen had cut fresh grass, laid it a foot and a half thick on the lowest deck, and covered the hay with tarps. Of the fifty-some originally wounded, several had elected to return to their units. Those that remained now eased their weary bodies onto the giant mattress and fell asleep. The officers and men who had assisted the invalids were given berths on an upper deck.

Comanche boarded last. Captain Marsh and Denny Lynch led the wounded hero through the stern back by the waterwheel. The captain had made a cozy berth between the rudders where the heroic horse immediately laid down and went to sleep.

⚌

News trickled to the telegraphs then flooded the country. Indian telegraph: drums, smoke, mirrors, wind whisperers, or whatever scooped all the newspapers. The details of many of the early reports were unreliable. On July 3rd, Libbie while shopping in Bismarck overheard two Crow scouts, Horned Toad and Spotted Cock, tell a crowd of the massacre, saying that the general had shot himself. She let out a yelp then quickly left the store.

Although the officers' wives suspected the worst, hope still lived in their hearts. That is until the morning of July 5th. Libbie accompanied the officers bearing the horrid news to each of the other widows. The Army was very efficient, and the women were Army wives; they knew how to behave. They supported each other, comforted their children, and packed up their homes. The Northern Pacific offered free rail passes.

In Monroe, Michigan, Libbie's hometown and where many of her relatives now lived, they heard the news shortly before noon on the 4th. Every church bell, firehouse bells, and even the bells on private homes, tolled all afternoon. Every resident of Monroe knew someone. Many of Custer's big family lived here, as did the relatives of Autie Reed and Jimmy Calhoun. By the end of the week, news traveled throughout America and reached Europe. Libbie never heard officially from the War Department. Nevin Custer, the remaining brother, thought this just as well because the President publically blamed George Armstrong Custer for the tragedy. The Custer family blamed President Grant.

The news hit Camelann hard. Everyone had met Tom and Toledo. At vespers Reverend Tuttle said a prayer for the loss of the soldiers. He told a story about Tom taking the children for rides on Toledo. They remembered. He and his brothers and Toledo became instant heroes.

However, the big event on July 4th happened when Summer walked out on the porch, looking lovely in a tan and white cotton robe, a gift from the Sisters of Charity, who had all worked feverously embroidering a band of bright poppies and frolicking lion cubs along the lapels and cuffs. She sat on the long swing and hugged all her older children. Then Louisa and Daniel carefully carried the new additions to their mother. Daniel had the foresight to hire a photographer to catch the poignant moment. As the sun sank behind the mountains, Hal and Lobo set off fireworks. First, Daniel locked the dogs—they hated fireworks—in the shed. For a better view, the children sat on the steps, the twins slept in their cradle; and then Daniel settled on the swing, holding Summer's hand. "Look at them. Aren't they precious? I'm the luckiest man alive."

—※—

Elliott, Will, and Bear decided Tom needed to rest, to heal. They moved their little camp uphill near the cottonwood trees and planned to stay for at least two more weeks, perhaps more. A flat area provided level ground for three tents and a spring gurgled nearby. They had a good view of the river in both directions. Fish and game were plentiful; the weather was perfect.

On the 14th Tom regained consciousness but seemed confused and didn't talk. He sat up, leaning against cushions from Abbey's wagon, while Dr. Cutter and Beau Farro cleaned him up, shaved his scruffy whiskers, helped him bathe, and changed his bandages.

Dr. Cutter held up a clean shirt of blue cotton, one of his own. "Let me slip this over your head, Tom." The patient nodded and further helped change his trousers to a pair of canvas breeches.

Emil and Alice brought a plate of pancakes with berry syrup and a cup of hot tea sweetened with honey Bear found. He ate every bite and drank all the tea. He smiled at the children, but did not seem to recognize them. Abbey watched from a distance.

⚌⚌

On the *Far West,* General Terry found Captain Marsh alone. Before the war General Alfred Terry had been a successful Connecticut attorney; today he chose his words with a lawyer's care. "Captain, you have on board forty-eight suffering men, a most precious cargo a boat can ever carry. These wounded soldiers are victims of a terrible blunder, a sad and terrible blunder. I know the Yellowstone is a dangerous river. Please use all your great skill to safely take these boys to the hospital at Ft. Lincoln."

The men were in good hands. Captain Marsh had thirty years of experience navigating these wild northwestern rivers, and the *Far West* was dubbed the greyhound of river steamers. At 190 feet long and a sleek 33 feet wide, with three decks, three boilers, two engines, and a waterwheel, she could haul

400 tons. Fully loaded, she only drew twenty inches of water. Her crew bragged, saying she could skim along on the dew. At different times the *Far West* served as a floating supply depot, a general officer's headquarters, and a hospital, whatever was necessary. As soon as her patients were safely unloaded in Bismarck, the *Far West* would be reloaded with supplies and reverse its journey.

Along the lower deck, further protecting the men, firewood was stacked four feet high. At full steam, the *Far West* burned nearly a cord of wood every hour. From their starting point on the Yellowstone to Ft. Lincoln was seven hundred miles. Traveling with the fast current, Captain Marsh expected to get his precious cargo home in less than three days.

<hr />

The women had bathed upstream in a warm eddy then washed bundles of clothes and carried the wet things back to the camp where they hung them on bushes to dry. Bear and another Indian had caught two big salmon which now roasted in the coals of the fire.

The children played catch with a ball from Elliott's pack. Will pulled Abbey down to the blanket in front of the fire and sat behind her. With Violet's sewing scissors he snipped the dark out of Abbey's hair, leaving just an inch or so of golden curls. Will leaned back studying his handiwork. "That's a hundred percent improvement." He handed her the little mirror the men used for shaving as he gathered the mess of cut hair. "You are not meant to be dark haired."

She held up the mirror, combing her short mop with her fingers. It felt cool and clean and she liked that it was blonde again. She smiled into the mirror expecting to see Will's face, but instead caught Tom watching her. Earlier he had wobbled out to the fireside with a walking stick devised by Bear, and he stood leaning against a rock. The moment she saw his face in the mirror, she knew he recognized her, and her breath caught.

She said nothing. Elliott came over and helped Tom situate into the camp chair. Despite the splints and bandages, he looked healthier in the borrowed clean blue shirt and canvas trousers.

"Thanks Elliott," he said with a loud sigh as he settled into the chair. "For the clothes, too. I feel human." He avoided looking at Abbey.

Long after dinner only the white adults remained by the fire. The Indians had left for guard duty or to their own tipi. Alice and Emil slept in their tent.

Abbey passed around fresh cups of coffee each laced with a teaspoon of whiskey. She settled down between Will and Tom. "Your memory is coming back, isn't it, Tom?"

He nodded as tears silently trickled from the outside corners of his eyes. Abbey reached over and took his hand. "I'm sorry. The memories must be horrid."

Tom nodded and said, "Everything happened so fast. Dust and gun smoke, the noise…. I hate those whistles." His voice hitched and an anguished sob escaped. "They were on top of us before we knew it. I saw them kill Autie." He lowered his head and shook it.

When he recovered, he said, "I remember Rain-In-The-Face coming at me with a hatchet. I had a pistol, but my hand wouldn't work. I couldn't fire it then everything went black."

Will spoke. "Crazy Horse stopped Rain. Beau Farro and I brought you here. He and Dr. Cutter somehow have kept you alive."

Tom's face contorted in agony. "Why me?"

Will kept his voice soft. "I asked him to save you if they could."

Tom shook his head. "The entire 7th?"

Elliott spoke. "We've only talked with the Indians. "According to them, all of the five companies with your brother were wiped out. They tell us some of Reno and Benteen's men survived."

Overhead bats swooped avoiding the smoke. Down by the river, frogs croaked, and at hand, the fire crackled and shifted sending sparks into the night. Tom lowered his head and rubbed his temple as if his head hurt. Violet poured hot water into a cup, then stirred in some honey. "Here, this is willow bark tea. It's bitter but it will help your headache. It's a lot to take in."

He nodded thanks and took a sip. "Hello Violet. Sorry for taking so long to recognize you." His eyes moved to Abbey. He smiled and his voice softened. "And Abbey. Alice and Emil have been so gentle with me." He nodded toward Will and Elliott. "Thank you. I guess." Another sob came out. "No one else survived?"

Elliott said, "We have lots to talk about, but we have lots of time, too. We plan to stay here for the next week or even longer. You need a healing time, both physically and mentally."

Tom looked from Abbey to Will. "I didn't recognize her until your cut her hair. He nodded to Will. "She's meant to be a blonde."

⚉

Daniel helped Summer walk down the pine needle path to the swimming beach. Mrs. Love followed with the babies in a buggy. Once settled in the shade, Summer looked out to the floating docks where all her children, Louisa, and Hal's boys gathered. They all swam like seals; she and Daniel had made sure they could all swim. Lilly never knew she couldn't swim. She just followed the boys and doggie paddled around like Owen and Mayo.

"Elliott sent a telegram this morning. I'm surprised he sent it to Morgan's Corner and didn't send it in code. He must have couriered a message to somewhere with a telegraph because they are camped along the Yellowstone sixty miles south of the Canadian border. Elliott's son, Todd, is with them. He was traveling across Canada and was injured. Somehow they connected. He cannot travel yet so they plan to continue camping for another week or two while Todd heals then come here."

Louisa and Lilly came running to the carriage to see the babies.

Mrs. Love held out towels. "Sit on the blanket and dry off. Don't drip water on the babies." She gestured toward a large picnic basket. "We brought sandwiches and lemonade."

The girls giggled. "I smell gingerbread. I'm starved."

From under the tree on the bench where they sat, Summer looked up to Daniel. "I thought Elliott's son died in a boating accident in Maine last year."

Daniel shrugged. "Must be a second son. Let's hope he recovers." He shook his head. "Imagine losing two children."

He took her hand and squeezed it; they sat in the dappled sunlight for a time watching their boys race and roughhouse from dock to dock, diving, canon balling, all brown as Indians; the girls giggled on the blanket with the twins, who wiggled and made baby noises. Daniel took Summer's hand again. "Did you ever imagine six children all those so many years ago when you bandaged that young soldier's leg?"

From beneath her wide-brimmed straw hat, Summer lowered her eyes. Looking both cool and radiant, she wore a pale pink striped skirt with a white eyelet blouse. The short capped sleeves and oval scooped neckline showed off the creamery skin of her lovely arms and décolleté. "I, no doubt, was thinking exactly what I'm thinking now."

"And what is that?"

Her cheeks pinked. "I was wondering how could I get this handsome young man to kiss me."

His kissed her cheek. "Was that so difficult?"

She arched a dark eyebrow. "I meant a toe curling kiss."

He checked all the children. No one was watching. Mrs. Love, who sat on the blanket intent with the girls and the babies, had her back to him. The girls were digging in the picnic basket. "Ray gave us an okay?"

"I thought you should ask? You're both men."

"You're the patient." He sniffed the air and grinned. "Do I smell gingersnaps?"

"That is gingerbread."

"Close enough. I'll talk to Ray."

She leaned her shoulder into his. "You remember toe curling, don't you?"

"If not, you'll have to teach me."

Chapter 27

THE ART OF DECEIT

"Are Violet and Elliott married?" asked Tom. Blistering sun and suffocating heat blasted eastern Montana. He and Abbey sat near the spring in the relative cool shade of the cottonwoods. Abbey wore a simple loose white muslin shirt and a tan poplin skirt, and although Tom appeared rested, he looked wrinkled and scruffy. He needed a shave.

Below them the Yellowstone River flowed north as it wound through the pines. Voices trickled up from the water. Violet and Elliott sat on a rock down by the river; Will and the children splashed in the shallow water by the pebbly beach. Elliott placed an arm around Vi and kissed the side of her neck.

"That sly old fox, who does he think he's fooling?"

Abbey grinned and shook her head, her blonde curls bounced. She looked and felt so much better since Will had trimmed her hair. "They're obvious aren't they? I think they're perfect for each other, and I'm happy for them. They planned to be married in San Francisco, but since we're no longer going there, they've changed the venue to Camelann." She sighed softly. "I think a small wedding there will be just as nice. You know Camelann is my favorite place in the entire world. I feel safe there, and I adore both of them. Elliott gave Will extra time and he saved your life."

Tom fidgeted in his camp chair. He seemed unsettled. Memories of the battle at the Little Big Horn materialized with increased frequency. He compared it to a jigsaw puzzle with missing pieces. Finally, he asked. "Why did Will go to the trouble to save me? I don't understand. He barely knows me."

Her eyes grew big and wet and she swiped her hands through her short hair. "I don't know if I can talk about it. I choke up just thinking about what Will is doing. He is by far the kindest person I've ever known." She pulled out a hanky and wiped tears from the edges of her lashes. "You see, he's dying. His heart is weakening. Elliott has kept him alive with digitalis and the proper diet and exercise, and it worked for a while, but he knows his heart is not acting as it should. He can feel it failing." She bent her head and brushed away more tears.

"Oh, God, I am so sorry, Abbey. Do the children know?"

She found it touching that he thought of her children. She shrugged. "We haven't told them, but I suspect they know something untoward is happening. Of course, we don't know when. It could happen tomorrow or three months from now." She took another deep breath. Her voice quivered. "He saved you, Tom, because he wants you to marry me...when he's gone."

Disbelief swept across Tom's face. No words came out.

Abbey took another shaky breath and said, "Sitting Bull is the problem. He's already put in a bid to marry me." She now sat up, her back straight as an arrow. "I know it's ridiculous, but Sitting Bull likes women, especially white women, and he's taken a fancy to me. At first, he joked about it, but ever since the Sun Dance he is adamant, and now he defeated the bluecoats and is a hero, he thinks he can have anything he wants which at the moment is to make me one of his wives."

Her voice dripped anger. "You know he didn't even fight in the battle. Crazy Horse and Gall both warned Will to watch his back. Sitting Bull has made quiet threats to speed up the inevitable."

Tom let loose a low whistle. Abbey, released a chilly laugh and said, "Will rescued you because he found your handkerchief under my pillow. He quickly figured out, as he so kindly put it, you were important to me. Oh, Tom…" tears streaked her face, and she wiped the wetness away with her wretchedly soaked hanky. "I felt like such a traitor. I still do. If he had beaten me, I'd feel better. He calmly confronted me." Her shoulders shifted, "and I told him about us. All of it."

She stood and filled two cups at the spring and handed one to Tom. As she sat back down, she said, "He's doing this for a lot of reasons, but mostly because he cares about my happiness, and you have the skills to protect me and our children." She took a long drink of water and set the cup in the dirt beside the cushion then wrapped her hands and arms tightly around her chest. "Don't worry, Tom. I won't make you marry me. I'm praying we make it to Camelann. We'll be safe there. Daniel will protect us."

Tom looked down to the river, checking to see if anyone was watching them; Will and the children were sprawled on the grass talking animatedly about something; Vi and Elliott were still in a world of their own. Tom leaned forward and offered his hand. When she took it, heat flashed through him, and he saw color rise in her cheeks. Words were not needed to know she felt it too.

A long moment passed. His voice came out in a slow drawl packed with emotion and honey thick. "Oh, Abbey, I had given up any hope that I might ever again hold you. Now, I have a reason to live. I just don't like that Will … he's a far better man than I'd ever hope to be. Death seems to be all around me. It's wrong that another's death has the power to give me joy. I'm numb with sadness and happiness all mixed together."

He placed his open palm against his heart, a smile nearly as wide as the big Montana sky opened on his scruffy face. His voice whispered. "Inside I'm all aglow. I never for a moment quit loving you." Tears filled his eyes. "I hate though that Will must die. It's not right. A path through the goodness and sadness seems impossible."

They both needed desperately to touch, to comfort one another, to center themselves, but they knew such a thing was impossible. Above all else, they understood they could not betray Will for they both loved him.

Suddenly, Abbey jumped to her feet and pointed south. "Look, look, it's a steamboat, a big one."

The wading party ran halfway up the hill to get a better view as Bear, Beau Farro, and the Indian guards all with repeating rifles appeared along the tree line. Elliott and Will signaled the Indians to lower their weapons; they waved to the steamer. The *Far West* blasted its deep steam whistle. An enormous flock of birds rose out of the low brush hugging the shore and darkened the sky; a small herd of antelope grazing in the lowlands on the far side of the river scattered.

"I'm going down in case they stop. I'll try to keep them away from you. If I can't, how is your Scottish brogue?"

For a moment, Tom looked puzzled then said, "Actually, our adjutant is Canadian. We bantered accents all the time...just for something to do. Riding a horse for ten hours a day is boring." His face suddenly crumpled. "Oh, God, Cooke must be dead, too." Devastating memories came back at the oddest times.

A breeze rustled the cottonwood leaves sending music through the air. Abbey touched his shoulder. "Elliott is planning on introducing you as his son who has been injured in a hunting accident. Todd was killed last summer. Elliott adored him. Of course he would talk to you first." She softened her voice. "Sorry to set this all on you at the same time. There may be some men on the boat who know Tom Custer. Elliott thinks you should change your name, your identity. We'll talk later about that. Elliott just has your safety in mind. It's ultimately your decision."

He nodded as they watched the *Far West's* crew hitch two long cable around two trees neatly docking the steamer alongside the beach. "I know Captain Marsh," said Tom.

Abbey ducked into her tent and returned with her ragged slouch hat, dark glasses, and a small red plaid blanket. "I'll do my best to keep them down by the water, but in case they come up here..." She looked him over: Elliott's wrinkled blue cotton shirt hung loose outside his tan trousers which had one leg rolled to the knee to accommodate the splints, no socks, bare hairy legs, Indian moccasins, and frankly he needed a bath. With the rough beard, he looked nothing like a soldier. "You're all scruffy. Good. Slump a little. You don't look anything like the well-groomed Major Tom Custer I remember. Cover up your arm. The tattoo."

He nodded and put on the hat and dark glasses then emptied Abbey's cup into the dirt, making mud. He then smeared it lightly over the tattoo. He chuckled. "Stage makeup."

She blinked and whispered, "Remember the accent," then hurried down to the landing, her tan skirt swirling about her bare ankles.

His heart skipped a beat. In just ten minutes his life had done an astonishing cartwheel. He stretched his good arm and leg, threw the plaid blanket over one shoulder. He felt alive for the first time since Rain had come after him with a hatchet, since that bloody day on another hillside.

※

After the dancing and celebration, the Indian village leaders, Sitting Bull, Chief Gall, Crazy Horse, Black Moon, and Rain gathered around Sitting Bull's fire. Now camped in the relative safety of the Big Horn Mountains, they passed the pipe; each had a story to tell. The Great Battle of the Greasy Grass Valley would live in legend for many generations. Each man also possessed some memento, a watch, a ring, a medal. One of Sitting Bull's braves had captured an officer's pistol and presented it to the great chief; Rain had Tom's Medals and an officer's hat. They knew they fought well, individually and as a cohesive force.

"We have too many ponies," said Crazy Horse. "They need new pastures daily. We must split up." He'd brought a puppy, a golden-red color, with big paws and pointy ears. It had played for most of the evening with a strip of rawhide, now it slept in Crazy Horse's lap.

"Nice pup," said Chief Gall.

Crazy Horse handed Gall the little dog. He knew his friend still exerted an immense effort to pull his mind out of the depression brought about by the brutal murders of two of his wives and three of his children. Gall had fought in a manic frenzy of hatred and blood.

The puppy woke for a minute and licked his fingers, then settled into the big Indian's lap. He stroked the soft fur, and his heart slowed. "We beat the bluecoats, but you know we did not win. Our way of life is gone. Now they will come after us with thousands and thousands of soldiers, and if we defeat them they will come again with thousands more. Farmers, loggers, and miners will flood our hunting ground. I plan to roam until winter then go north. Next summer I may plant a garden."

Sitting Bull held up an old medal. "This is from when the British ruled." He fingered it lovingly. "They gave it to my great grandfather's father. I will roam too, but we will go to Canada." He held up the ancient medal. "I'll claim British citizenships. I want to find that pretty blonde wife of Thunder Cloud first though." He laughed an ugly laugh. "She will keep me warm during the long Canadian nights." He nodded toward the puppy. "And lick me like that mutt licks you."

Crazy Horse ignored Sitting Bull and took a long draw on the pipe. He shook his head. "You're just exchanging redcoats for

bluecoats. They will have to kill me to get me on a reservation."
He looked at Chief Gall. His tone and expression mocked. "Are
you growing turnips in your garden? Carrots? Maybe chickens?
The whites will buy eggs."

⚏

"Captain Marsh, may I present my wife, Abbey DuPree," said
Will.

The captain took her hand and bowed slightly. He was not
immune to a pretty lady. "I'm pleased to meet you, Mrs. Dupree.
I've been telling your husband and Dr. Cutter and Mrs. Montour
about our precious cargo. We have forty some wounded and
Captain Keogh's Comanche on board." He motioned for one of
the crew to bring out another chair and lemonade.

Dr. Porter stepped down the gangplank and joined them.
The captain made introductions. They spoke for a good half-
hour. The children sat spellbound, one on each side of their
father. They knew the names they spoke of because they'd lived
in the Indian camp and ridden the train with the Custers, but
they knew to be quiet.

"We heard," said Will, "from some passing Indians of their
victory, but I'm glad to hear the Army's version. General Terry's
words, *a horrid blunder,* sounds appropriate."

When Captain Marsh told of the death of all the Custers,
Will tightened his grip on the children. Alice leaned her head
against her father's arm but Emil didn't even twinge. Finally, the
captain rose to leave; he looked up the hill.

Abbey answered his quizzical look. She'd never been good at telling falsehoods, but she knew if you intend to lie, keep it as close to the truth as possible. "That's Dr. Cutter's son. Todd was hunting north of here and is recovering from an accident with a horse. We will stay here while he recovers, then we will continue to Bismarck and take the train east."

Dr. Porter and Dr. Cutter spoke for a moment about the extent of his son's injuries. "How are you for medical supplies? I could spare some."

Violet answered. "We are all set with medical supplies, but we are low on coffee." She smiled at the captain. "Do you have some we could purchase?"

Captain Marsh walked over to one of his crew and spoke quietly to him. Five minutes later, another crewman returned with two bulging gunnysacks and set them at the captain's feet.

"Thanks, Jerry." He looked to Violet. "We have plenty of supplies, Madame. Enjoy this with our compliments."

Abbey could smell the fresh bread. Her stomach growled and she smiled ear to ear. "That smells marvelous. Thank you, Sir. We'll have a delicious dinner tonight."

Grant Marsh returned her smile. "Consider it a gift from the *Far West*. Be gentle. I asked the cook to spare a few eggs." He moved to shoulder the gunnysacks. "Allow me Madame. The hill is steep."

Abbey deftly reached out and lifted the bags. "Thank you, Sir. Emil and Alice are strong." She motioned with her chin for the children who readily took the bags and raced up the hill. "Now don't," she hollered after them, "don't get into that until

I'm there." She turned to Captain Marsh. "Your generosity is appreciated. That bread has my mouth watering."

Captain Marsh turned to Dr. Cutter. "I thought your boy might enjoy the bread. There's a quart of beef broth, too. Nothing like beef broth and toast to help heal the body. He's lucky you were close by...a miracle really."

"Yes," replied Dr. Cutter, smooth as if he'd rehearsed his lines. "We planned to meet further upriver. His friends with the help of some Crow scouts brought him here by canoe. Thank God he's safe."

"We'll stop by on our return trip and check on you. I always carry extra supplies," said Grant Marsh. He shook hands all around. "Nice meeting all of you. Good luck to your son, Dr. Cutter."

⚓

That evening Abbey made omelets with wild chives, glorious toast with elderberry jam she'd made days ago from berries the children had picked, and wilted watercress with bacon and vinegar dressing, all from the *Far West's* generous provision of bread, butter, eggs, and a small bottle of apple cider vinegar. Dinner was an enormous success. She gave the broth to Tom who said it really did help.

While Abbey and Violet cleaned the dishes and put the children to bed, the men talked long into the night about Sitting Bull's threat, Will and Tom's health, and Elliott's intelligent suggestions.

"I realize, Tom, giving up your name and identity may seem daunting. However, you can always go back to being Tom

Custer. You can claim amnesia. More soldiers injured in battle than the public realize suffer from memory loss. After weeks, months, they awaken and realize who they are.

"I thought of this deception when I realized how close Todd's name was to yours. Thomas Ward Custer, Todd Wallace Cutter. You even have the same middle initial." Elliott leaned back. His voice thickened with emotion. "Todd planned to study English Literature at Oxford. He loved Shakespeare. Todd was about your height and build, and he was athletic like you, and with your coloring. Tom, I'd be proud for you to use his name. I still have all his papers."

"I appreciate your concern, Elliott. I think of how devastated my parents, Libbie, my sister, Maggie, the rest of the family, must be. My parents lost three sons, a nephew, and a son-in-in law. Would my return to life be a help to them? I don't know."

Will sat up. "Using Todd's identity gives you options. Don't rush into anything. Remember Abbey, Emil, and Alice are involved now. I do not, and I don't think you do either, want them in harm's way. You'd gain national attention as the last survivor of the Little Big Horn. Some hot shot may want to put a notch on his belt—the last Custer. Do you really want to continue being a soldier after what you've been through?"

Tom held up his splinted arm. "When will these come off?"

"Another two weeks, three at the most. Why don't you give yourself until then to decide? I'll tell you about Todd and we'll touch up that brogue of yours."

"Aye, I thought I sounded jolly good."

Elliott chuckled. "To a Scotsman you remind me of a bloke who learned English from a German who grew up in Japan."

"That bad, eh?"

Later that night as Will lay down by Abbey, she awoke and snuggled against her husband.

Will put his arm around her. "Do you find it difficult to be around both of us?"

She didn't answer for a long moment. He thought she might have gone back to sleep but then she said, "Will, I'm so grateful you are both alive. God definitely is smiling on me." She nuzzled his neck and added, "But if you're asking another question... I know to whom I'm married, and I have no urge to crawl under his blanket, but it's nice to know he's there in case my husband keeps asking silly questions."

Chapter 28

A MOMENT IN TIME

S ummer shook out her cardinal red riding habit. She smiled fondly, remembering the time she'd worn it at the falls. *Yes, Daniel will remember this.* She laid everything out on the bed: black corset, black silk stockings, blouse, the gaucho trousers, the bolero jacket, hat, gloves, and black leather boots. After a bath, she reluctantly asked Mrs. Love to help her with the laces.

Mrs. Love had reared nine children and had thirty some grandchildren. Two of her granddaughters helped with the cleaning and laundry here. However, she often frowned on Summer's clothes. Tonight, she didn't disappoint. As she tugged the laces, she muttered, "You know, Mrs. Charteris, you're just asking for another baby. Don't you have enough?"

Summer groaned. "Daniel asked me the same question. I'm not ready for a convent yet. Let's see if he still feels that way." She donned the stockings, gaucho trousers, the silk blouse, and short jacket then her boots and hat. After checking herself in the bathroom mirror, Summer walked through to the kitchen.

Mrs. Love halted her in the middle of the room and handed her carrots for the horses. She smiled. "You look lovely, Miss Summer. He doesn't have a chance. I'll stay the night and take care of the children."

She, Daniel, and Ray had decided on a late evening ride up to the site for Camelann's proposed hospital, the one Daniel had promised to build if Ray kept Summer alive. When she stepped outside to where Ray and Daniel waited with the horses, Ray's chin jerked and he said, "Good Lord, Summer, you're like a rubber band. You snap back quicker than any of my patients."

Daniel's eyes crinkled at the corners. "Isn't it about time I wrapped my hands around that elastic band?"

Summer blushed, but Ray turned professional and said, "Yes, whatever feels right. However, stay out of the lake for another month. I'm erring on the side of caution. I doubt if your incision could be infected now but, the water in the bathtub has to be more sanitary than lake water."

Nonchalantly Summer handed carrots for the horses to the men then fed one to Rabbit, leaning her cheek against the mare's neck and combing her fingers through the horse's black mane. Ray and Daniel had been treating her like a fragile antique vase for the past six weeks. Before Daniel could maneuver to give her a gentlemanly leg up, she pulled herself into Rabbit's saddle then smiled down at her husband with her old devilish wink. "I'm ready Daniel, ready to race. Last one up the mountain is a rotten egg."

All romantic notions took a bad turn for Chester stepped in a foxhole and Daniel spent the night in the barn icing the stallion's ankle.

They did decided to place the hospital on Christmas Tree Ridge. The views from there in all directions took one's breath away, and a breeze most days whistled through the pines. It would be an ideal place for anyone to convalesce, and once a road was built, the access would be easy. Now the climb winded the horses.

Daniel's frustration grew. Weeks before she suggested, they invited Frank Furness, former Captain Furness of the 6th Pennsylvania Cavalry and Medal of Honor recipient, and his wife, Fannie, for a weekend. Captain Frank Furness who fought at Gettysburg with Daniel and Hal graciously accepted. Frank's wife Fannie (with an i) and Hal's wife Fanny(with a y) had attended school together as girls and were great friends. Frank had gained fame for his design of the Philadelphia Museum of Fine Arts for the Centennial Celebration, and now he was one of America's most sought-after architects.

After an afternoon tour of Camelann, hearing their plans, and dining on Mrs. Love's sweet onion smothered chicken dinner with roasted vegetables and fresh rolls, he volunteered to design the hospital and to supervise the actual construction.

"Are you sure Frank? The design is all I hoped for," said Daniel. "I'm aware of how valuable your time is."

Frank stroked his magnificent moustache and beard then smiled. They were sitting on the newly screened porch enjoying views of the lake where three of the boys fished from the dock. He patted Fannie's knee. "My wife always is trying to drag me to London or Paris." He nodded toward the lake. "I'd much rather fish. We'll build a kiln and make bricks from Camelann's own clay, which will save you immense amounts of cash. And," as Mrs. Love served peach pie with blueberries and whipped cream, he added, "we will use Amish carpenters."

※

The night sky stretched above them like an enormous indigo tent; stars thick as grass and a sickle moon reflected in the smooth waters of the Yellowstone as the three long canoes, each guided by an Indian, stealthily floated with the current.

Dr. Cutter had removed Tom's bandages and splints two days earlier, and now Tom reveled in the freedom to stretch those long muscles, feeling his old strength return. He also loved being on the water. A storm had passed through the valley yesterday bringing clear skies with it. Pungent pine and the rich earthy scent of damp soil mixed with a chilly north wind, so fresh it hurt to breathe. The skill of the Indians in moving the canoes impressed him. They made no noise and it appeared effortless, but he realized it wasn't. Beau Farro sat in the stern of the lead canoe, guiding it through the waters with Will, Abbey, and the children. Little Wind guided the second canoe with Dr. Cutter, Violet, and Tom. Bear steered the third canoe full of their gear.

Will, Bear, and Beau Farro had made the decision to leave their camp at Black Rock that last week in July. The Yellowstone, still flush with spring rains and snowmelt, could dry to a trickle any day soon. And since Little Wind *found* two more canoes, they sent the horses north with Little Wind's brother, Rock Hard Head.

Two days earlier while checking Tom's flexibility and strength Elliott announced, "You're annoyingly fit, and you sound like a true Scotsman, Todd. Now follow me about and start walking like a kin of Bobby Burns."

Under his breath, Tom/Todd muttered, "Next you'll have me quoting poetry and wearing a bloody kilt!"

Tom had just about decided to use Todd Cutter's name and identity. He knew he wanted no more of soldiering, no more killing, and he definitely didn't intend to allow some politician to drag him from whistle stop to whistle stop during the upcoming Presidential campaign, or, heaven forbid, he would be subpoenaed to give evidence before a congressional committee. He remembered the ugly newspaper articles when Autie testified before Hiester Clymer's congressional committee. He particularly remembered how Sherman, Sheridan, and especially President Grant had betrayed Autie. Deep in his heart he knew he would never forgive them.

And if that wasn't enough heartache, every night he awoke in a sweat reliving the horrors of the Little Big Horn. He did not want to relive those last minutes of the 7th Cavalry's glory before a Board of Inquiry about who committed suicide or who shot whom, or how the 7th fell apart. His family remained his biggest concern. He'd allocated $40.00 a month to his mother for years. He worried if and how they'd survive without that money. He did know, nothing he did, not even his return, could remove the sting of Autie's death for his mother. The sun rose and set on Autie.

And, the primary reason to shed his Custer identity: Abbey and the children's need for obscurity seemed even greater than his. Abbey assured him Summer and Daniel and Camelann would protect them. Other than spending time with horses and his new family, he didn't know exactly what he wanted, perhaps to just fade into anonymity for a while. Memories of Camelann beckoned him. He felt he might heal there. More than anything on earth he wanted to learn to be a good father and husband for he had no doubts he could love them. He already did. That she or the children wouldn't want him haunted him.

He'd always enjoyed playing the bit parts in Libbie and his sister Maggie's amateur theatrical productions during the long Ft. Lincoln winters. The girls had told him he was a natural actor. Could he do it for real now? *Well,* he said to his new self, *Todd Cutter, my lad, you'll get a chance soon.*

Now, they headed to Ft. Buford, an outpost on the Canadian border, where they'd surely be questioned, then to Bismarck, which might prove more difficult. *How many citizens, clerks, bartenders in Bismarck will remember Tom Custer? How many girls? I danced with a lot of Bismarck ladies. Now, I'm praying they don't remember me. I've gained fifteen pounds; my hair is almost to my shoulders and lightened by the sun. I'm not at all fond of this full beard, but Vi tells me to keep it. Without shaving she tells me I look like a mountain man, and I'm practicing how to not walk like a soldier. And I smell like a goat. Good Lord, I need a bath.*

❧

The day Ezra fitted the last window screen in the house, the Charteris' children had a fly assassinating mission. Armed with swatters, the children destroyed every fly, mosquito, and bug that dared to cross their doorstep. They actually fought over who used the broom and dustpan. Daniel made a dramatic ceremony of removing the disgusting flypapers, sticky traps for unwanted insects, that hung over doorways and from the kitchen ceiling from April until frost.

After baths and celebratory shoofly pie, the children climbed into their beds. Daniel, feigning exhaustion, asked Mrs. Love to stay the night. Of course, he was not exhausted, just the opposite. He didn't know either that Mrs. Love had already decided she'd be needed overnight.

Excited and energized like a college boy, he lit at least twenty candles in the bathroom and bedroom, uncorked a bottle of iced champagne while Summer filled the tub with steaming water, bubbles, and rose pedals.

Daniel slipped off his shirt and said with a smug smile, "I guess our nocturnal swims aren't a secret. Ray suggested we stay out of the lake for a time, but thought splashing in a tub instead would be safe. He still is concerned about infection."

He pulled a table near the tub and set the champagne and glasses on it, and after helping each other with their nightly ritual of pulling off boots and unlacing laces, they left their clothing in a heap on the bathroom floor and eased into the steaming water.

As she took the champagne glass from her husband, she asked, "I haven't mustered the courage to really look at my scar yet. Does it look terrible?"

He reached beneath the bubbles and caressed her scar. "How do you feel about that huge scar on my leg?"

She took a deep breath and leaned her head against his shoulder. "Oh, Daniel, I'm so grateful for that scar. I dug a bullet out of your leg and made that scar, sewed it up with a hair from Chester's tail because I had no strong thread. It's a wonder you're alive." She reached beneath the bubbles and caressed his leg. When I see it, I'm so glad you have your leg. I was only eighteen. I doubt if I could have amputated it. You'd probably be dead."

He topped off her champagne glass. "I haven't seen your scar since Ray first cut you, but I know I'll be eternally grateful for that minor imperfection because it kept you alive and gave us two more beautiful babies. Set your glass on the table, sweetheart."

She arched her eyebrows with a question poised on her lips.

He grinned. "I don't want you to spill the champagne—it's expensive stuff. I'd hate to see it go down the drain. I've waited six weeks to touch you and I cannot wait much longer."

"Daniel, the tub's full. This is not the lake. You'll have water all over the floor!"

He set her champagne glass on the table then made a huge splash as he gathered her close and laughed. "You don't think I plan to sit here blowing bubbles, do you? With what I have in mind, sweetheart, I may empty it, and by the time I'm finished with you, you won't care."

❧

"Thwack!"

Terror struck Tom like a blade stuck deep in his spine. The sound of an arrow piercing flesh once heard remains unforgettable. A small cry came from Abbey and a gasp. "Will's hit!" Tom's rifle snapped to his shoulder; a bullet chambered.

The Indian guides immediately knew. Expertly they slid the canoes into the shadowed part of the river and beneath an overhang of willowy branches. At the same time, Beau Farro in the lowest of voices whispered, "Hold your fire. No flash. Let Bear use his bow." Tom lowered his rifle, allowing it to rest in the crook of his arm; no way did he relax.

The very air beneath the thin veil of limp branches quivered with fear and expectation. In the dim predawn light, he could see her blonde head bend toward Will. As if she read his mind, she pulled up her hood and covered her hair.

Tom watched in amazement as at least a dozen arrows flew from Bear's bow, powerful and fast. He'd heard of Bear's prowess as an archer. Red Cloud told of how Bear once shot an arrow clean through a buffalo's chest, and how he could fire off eight arrows before the first found its mark. Two more unmistakable *thwacks* came from across the river; Bear's arrow hit true. And a loud splash cut into the silence of the night.

Dr. Cutter motioned to Little Wind to pull their canoe alongside Beau Farro's. Then the Indian guides and Tom held the boats steady while Elliott maneuvered into Will's canoe. Abbey slid out of the way and with sign language moved a terrified Emil into Tom's arms. At the same moment, a huge Indian, by the looks of him a Hunkpapa, rose out of the water like a great fish. He grabbed Alice who let out a high-pitched yell before the huge hand covered her mouth. Abbey screamed as another fierce native emerged behind her.

Tom's fighting instincts came back in a flash, all those years of training as a soldier roared to life. He pressed Emil to the floor of the boat, shot the Indian behind Abbey. "Stay down," he told everyone then graceful as a thoroughbred, he leaped over Emil, Dr. Cutter, and that canoe. His body struck both Alice and the Hunkpapa, and knocked Alice free. As Tom rose out of the shallow water, he bellowed, "Abbey, lay flat! They're Sitting Bull's braves. They're after you. Bear, grab Alice."

Once on his feet in the knee-high water, Tom used the butt of his rifle and cracked the attacking Indian on the bridge of his nose. Blood erupted, but failed to faze the big Hunkpapa. He slammed his head into Tom's chest. Tom whipped about smacking his opponent a cracking blow to the ear with his elbow and finally smashing another powerful blow to the base of his skull, breaking the brave's neck. Bear, now standing in the shallow water, lifted Alice as if she were a wet sack of flour and hugged her hard until she vomited then sputtered for breath. Tom took her into his arms. "You're all right. I have you."

Just as dawn broke, a shaft of sunlight shot across the water, and the sound of the *Far West's* engines chugged round the bend toward them; sitting deep and fighting the current she inched toward them at a snail's pace. Captain Marsh returned Abbey's frantic wave with a blast of the steam whistle. Hundreds of crows blackened the sky; the ominous flutter of their wings flushed the attacking Indians from crevices in the rocks. They scattered like the birds. The sixty fresh recruits headed toward the Little Big Horn to fill some of the losses of the 7th Cavalry, aiming their rifles from the *Far West's* upper decks may have motivated them, too. Once abreast of the gathering on the shore, the crew tied the steamer down.

Beau Farro and Tom at Elliott's direction lifted Will Thunder Cloud to a blanket on shore. Abbey knelt at Will's side, holding his hand. A wide swath of red streaked her tan skirt. Blood at a trickle pumped from the arrow wound in Will's chest just above his heart. The children, shaking and pale, knelt at his other side.

Silent sobs and tears choked Alice and Emil for they knew their father was dying. No one could live with such a wound. Captain Marsh came down the stairs from the pilot's house. He and Violet stood behind the children. Only Abbey's soft words made any sound. Will caressed her hair and murmured something. She beckoned the children to come closer; he whispered to them and touched their faces. Only the soft purr of the idling steamer and the awakening wildlife broke the silence of the primal forest.

Finally, Elliott removed his fingers from Will's throat and shook his head. The blood no longer trickled. Silent tears stained every face. Time seemed to choke and stand still. After an immeasurable amount of time, Bear stood and raised his arms to the rising sun; his deep bass voice chanted in Sioux. All the natives faced the sun, raised their arms, and joined their voices with Bear's.

Abbey, with an arm around each of her children, stood and said, "We want to take him to Camelann. How can we do that?"

Captain Marsh wrote something on the back of his card and handed it to her. "In Bismarck ask for this man at the telegraph office. Pete Newton is a good man for information. He knows everyone and can fix most everything." He added. "Pete's wife, Henrietta rents a few rooms in her home for travelers. Use my name. They're good people and will help you with anything. I wish I could turn around and take you to Bismarck, but General Terry needs these recruits and supplies."

To Elliott, he softly said, "There's only one undertaker, Josh Cardin, and he's honest. You'll want a coffin for the train."

⧉

Violet led Alice and Emil to collect wildflowers while Abbey and Elliott prepared Will's body. Elliott removed the arrow then Abbey bathed her husband with warm water made fragrant with sage and lavender. The natives gently dressed him then wrapped Will in Indian blankets and a buffalo robe, the children and Abbey tucked the flowers around him.

Elliott walked Captain Marsh over to Tom. He slid his arm onto Tom's shoulder. "Captain, I'd like you to meet my son. Todd Cutter, and Todd, I'm pleased to introduce Grant Marsh, the finest riverboat captain in the Northwest."

Tom was still wet and bloody with a torn sleeve and sick with the death of Will Thunder Cloud. Elliott's hand on his shoulder felt like that of a good father, and the ex-cavalry officer needed a good father about now.

He extended his hand. "Pleased to make your acquaintance, Sir. Bloody sad business, isn't it?" he said in his best brogue, and Tom Custer fit into the role of Dr. Cutter's son, Todd Wallace Cutter, as if he'd been born to the part. No one, not even Emil or Alice, had trouble making the transition from cavalry officer to Scotsman. He was Todd Cutter, Scotsman and Shakespearean scholar. Violet who always had anything anyone might need tucked somewhere in her needlework bag handed him a small slim volume of the Bard's *Macbeth*.

᚛᚜

Captain Marsh and Todd devised a short flagpole and a small U.S. flag at half-mast for the bow of the lead canoe. Captain Marsh gave each of the men and Emil black armbands. The Indians understood the armbands as good medicine and wore them proudly. The women wore their black capes.

Guilliaume Emil Thunder Cloud Dupree resting in the bow of Bear's war canoe, rode to Bismarck like an ancient warrior. At Ft. Buford, where the Yellowstone flows into the Missouri River, Elliott handed the guard the letter Captain Marsh had quickly written. After the captain in charge of the dock read it, he waved them on their way.

Bismarck, a river port and railroad terminal, bustled with commerce. Todd spotted a few people from his former life: soldiers, a clerk, townspeople, but no one took particular notice of him. They pulled into the busy harbor, bypassing Ft. Abraham Lincoln, the home of the 7th Cavalry. While Abbey and Dr. Cutter spoke to the harbormaster, the children discovered the big sign over the livery stable: *Comanche - The Lone Survivor of The Little Big Horn.* Todd in hope of diverting their sadness took them inside.

A grizzly old man shook a horny finger at Emil. "Now don't you go plucking any hair out of that poor horse's tail. Every kid who comes by here wants a piece of him. Soon he'll be tailless."

Todd nodded. "Aye, I ken horses, and they ken their manners. We'll be kind to the old warrior." He motioned for the children to perch themselves on the fence while he opened the gate and walked inside.

"Here, here, you can't do …" But the old man's words trailed off as Comanche whinnied and nuzzled against the former Tom Custer, smelling him all over, and softly nickering. They had ridden together for almost ten years. The horse recognized a kindred soldier of the 7th Cavalry.

Emil and Alice silently watched as Todd Cutter picked up a brush in the stall and gently groomed Myles Keogh's horse for a long time. Lone survivors of Colonel George Custer's five companies of Cavalry, they'd bonded years ago. Comanche didn't notice his less than military grooming. Rather than the layers of grime and sweat, the horse smelled the soul of a Cavalryman. Very low, with his cheek resting on Comanche's withers, Todd hummed **Garry Owen.** The horse kicked the back wall. The old timer started to complain, but stopped as Comanche again nuzzled the man. Instead, he said, "You two seem to understand each other."

Todd smiled up to the children. "Aye, he's my brother. Aren't you boy?"

Comanche nickered and nuzzled Todd's neck.

Chapter 29

COMING HOME

The six-day stay in Bismarck passed like a prison term. As recommended, Todd and Abbey went to the telegraph office to request Peter Newton's guidance and secure lodgings from his wife, Henrietta. While Peter with his lumberjack build and flamboyant personality tried to make their stay enjoyable, Hennie's toothpick-thin body matched her pinched and prissy attitude and had them staying in their rooms or making excuses to go for long walks.

The Newton's rambling house itself did give comfort with its polished pine floors, covered with hand-woven rugs, and its cozy fireplaces in the thick log and adobe walls.

And Peter also saw to the coffin; he stood with Dr. Cutter and Josh Cardin as the Indians transferred Thunder Cloud's shrouded body to the coffin. The undertaker explained. "Lots of hatred toward the Indians in these parts. Fire and brimstone preachers insist that heathens be buried face down so they can't look on the face of the Lord at The Rapture." He nodded to Bear and Beau Farro. "They won't let that happen."

Peter spoke with Beau Farro and suggested they take the casket to his icehouse which stood next to the stable and gave directions. He sold the canoes and helped with travel arrangements. Violet and Elliott requested a private railcar if at all possible. Peter knew who to see to grease the ropes. One was found in Denver and would arrive in Bismarck, Dakota Territory on August 2nd.

Hennie suggested the bathhouse near the livery for the men and Emil. "May I also advise haircuts and shaves or at least a whisker trims. I run a clean house. We don't want bugs," she said, looking directly at Dr. Cutter and his son. "And gentlemen, you might want to consider fresh clothes at the Mercantile Mart."

For the women and Alice, she provided steaming soaks and shampoos in her large copper tub in the curtained-off corner of the big kitchen. She sniffed at them and asked, "Do you need clothing?"

Abbey shook her head. Alice, who sat in the tub, groaned as her mother rinsed her hair. In a voice laced with sarcasm, a highly unusual tone for this seven year-old, she said, "We have clean clothes. Mother insisted I wash MY THINGS!" Under her breath, she added, "Emil could get away with murder." Her voice sounded close to tears. "I'd love something new."

Abbey hugged her daughter. "Can you wait until tomorrow, darling? I think we all deserve something new."

Violet nodded. "Me too."

"Do we have enough money to buy me something?"

Abbey bent down and kissed her thoughtful daughter's wet hair. "Oh, Alice, I can write a check, and Elliott offered to pay for anything we need, and Uncle Danny would wire us money if we asked. You worry too much; Daddy took good care of us, and we have family to help us."

When the men returned in their stiff new clothes, black frock coats and trousers, white shirts, and western style boots, they joined the women who now sat on the back porch chattering and combing each other's hair as it dried. Hennie arched her eyebrows and looked them over. "Much better gentlemen, you no longer look like you escaped from jail."

Tom ignored her and handed a pale blue box to Alice. "Elliott and I thought this looked about your size."

The girl's face smoothed in a mix of expectation and joy. She untied the silk ribbons and reached below the tissue paper. A tiered skirt of multi-colored polka dots on white polished cotton fell into her lap, along with a blouse of cornflower blue cotton.

Alice beamed and so did everyone else on the porch except Hennie. Her rough fingers grabbed at the material, and she frowned. "You didn't get that at our mart."

Elliott shook his head. Still angry about the "bug" comment, he said, "We found it in *The Silver Needle*, a charming little shop around the corner from the mart." And although he knew the answer, he asked, "Who owns the mart?"

"We do," said Hennie, with her mouth curling down at the corners. "My father started the mart for the common folk." Her rough hand fingered the silk ribbon. "Not many around here have money to waste at The Silver Needle. . Some officers and their wives shop there or order their clothes from New York."

She squirmed in her chair, smoothing her apron. "Think they're too good for the likes of us. You should have seen how those Custer brothers dressed, cashmere jackets lined with silk taffeta, patent leather boots, regular dandies they were. Now, I hear the government is going to give the younger one's pension to his mother. Can you imagine? If the federal government has so much extra money I wish they'd sprinkle some of it around here."

Abbey watched red splotches gather on Todd's face. *Thank God,* she thought, *he has that beard.* She stood abruptly. "Todd, will you please help me with the lock on my valise. I think it's jammed." With her back straight as if she balanced a book on her head, she left the porch. Todd followed.

As they exited the porch, Hennie's voice trailed behind them. "I suppose I shouldn't speak ill of the dead. It makes me so dang mad, though, to see her get something for nothing when I work my fingers…." Hennie took a shuddering breath. "Give me ten minutes and I'll have a feast on the table."

Vi also stood and motioned to the children. "I can help in the kitchen, and these two can set the table."

⧜

Abbey pulled Todd into the room she shared with Violet and the children and closed the door. The lock clicked.

Todd punched his right fist into his left palm and let out a long harsh breath. Abbey watched the bright spots fade. "Thanks for getting me out of there. This masquerade is far more difficult than I expected."

She pulled him into her arms, her cheek against his chest. His arms came up, and held her as he kissed the top of her head. She murmured, "I realize it's hard, but know this Tom Custer or Todd Cutter, it's worth it. I do not want to share you with the world. No matter what name you use, you will always be Tom Custer to me. I loved Will Thunder Cloud, I always will, but you, too, have crept into my heart. I love you, Tom. I consider myself blessed to be part of both your lives. I know this charade is difficult, but in the end it will be a good thing. I'm so glad someone is helping your parents." Her fingers found his cheek; she brought his face down to hers and kissed him with the fire she felt.

A soft tap on the door and Violet whispered. "Dinner is served. Is that lock fixed yet?"

Todd stepped back and opened the door. "It just needed a hug." He turned to Abbey. "After you, Mrs. Dupree."

The Indians placed Will Thunder Cloud's simple coffin in the icehouse and told Todd and Elliott they intended to stand guard. With great seriousness, they asked if the Newton's would send dinner to them. Peter set up a wooden table in the shade of a maple tree near the stable and Hennie sent out bowls of steaming buffalo stew, fresh bread, and an entire elderberry pie.

After dinner Dr. Cutter told the women what Josh Cardin related regarding burying Indians facedown.

Abbey said, "That is just plain mean. And ugly. I'll have to tell them how much I appreciate their vigilance. Have any of you heard of this?"

Todd started to respond. He'd heard of this practice often, but he realized, fortunately that a Shakespeare scholar from Scotland wouldn't know such a thing. The responsibility increased a notch; taking on another's identity required more than an accent or the proper clothing. He needed to step into a different history.

⚜

Bear and Beau Farro, one or the other, stayed with Thunder Cloud at all times. They let it be known to Abbey and the doctor they did not intend to leave him until he was safely buried in the white man's way.

Painful goodbyes were said to Little Wind, his brother, Rock Hard Head, and to the ponies Chief Gall had given Emil and Alice. How could they possibly need more horses at Camelann?

Abbey and Todd found a small empty church. They sat in the last pew. The dark cool interior welcomed them, gave great peace to the sadness; they sat, holding hands, and talked long into the afternoon, getting to know each other again. Often they took the children to visit Comanche. They wished they could buy him and take him to Camelann, but, of course, they couldn't. He was a national treasure now.

The six-day wait for the railcar passed; goodbyes to Comanche became ridiculously difficult for Todd. "I want," he whispered to Abbey as the old man watched, "to steal him."

She could tell he meant it; his eyes looked desperate. "Don't even think of it. They still hang horse thieves."

Since they had no horses, Bear and Beau Farro rode in the stable section of the car with Will's coffin fortified by big blocks of ice, which Peter and a crew cut out of the river during the Montana winter and buried deep under sawdust and dirt beneath the icehouse. The other six passengers settled into the long ride to Camelann. The train stopped for several hours in Pine Ridge where Red Cloud, his family, and the Reservation Indians paid homage to Thunder Cloud by lining the railroad tracks to say goodbye.

In most major cities, Todd bought stacks of newspapers. His appetite for information about the Massacre at the Little Big Horn seemed insatiable.

"You are making yourself sick," said Abbey as they pulled out of Chicago. "What are you trying to discover?"

Todd shifted his shoulders. "I lost two of my brothers, Autie and Boston, my nephew, Autie Reed, my sister's husband, Jimmy Calhoun, most of my friends, my horse."

His voice stayed a raw whisper so full of anguish it hurt Abbey to hear it. "I was so proud to be part of the 7th. My life, since I turned sixteen, wrapped around the U.S. Army and later the 7th Cavalry. Now—like a puff of smoke---- the 7th I knew is gone. How did that happen? I was there and I don't know. I cannot be the only human to survive, and if so, why? Why me?" He looked into her eyes and his voice broke. "It haunts me, Abbey."

Abbey stood and folded a red trader's blanket over her arm. Long past midnight, Alice and Emil had been asleep for hours. "Vi, please keep an eye on the children. We're going up." She pointed to the ceiling and nodded to Todd. "Come and make sure I am not conked by the bridges. I want to show you something."

On the ladder Abbey looked back at the new Todd Cutter. He looked tired, troubled, and unhappy. His reaction to the happenings and the reports of the Little Big Horn pushed him to the verge of severe depression. In an attempt to add levity to the moment and cheer him up, she asked, "Where did the word conked come from? You have to admit it's a funny word."

Todd, who stood tight behind her to keep her skirts at bay, said, "I don't know it's origin, but Keogh always made sure a new recruit was conked by a low hanging tree branch. We old timers waited for their rude awakening." He didn't smile. "We thought that was funny."

By the time they reached the roof, the train had cleared Chicago. The night was August balmy with no moon, but a brilliant blanket of stars spread in all directions. A brisk but comfortable breeze whipped her skirts and kept smoke and ashes from them; and from a forward car, drifted a baritone voice with a guitar singing *Beautiful Dreamer*:

Beautiful dreamer, wake unto me,
Starlight and dewdrop are waiting for thee;
Sounds of the rude world, heard in the day,
Lull'd by the moonlight have all pass'd away!
Beautiful dreamer, queen of my song,
List while I woo thee with soft melody;
Gone are the cares of life's busy throng,
Beautiful dreamer, awake unto me!
Beautiful dreamer, awake unto me!

She leaned into his shoulder. "Oh, Todd, it's all so beautiful." The golden wheat, silver now in the starlight, rolled like ocean waves, the patchwork quilt of fields seems to stretch forever. Stephen Foster's music twined around them.

Todd spread a big, thick buffalo robe then the blanket. "Sit facing where we are headed. That way, we won't get conked." He took her hand and squeezed it. "Sorry, I'm so miserable. I can't seem to shake this sadness." He smiled a little. "How are you? You listen to all my woes, and everyone worries about me in my new character. You've lost your husband and best friend, your children are taking it hard, and then there's me clumsy as a foal in my new role."

Abbey sat and patted the blanket beside her. He didn't move.

"Train rides give one a lot of time to think. I imagine your long days on horseback did the same. Please sit Tom, I want to tell you a little story of how I met Will. I want no secrets between us."

When he sat down, she rested her head on his shoulder, enjoying the wind in her hair, the scent of him. She kissed his cheek. He placed his arm around her, she snuggled her hand into his. "Know first, Todd Cutter I am still in love with Tom Custer."

He squeezed her hand. "He's happy to hear that because he hasn't gone anywhere. And he's still wild about you. Every night Tom has to control the urge to slip into your bunk. He's having a great deal of trouble keeping his hands off you, and the only thing keeping him civilized is respect for Will Thunder Cloud."

She smiled into his shoulder. "It's a good thing Tom controls his hands, because I'd more than likely melt if he touched me."

She laid back; he leaned on his elbow beside her. "First, let me tell you how I met Will. I think it's important.

"The night was clear like tonight, but icy cold, Colorado in winter. I knew for a day or so that Ed and Jake Hunt were lovers, homosexual lovers. They had been since West Point, and apparently marriage to me made no difference.

"Jake became a raging wild madman, jealous of my pregnancy. He came to our quarters when Ed wasn't there. I'm sure now they planned that. He tried to rape me but failed, then he beat me terribly, punching and kicking me all over but especially my stomach to kill the baby. How I stayed clear-headed, I do not know, but I did. I weighed my options. My life and my unborn child's life were in danger. Jake was insane. However, if I told the post commander, Jake and Ed would be drummed out of the army, or more than likely, be set up to be killed by the Indians."

The lines of her jaw and neck grew tight and her voice bitter and harsh. "Two West Point graduates who were homosexuals?" A chilling laugh escaped her throat. "Good Lord! How would the Army handle such a thing? They abhor homosexuals. I could easily have exposed Jake without any remorse, but, at that time, I felt sorry for Ed.

"I chose to run away to Red Cloud's winter camp. They knew me. Mary and I taught the children. Wakanda had invited Mary and me to visit them. At the time I thought it a good decision.

"I only had a vague idea of where their camp was." She sat forward and hugged her knees.

"Good Lord, Abbey. You could have died. Wolves …winter." He rubbed her back.

"I was desperate. My marriage was over. Ed had no back-bone. He didn't beat me, but he allowed Jake to do his dirty work. My body was bruised, both eyes black, almost swollen shut, my nose bleeding...shaking... scared...I had to protect my child. Snow threatened from Canada, but when I left the skies were clear. I made it part way up the mountain then I started cramping so I decided to camp for the rest of the night. I managed a little fire then fell asleep.

"A sharp cramp awakened me. I sat up and looked across the dying embers of my fire to see this big Indian in buckskins and furs, armed to the teeth--two tomahawks, a long knife, a rifle strapped to his back--sitting across my campfire, staring at me. I recognized him, Wakanda's son, which helped a little, but I knew I was in trouble. The pain became fierce. He helped me stand and a mass of blood and ... I lost the baby.

"The next thing I knew his hands pulled off my clothes, he cleaned blood and other stuff off me, he pushed rags between my legs, and bundled me as if I were the newborn. I lay there terrified but grateful. I knew he saved my life. Over the howl of the wind I heard the wolves. He buried my tiny baby, even performed a small funeral, fed the pony, and took care of the dog."

"You took the dog...?"

She nodded. "Owen was a puppy. He'd have followed me... when I left the fort he was my only friend. He fit in my saddlebag.

"Later that night after he built up the fire and made coffee and biscuits, when my heart quit pounding so hard, but the tears wouldn't stop, he bundled his big body and Owen inside the bearskin with me. I never felt frightened of him. I just knew he would never harm me. He pointed up to the stars. He said,

'Your baby's up there watching over you. Pray to him. Ask him anything. He'll always be with you.' He pointed north. 'There's my grandfather, all my ancestors,' he said. 'We're never alone'.'"

Todd rolled toward her. "You are one incredible woman, and Will Thunder Cloud…"

"'Kiss me, Tom." Her voice wobbled and grew raspy; her breath whispered against his cheek. "I need to know Todd Cutter. I know Will won't mind. Do you think they will?"

She turned and pointed to the sky; he looked up. The heavens, the enormous bowl of the sky, exploded with shooting stars, more than he could count. His chest filled, his heart felt as if it might shatter, and his breath locked; he couldn't breathe. His mind knew they were just shooting stars. These came every August, the Perseiod meteor shower, and soldiers who slept under the open skies knew them, looked forward to them every summer. But tonight with Abbey's cool hands holding his cheek, her lush body pressed against his, these shooting stars became his brothers, his brave band of star riders, Autie and the men of the glorious 7th Ch avalry.

The music of *Garry Owen* played in his mind as she pulled him tight against her and kissed him, then held his cheek tight against her chest as they both cried.

"Will's up there, too," she whispered. "I know he doesn't mind if we kiss. He'd want us to have the magic. That's what he called lovemaking—magic."

"What if I don't stop with a kiss?" His one hand moved to her waist.

"I don't want you to stop with a kiss. Will knows we both loved him. Just don't let me scream and wake the entire train or lose my clothes." She giggled as she felt his hand on her skin. "And don't let me fall asleep and roll off the roof!"

Todd laughed, too, a gentle sweet laugh with no sadness whatsoever. "I guarantee lass, you'll not fall asleep, but oops... something lacy just flew away...your undergarment?"

Chapter 30

THE ARMS OF FAMILY

Lilly and Louisa were mixing pieces of toffee into cookie dough when Daniel came into the kitchen waving a telegram. "Abbey, the children, Vi, Elliott, and his son arrive tonight. They are bringing Will here for burial." They'd known of Will's death for several days.

"What a sad journey, " said Summer. "I suspected they might want to bury him here. Have you told Wakanda?"

Daniel nodded. "They are coming into Emmitsburg around ten o'clock tonight. Who should meet the train?"

Lilly looked horrified. No way was she not meeting Emil.

Summer noticed her daughter's set jaw and said, "We all will meet the train and bring Will home to Camelann."

She clapped her hands. "As soon as you finish the cookies will you two run over to the chapel and tell Howie and your grandmother what is happening? I suppose the funeral will be tomorrow or the next day. And on the way back gather enough flowers for a huge bouquet. We have snapdragons, daisies, late roses, and asters in the garden, and Queen Ann's lace by the bridge.

"Daniel, please start the boys grooming all the horses, especially the Percherons, and the big wagon needs to be cleaned. I'll walk over to the Indian School and see how Wakanda is." She breathed deeply " Then I'll help Mrs. Love with the beds and cooking. I know ..."

⚎

"May we have a party after the funeral?" Lilly asked her mother as she maneuvered Sooty behind the big red wagon along the mountain track on the way to Emitsburg. She wore her hair in thick braids and her favorite outfit: a cream-colored doeskin riding skirt and blouse, both fringed on the hem and sleeves with her red bandanna and cowboy boots. All the children sparkled and wore their red neckerchiefs; the adults all wore dark clothing. Summer had decided that tomorrow would be soon enough for the children to wear mourning clothes. Stars twinkled through the canopy of leaves, and night animals rustled the underbrush. "Remember Lilly, this is a sad time for Emil and Alice. Do you think a party is the right thing?"

Lilly shrugged and pressed her knees hard against Sooty in hopes of moving ahead of her mother who just didn't understand. *I've waited and waited for eons for Emil! I want a bonfire and fiddlers and dancing and fireworks. I want to celebrate Emil's homecoming.*

It didn't work. Rabbit trotted up beside Sooty. Summer leaned down toward her daughter. "Lilly, I've found it best to see the lay of the land before setting my heart on something. Let's see how Emil, Alice, and Abbey are before we think of a party. They need comfort and nurturing. Let's wait and see. "

Lilly shot her mother a glare. *She just doesn't understand; I've waited and waited.*

⚏

The village of Emmitsburg looked like a drawing from a book of fairytales, its white frame houses, the church steeples, silent storefronts all gleamed in the starlight. The town seemed asleep as they waited for the train. They heard the distant whistle, and Gussie, an expert at listening to the rails to calculate the train's location, leaned his ear on one track and announced, "It's only four miles away."

The stationmaster sputtered and glared at him, but Daniel, who had developed a formidable look during the war, scowled back which put a stop to that.

Lilly felt eyes on her and surveyed the houses. They looked back, with their windows all dark, but she knew the citizens of Emmitsburg hid in the shadows and watched.

They were quite a troop: Daniel, Hal, Summer, Wakanda, the Reverend Howard and Mrs. Tuttle, seven children, all on horseback, Lobo, driving the wagon with Romeo and Juliet, the huge gleaming black Percherons, stomping in their traces. Summer held a finger to her lips.

When the train finally steamed into the town, nothing happened at all like Lilly supposed. No other passengers detrained. Abbey and Violet eased onto the platform with Alice and Emil.

No one waved or shouted hello. They kept their eyes on the doorway into the train. Everyone else's stared at it, too. Lilly slipped her hand in her mother's. Bear and another Indian, dressed in a long sleeveless gray coat and a heavily feathered stovepipe hat, with Dr. Cutter and another man, carried the coffin. Her father and Hal stepped forward and helped lift it to the bed of the big red wagon. The yellow wheels appeared garish, inappropriate. The big bouquet of asters, snapdragons, roses, and Queen Ann's Lace softened the harshness.

Louisa squeezed her other hand as tears leaked from Lilly's eyes. Memories of Will Thunder Cloud lifting her onto his horse and parading her around the lake hurt her heart. He had always been kind to her, his shining black hair blowing in the wind, his handsome face smiling. What if it was her father in that coffin? Her heart cried for Emil and Alice. The Indians chanted and the one with the tall hat waived a smoking brazier of burning sage and cedar.

Abbey, and her children hugged a visibly shaken Wakanda and helped her onto the wagon. Dr. Cutter, Mrs. Montour, and the young gentleman sat on the wagon's benches around her.

The journey home from Emmitsburg to Camelann moved at a tortoise's pace and was inexplicably sad. Lilly nudged Sooty beside Rabbit and reached up taking her mother's hand. Summer bent down and brushed her lips against Lilly's hair. A knowing worth a million words passed between them in that squeeze of their hands.

⚶

Will Thunder Cloud's service was a blend of Bible passages, prayers, native chants, drums, and Presbyterian hymns. The funeral was poignant, pious, and private. Only residents of Camelann and Will's father, Nicholas DuPree from Toronto and Will's half-sister, Tilley, the lady doctor from Philadelphia, were invited. Major General Phil Sheridan, although uninvited, rode into Camelann without his usual entrouge the morning of the funeral. Of course, they couldn't escort him off the premises. He was an old friend and a major general.

Todd buried his anger and shook hands when introduced to the general. For a few moments they spoke of the great hunting in Montana and about the journey home from the gorgeous countryside along the Yellowstone. No one mentioned the tragedy of the Little Big Horn.

Summer, who had recognized Tom when he stepped off the train, rescued him. She shook hands and kissed Phil Sheridan's cheek then said, "Excuse us General. Todd, I need some chairs moved. Would you be so kind?"

To Phil, she added. "Abbey, I'm sure, wants to speak with you." She hugged him again. "Don't you dare leave without talking to me. I want to hear about your marriage. I'll see you after the service."

As Summer and Todd walked toward the cemetery, Summer asked, "Thank you for not making a scene. I'm sure he didn't recognize you. "Was it difficult?"

Todd massaged his fist. "I wanted to …"

Summer patted his arm. "How in the devil did he learn about Will so quickly?"

He shrugged. "The agent at Pine Ridge probably wired him when we stopped there." He grimaced. "Imagine what our world will be like when Mr. Bell's new telephone reaches all over the country. We won't have any privacy at all."

"You know, you sound like a Scotsman. Will you wear a kilt when you marry Abbey? " Last night, when Will, the Indians, and the children were all settled. Tom and Abbey told Summer and Daniel everything, including their desire to marry quickly and quietly once Will was buried. "I mean," said Abbey, "no disrespect to Will, but we've lost too much and we love each other. Will understood. In fact, Will urged us to marry. It's a long story. We will tell you later."

Summer and Daniel understood.

Now, Summer, sensing his reluctance to wear a kilt, hooked her arm in his and leaned her head against his shoulder. "Now Todd Cutter, why on earth would you not wear one?"

Chapter 31

LONG OVERDUE

In October Hal and Daniel ran telegraph poles and lines all the way to Camelann, completely bypassing Morgan's Corner. They knew Mr. Bell's telephone would reach Camelann in a year or so. In the meantime, they installed a private telegraph. All the children learned to send and receive Morse Code. Alice showed amazing promise.

Martha Graves did not take well to her source of gossip drying up. She had no foresight and the concept of how valuable the telephone would be to her hobby escaped her. Instead she sulked and daily grew angrier about the loss of Charteris lore to spread around Morgan's Corner. Furthermore when Alice, Louisa, and Lilly spotted her in a sycamore tree on Camelann land cutting the wires, she threw rocks at them. They told Daniel.

"I don't care if her aim is lousy, she knows she shouldn't throw rocks at you. Good Lord, what if she hit you." He wrote her a scathing letter, which threatened to have her fired if she cut the wires again, and he reported the incident to the new Sheriff, Todd Cutter.

Todd and Abbey had just returned from their three-week honeymoon in Cape May, New Jersey, when Daniel pinned a star on his chest. They seated themselves with Abbey and Summer on the porch. Daniel spoke to his sister. "Now don't go looking like that, Abbey. A sheriff in the East is not at all like a sheriff in the Wild West."

Abbey smiled broadly and winked first at Summer then the three girls who played with their dolls on the porch floor. The girls wore calico dresses, navy, burgundy, and forest green, with white pinafores and dark stockings. Summer and Mrs. Love had made matching dresses for their dolls. Daniel thought his sister looked healthier and happier than ever, and prettier, too. The sun and the salt air and perhaps the honeymoon had been good for her.

"You have no idea," she said, "how wild Cape May can be in an election year. No knight from King Arthur's court or even Wild Bill Hickok could have protected me better than your new sheriff. See his new walking stick?"

Todd lifted the beautiful polished cane of burled walnut with a silver dragon's head for a handle. "My wife bought it for me. Made in Germany, it's almost as useful as a sword. She already had me wearing tweeds and carrying a dirk in my boot, but thought I needed to look more Scottish so ..."

Abbey blinked. "You have to admit; it certainly came in mighty handy. Tell them Todd."

"Two nights ago, after dinner at this little cafe, we were walking along the seawall back to the hotel." His face softened.

"Giant waves crashed on the rocks, the moon cast the sea in silver, the night was gorgeous, very romantic... when these five college boys-- punks from Yale-- I learned later-- surrounded us. They were drunk and all sported Rutherford Hayes for President buttons. Wanted to know for whom I would vote.

"Before I could think of what to say, one grabbed Abbey." He ran his hand down the burled walnut and said, "I dropped three in less than fifteen seconds, two broken noses, a knee, a lot of blood. The other two ran away."

"Tell them the best part!"

Todd grinned at Abbey. "You tell them."

"A carriage stopped and guess who got out?"

All shoulders shrugged. The girls put down their dolls.

Abbey couldn't contain herself. "You'll never guess. President Grant, Generals Sherman and Sheridan."

"What happened?" asked Summer.

Abbey beamed. "They first congratulated Todd. President Grant asked to see his cane and complimented it. Their guards on horseback collected and arrested the ruffians. Little Phil introduced us. General Sherman remembered me and mentioned I was your sister. Little Phil noticed my ring and congratulated us on our marriage. Our hotel was only a few yards away. We said good night." She shrugged. "That was it."

"They didn't recognize you, Todd?" asked Daniel.

"The President didn't. General Sherman may have. He's pretty sharp. During the war, Tom held his horse for him several times. He kept looking from me to Abbey." Todd glanced at Daniel. "Most men remember a girl like Abbey."

Lilly jammed the doll's arm into the little sleeve and whispered to the other girls, but everyone heard her. "They remember her bosoms."

Todd Cutter stood and slapped his new walking stick against his palm. He tried to not smile but failed. His wife's face turned beet red; Summer choked. Daniel shook his head.

Todd finally managed to smooth his face. "Now someone tell me about this woman I'm supposed to arrest."

Daniel stood also. "Girls, run and tell everyone to meet at the bridge. Todd and I are going to toss Mrs. Graves in the lake. It is long past due. No one throws rocks at my girls." He put his arm around the shoulder of his new brother-in-law. "Did you ever hear the story about how she whacked Louisa with a Genoa salami?"

Chapter 32

MEMORIES

September 2, 1880

"Mother," called Maggie Custer Calhoun as she entered her home in Monroe, Michigan. "There's a large envelope for you. I wonder…"

"Open it for me, dear. Is it from Libbie?" Armstrong's widow resided in New York City now. Maria Custer lived for Libbie's letters.

Maggie removed her gloves and unpinned her hat, an elaborate affair of straw, laden with summer flowers made of silk. It soon would be stored away with all the summer things, another year passed. She put the gloves in the hat and laid both on the hall table beneath framed photographs of her husband, Jimmy, her brothers, Autie, Tom, and, Boston, and Autie Reed, her nephew. It had been four years since that day, the horrible day on the Little Big Horn. Memories still cut like a dagger into Maggie's heart. They had been so happy, her brothers, her handsome

Jimmy, the Custer Clan, The entire U.S. Army envied them: tenting on the plains, picnics, riding with the men at the head of the column, seeing parts of America few white eyes had ever seen. Not a day passed that she didn't relive those halcyon years.

"It's from Pennsylvania. Why look, Mama, it's a photograph and a letter from a Mrs. Todd Cutter. Do you know her?"

Maggie studied the picture for a moment, her fingers touching the faces, her eyes suddenly filed with tears, but her mouth smiled uncontrollably. She pulled a lace hanky from her sleeve as she handed the photograph to her mother.

"Read the letter to me, Maggie. My eyes are so weak."

Maggie, still smiling, fussed with her handkerchief, mopping her eyes, blowing her nose. Finally, she tucked it back in her sleeve. She read:

Dear Mrs. Custer,
Ever since the tragedy of the Little Big Horn, I have wanted to write and express my sorrow for your loss. You more than likely do not remember me. A few years ago, your son, Tom, introduced me to you and your husband. I was Abbey Dupree then. We lunched at a German delicatessen on the docks in Toledo. I remember we ate wonderful warm brisket sandwiches on black bread with tangy mustard, potato salad, and garlic pickles. Nevin and Ann came with you.

Tom was escorting me across country. I remember you admired my blonde hair, and you told how you loved tow-headed babies, how Autie and Tom had been so blond as boys. I was married at that time to a half-breed and my children were dark haired. You couldn't understand how

I could marry an Indian. Let me assure you Will Thunder Cloud was a marvelous husband and father, and he became a great friend of your son, Tom.

Will died about the same time your boys were killed. That was such a heartbreaking tragedy. I remarried and have been blessed with three more children. The enclosed photograph reminded me of how much you love blond children, how proud you were of your boys. My husband, Todd, sits to my right. Will Thunder Cloud's children, Emil and Alice, stand to my left. In front of Todd are our tow-heads: Samuel, Thomas, and William. When you spoke of your love for your little tow-heads, I didn't understand. I certainly do now.

I remember your son, Tom, fondly. He was very kind and considerate to me, a true gentleman. On several occasions he mentioned to me how much he loved his family. I'm sorry for your loss.

Cordially,
Abbey Cutter

"How strange! Why on earth would that woman think I would want a photograph of her children?" Maria Custer laid the photograph on the table and pushed it away from her. "I vaguely remember her. Golden blonde hair, a gorgeous brown riding habit, a silly hat with a plume. So out of place in Toledo. Seems cheeky to me for her to send such a thing. Maggie, just toss it in the bin, and is it time for my glass of sherry? I do so like my sherry. Your eyes look red, Maggie. Is it that ragweed again? Or are you upset about my wine? Remember, the doctor ordered it. I only have one glass a day. It helps ease the pain of …losing Autie.

"On second thought, don't throw that photograph away. Show it to Nevin and Ann. Maybe they remember her. What was her name again?"

"Abbey, Abbey Cutter." Maggie pulled out her handkerchief again and blew her nose. Tears streamed from her eyes. She took the photograph and held it against her heart. *I know it's Tommy. That middle boy looks just like him. Oh my God, he's alive.* She mopped her eyes again.

"You'd better do something about that ragweed. Your looks will be ruined and you'll never get another husband if you keep sniffing. Oh Maggie, why hasn't our dear Libbie written? Where's my sherry?"

AUTHOR'S NOTE AND
ACKNOWLEDGEMENTS

The great era of American Indian tribes ruling the Northern Plains ended within fifteen years after the Battle of the Little Big Horn. Crazy Horse arrived at the Red Cloud Agency, located near Fort Robinson, Nebraska, on May 5, 1877. The meeting was to be a respectful and solemn ceremony with First Lieutenant William P. Clark as the first step in his formal surrender. However, over the next four months rumors and horrid lies caused Crazy Horse to be arrested and accidentally stabbed in the back by a guard. Much controversy remains today over Crazy Horse's death.

Sitting Bull and Gall took their people to Canada very soon after the Battle of the Greasy Grass. Gall and Sitting Bull had a falling out and Gall returned to the reservation. He became a Christian and a farmer and urged his people to assimilate in the reservation culture. He died in 1894 and is buried in St. Elizabeth's Episcopal Cemetery in Wakpala, South Dakota.

To avoid starvation, Sitting Bull and his followers left Canada in 1883 and surrendered to the U.S. authorities. He became involved in the Ghost Dance movement. Fearing an uprising, the U.S. government arrested Sitting Bull. During the ensuing fracas, Sitting Bull was accidentally shot and killed by an Indian policeman.

The death of these three American heroes changed a way of life on the plains. Threatened with starvation, the Indians ceded *Paha Sapa* to the United States. However, the Sioux never accepted the legitimacy of the transaction. After lobbying Congress to create a forum to decide their claim, and subsequent litigation spanning forty years, the United States Supreme Court in the 1980 decision *United States v. Sioux Nation of Indians* acknowledged the United States had taken the Black Hills without just compensation. The Sioux refused the money offered, and continue to insist on their right to occupy the land.

Did Tom Custer die on that battlefield? History reports the original burial crews bungled the battlefield identification of remains. The heat, the mutilations, and the fear for their own lives caused the burial parties to create confusion. Shallow graves uprooted by animals created further loss of information. Tom Custer more than likely did die at the Little Big Horns, but some controversy exists. I like to think he survived as Todd Wallace Cutter and spent the rest of his life with Abbey at Camelann.

Heartfelt thanks go to Kathy Martinides, Cheryl Krass, Jackie and Dick Kurtz, and Mary Keifer who edited *Star Riders*. Without their guidance and enthusiasm, I would have fireflies flickering in April, geese migrating north in July, and bats flitting about in January. Also, great appreciation is sent to Ed

Gagnon and Carol Olescyski. Ed, a Canadian author, read *Star Riders* early and offered many excellent suggestions. Carol, a longtime friend and an obstetrics nurse, checked out the birth of the twins. Encouragement from family, friends, and fans has been enormous. Thank you.

Caroline Hartman
carolinehartman5@gmail.com

RESOURCES

Connell, Evan, *Son of the Morning Star*, New York, 1984.

Custer, Elizabeth Bacon, *Boots and Saddle*, New York, 1985.

_____, *Following the Guidon*, New York, 1893.

_____, *Tenting on the Plains*, New York, 1890.

Day, Carl F. *Tom Custer, Ride to Glory*, Univ. of Oklahoman, Norman 2002

LaPointe, Larry, *Sitting Bull, His Life and Legacy*, Salt Lake City, 2009.

McMurtry, Larry, *Custer*, New York, 2012.

Mestermaker, Albert J., *The Other Custer*, Colorado, 2014.

Paul, R. Eli, Editor, *Autobiography of Red Cloud, War Leader of the Oglalas*, Helena, Montana, 1997.

Stevenson, Joan, *Deliverance from the Little Big Horn*, University of Oklahoma, Norman, 2012.

Made in the USA
Middletown, DE
13 November 2015